[0]

First edition: September 2018

ISBN: 9780990487319

Cooper, Garry

By: Wind's Path

# EDGEWATER

## A NOVEL- BY GARRY COOPER

## ~ PROLOGUE ~

Edgewater—It's a town-- a small river delta town. You'll see though, it is your town. It is every town, big or small. After all, a big city, besides the traffic, is really made up of groups of people. The people interact the same. Some are pure, some aren't. Some love deeply, some won't –some can't.

Were you the loved or unloved? Were you the betrayed or the betrayer? Did you hate or were you hated? Did you hurt or were you hurt? Were you treated unfairly or were you unfair to others? Were your dreams crushed or was your love stolen by others—or by death? Did you hide your feelings?

Yes, Edgewater is us all. You already know the characters. You will live their lives here in this story. It's okay to cry—both happy tears and the sad ones. You will laugh, you will feel anger and hate. You will feel true goodness and love. You will feel aroused. You will feel all of your emotions.

Watch Abel suffer the unimaginable as a child. Watch him heal, learn to trust, learn to love -- but watch him!

Feel Layla's pure love for Ian and his for her. There is no purer love. Feel her worry, her pain, their intense compassion for their family. But, brace yourself for unspeakable tragedy.

Follow Mylee and Tony's high school love as it evolves and then dissolves while it brings to light a true love match that was made too late. Mylee needs your love—she deserves it. Love her to the end—like Seth did.

Follow Seth. He is a good man. A simple man whom could only love one person—and she was taken—twice!

Then, follow sweet Samantha, the victim of revenge, as her life becomes more complex at each turn.

[5]

Be prepared for the ending. Have a tissue in hand. Read on and experience life in EDGEWATER!

# CHAPTER 1

"Got a kit?" Abel heard a man ask. The unfamiliar voice was a rumbling bass-tone from decades of smoking cigarettes. His mother arrived home at two in the morning with the man. Abel cringed in fear against the wall at the inside edge of his bed.

"Yeah, in here." he heard his mother answer. He felt the paper thin wall shake as she flung her bedroom door against it causing dust from the wall to salt the side of his face. Torturing pangs of terror swirled within him.

"Hang on a sec." he heard his mother say. He heard her nightstand drawer scrape open, its rollers having never been in place since she scavenged it from their flophouse's dumpster. The room was silent but for his mother's bent spoon clanking to the nightstand and readying to be filled with a methamphetamine/heroin mixture. He listened as paranoid secretive mumbles were shared between them.

"Oh, God!" Abel thought. He covered his head with his pillow and squeezed it tight to his ears. He strained to silence the near-nightly sounds of his mother exchanging sex for drugs. Abel curled into a pitiful fetal position recounting the untold times his mother had shared with him that such an exchange had led to his birth. The sexual sounds unmercifully wore their way to his ears through what was left of his ancient pillow.

"Ugh!" Abel sounded while pressing his index fingers deep into his ears. He struggled not to hear the rhythmic squeals of the worn springs from his mother's dilapidated mattress. Abel felt an uncomfortable hope from the sickening sounds, hoping that his mother would be satisfied for the night and not force him to her room later to relieve her drug-induced, over-amped body from its agony by forcing him to perform oral sex on her until she passed out from exhaustion.

"This is what mothers and sons do," she would say after abusing him. She'd then warn him of he being taken to prison if he were ever to share their secret. His seven-year-old mind, when the abuse began, was unable to realize its foulness. Now in his teens, he recognized its wrongness.

"Abel! Get in here!" His mother screamed through the paper-thin wall. Abel held his breath and laid silent, praying his mother would lose her train of thought. He heard the man

[8]

coaxing his mother in a half whisper. "You want the hanger, Abel!

You get your ass in here, NOW!" his mother screamed. Abel knew

that if he didn't respond this time she would prance in, armed

with a wire clothes hanger, and beat him unmercifully.

"Please mama?" Abel begged, meeting his mother in the

hallway, hanger in her hand. She grabbed him by the wrist and

drug him to the dimly lit hand-rolled-cigarette-smelling room.

"Now Abel!" she ordered. She stood naked pointing the

wire hanger towards her open bedroom door. The nipples on her

prematurely flattened breasts were aimed downward to the floor.

A half-smoked cigarette dangled from her mouth. "Get in there

with Steve!" she ordered as Abel entered the room. She

motioned toward the naked bearded man lying on the bed with

the hanger. His entire body was painted with jailhouse tattoos. A

black teardrop inked at the side of one eye indicated the murder

of one of his close gang members. He had an evil and nasty smile

on his face as he pointed his large erect penis towards Abel.

"Make him take his pajamas off," the man said, staring in

anticipation.

"You heard him Abel, get them off and get in there!" his

mother said. She motioning to the man's groin with the hangar

and belted Abel across his back with it when he hesitated. "I'm going down to the corner to get some cigarettes." She pushed Abel to the bed as his pajamas fell to the floor. The over-muscled jailbird grabbed him and forced his mouth downward. Abel complied to make the terror as short-lived as possible.

"This is the last time!" Abel promised himself. His mind raced on what to take, where to go, and how to live when he ran away. He swore to himself to leave the following morning.

"You say anything to anybody you little dickhead, and I swear, I will torture you in ways you would never imagine!" the jailbird whispered in Abel's ear while wrenching his head back by his hair to the point of nearly breaking his neck while painfully raping him. His mother returned and watched as the man finished himself in Abel. The man stood and glared through him. "Get him out of here," the man growled.

"You heard him Abel. Get the hell out of here now," she said. She turned and began treating herself to another injection of the man's drugs. Abel retrieved his pajamas from the floor and limped to his room.


"Maybe I should join the military," Abel contemplated to himself a year later as he sat on the ledge of a window at school. He felt that he might be imposing on his aunt and uncle who had taken him in when he left his home the day after his last molestation. He had shown up helpless and with only the clothes on his back to their doorstep. His aunt and uncle knew that his mother was a drug fiend and that Abel was often hungry and mistreated.

"I have to do something; if any of the other kids find out about what I've done-- Somebody probably already knows!" Suddenly seeing his friend Seth and a girl named Sandy walking towards him, he forced a façade of composure upon himself.

"What's up, Abel?" Seth chimed cheerily. He noticed the pain on Abel's face.

"Hi Abel," Sandy added, noticing Abel's unusually large and exotic green eyes focused blankly towards the ground. She saw them reddened as he looked to her. "You okay?" she asked.

"Yeah," he responded, "Damn allergies are killing me though." Sandy smiled warmly. He turned towards Seth and unfolded his arms which he'd clasped to his stomach to suppress his abdomen pain. He sat erect and acted as normal as he could. His face blushed, seeing Sandy smiling at him and staring into his eyes.

"Come by and shoot a few hoops with me later at my gramps' place, Abel," Seth said as the bell rang for their first class of the day. "I'll kick your ass again!"

[11]

"Maybe I will," Abel responded, "But the ass kicking I'm not too sure about. I think it was your ass that got kicked last time, if I recall." Abel's face relaxed and his eyes cleared. He smiled at his friend.

"Just me and you Abel, one on one-- new day, new game!" Seth said, staring at Abel with a broad grin. "Unless you're chicken!" Seth turned to walk towards his class, giving Abel a challenging glance over his shoulder.

"See you later Abel," Sandy said in a flirty voice that aired the smell of the fruity flavored lollipop that she was nursing. Her face reddened after reaching and combing Abel's surfer-cut blonde hair back from his face with her spread fingers. She also glanced back at him over her shoulder, but hers was with a coy smile and a wink.

"Bye," Abel said, his voice unintentionally silenced by his shyness. He felt tenseness leave him as he was left alone.

"I hope she doesn't know," Abel thought. "I can tell she feels sorry for me." He walked past two of his classmates cuddling in a corner near the snack-bar as he walked to his class. He noticed goosebumps on the girl's arms as they kissed when he passed. "It'll probably be OK someday. I probably should get away from here though." Thoughts of joining the military after

[12]

he graduated reentered his head. He entered his auto shop class and sat at his desk, the knots in his stomach having returned to his everyday usual ones. He bore his pain, his thoughts, his memories, and his fears throughout high school.

Abel picked up his backpack and slung it over his shoulder one afternoon during his senior year. Two arrogant football jocks from wealthy families walked passed him, giving him their usual "We matter, you don't," looks. They wore their usual matching degrading sneers, born from the fact that Abel's natural physique dwarfed their hard-earned boyish ones.

"Hey weirdo dickhead!" one of them said, the other snickering as he did so.

"Assholes," Abel thought, ignoring them purposefully. He recalled how they had spread rumors of him being the killer of a girl in their class who was found murdered a couple years earlier. He was questioned twice by the local police concerning the incident. He hadn't even been in town the weekend that she was killed, but their rumor gained footing by the day in the small town.

"I wish those two fuckers would graduate and go off to where ever their arrogant families are sending them to college!"

he thought. He shook his head in disgust. He felt his blood pressure rise as they passed. He surmised that he being a "loner" fit the police profile for someone that could commit such a crime. He understood why he had piqued their interest. Only recently had he learned from Seth that nearly every person that knew the girl had been questioned as he was.

"At least these assholes finally stopped with the 'hey killer' and 'Boston Strangler' comments," Abel thought, attributing it to him threatening one of them with a closed fist one day. "I wish those assholes were there when the cop put his hand on my back and told me that I was no longer a suspect," Abel thought. "One of them probably did it!" he opined to himself. He yanked the door to his class open. A slight grimace of anger still remained on his face as the bell sounded. He wondered what had happened to the girl's single-mom mother who had come to town just a few months before her murder and left just after. He took his seat at his desk and the teacher began to point at the blackboard and speak.

# CHAPTER 2

Seth awakened one morning when he was nine years old after being left at his grandparents' house. His parents had attended a comedy show forty miles from Edgewater in Old Sacramento the night before. He heard sobbing from the kitchen and the scrape of his grandfather's chair on the floor as he rose from it when he came into their view. His grandmother and grandfather's faces were contorted in anguish. Their eyes and faces were reddened and swollen from what he could tell was crying.

"What's wrong Gramma?" he asked as tears began gathering in his eyes. His imagination of what terrible event had happened began to run wild. His grandmother's eyes met his for a brief moment before collapsing head first into her folded arms on the kitchen table. Her pitiful wails penetrated his soul. His grandfather slid a chair between Seth and his grandmother, allowing him to embrace both of them at the same time.

"Your mother and father were in an accident last night, Seth," his grandfather said with tears welling in his eyes. "A big truck had a tire blow and crossed into their lane when they were on their way here to pick you up and hit them head-on. Seth, they were both killed," his grandfather said. His crying became wails of sadness as he held his grandson. Seth began shaking—his skin paled to a deathly white.

"No!!" Seth screamed. His grandfather grabbed him as he collapsed towards the floor. "Please Grampa, no!" he pleaded. His grandfather hugged him tightly. The elderly man's tears flowed in torrents as he longed for a way to sooth his grandson's pain. He could find no such way. Seth sobbed in his grandfather's arms, soaking his jacket sopping wet with tears. He cried in his grandfather's embrace for most of the day.

"It will be okay Seth," his grandfather consoled each day. He did the same for nearly a month until Seth found the strength to begin to accept his terrible loss. Only much later did he realize that his grandfather was suffering the terrible pain of losing his only son. Seth ached and cried daily from his loss for over a year, his only solace being his grandparents' love for him. They nurtured him with love until they both succumbed to cancer by his eighteenth birthday. His grandmother died only a month before his grandfather. Seth was haunted by the memory of watching his grandfather grieve for his wife of many decades until his own death, which Seth attributed to a broken heart.

[16]

"You be a good man, Seth," his grandfather said to him a week before he lapsed into a coma. "You be honest and kind to others and never be afraid to love people. They all deserve it."

"I will, Grandpa," Seth promised. He was already instilled with such respect by the examples that both his grandfather and father had set.

Seth finished the last few weeks of high school, living alone in his grandparents' house. A lawyer had visited him and told him of the bank accounts and other assets left to him by his family. The house was paid off and Seth was the sole beneficiary of his family's trust. His finances were of no worry. His reputation and work ethic allowed him a job at his first asking.

"Seth, wake up! What the fuck are you doing?" Seth's co-worker screamed one morning two years later. He continued shaking him firmly to wake him from his hangover-induced sleep.

"Huh?" he mumbled. He mustered the strength to open his eyes. They felt like they had been sanded with sandpaper. He heard his coworker once again confront him excitedly.

"What the hell," his coworker exclaimed. He grabbed Seth's right hand and exposed the tip of his index finger to Seth's barely focusing eyes. Seth awoke rapidly to the sight of his finger

[17]

being a dark blackish purple and suddenly felt a toothache-like pain emanating from it. He lifted it closer to his bloodshot eyes and saw that the blood to it had been cut off from the dental floss that he had wrapped around it the previous night before he passed out. He drew it closer to his face and into better focus.

"Aw shit!" he said, realizing he had to get to the doctor. The doctor had to remove his finger from that knuckle on to save the rest of the finger—if not his hand.

"I'll just tell people what happened, fuck them if they can't take a joke!" Seth thought after returning from the doctor. He considered trying to save face by telling them some convoluted story about cutting it off with a table saw instead of from his over-drinking but savored the thought of eliciting some humor from his friends with the truth. He loved to see people laugh and to be the butt of his own jokes.


"Seth, you know you would probably feel a lot better in the mornings if you didn't drink so much," his friend Mylee said. She lifted his hand to the table and began changing the dressing. "You had that bicycle wreck on your way to the store to get more beer that time – then that burn from when you spilled that pot of hot water on yourself. I swear, it's going to be the death of you!"

[18]

"Yeah, I know," he said, looking guilty and smiling. She smiled back and shook her head, lovingly scolding him with it. She admired his innocent laid-back surfer look as he stared at her with his ocean-blue puppy-dog eyes. He peeked at her from under the brim of his camo baseball cap. His shoulder-length blond hair mushroomed from all sides of it. He milked a loving grin from her with his own, his perfect white teeth nearly blinding her as he did.

"You're a peach!" Mylee exclaimed through laughter. She couldn't help admiring Seth's most attractive feature, it being the comfortable and easy way that he carried himself. He lacked a hint of evilness, ulterior motive, or dishonesty. "Well, take it easy until this heals, buddy!" Mylee scolded. She gently returned his hand to the arm of the chair after replacing the bandage. She noticed the uncanny smoothness of Seth's dark tanned skin, given his near-daily work in the sun and other elements. "And you should wear some sunscreen—and no farm work until this heals!" Mylee ordered. She patted the top of his arm gently.

Seth wondered if her concern for him stemmed from him saving her from being gang-raped by a bunch of guys at a party one night when she was a freshman. It had happened the one and only night that he had ever seen her drink too much in school. He sat, picturing the guys fondling her and beginning to undress her, and only stopping after he had attacked them and threatened

[19]

them to call the police. He suffered a broken nose during the incident. "Come on, Seth!" one of the guys pleaded, as he groped her, adding, "She won't even remember being fucked, leave alone who fucked her!" Seth felt sick at the memory, recalling taking her into his arms that night and carrying her home and staying with her until her parents arrived. Seth heard that one of her friends had shared the story with her years later.

"Only if..," Seth thought. He sat thinking how much he had always been attracted to her and how she had fallen for the popular football star, Tony, early on and become unavailable before he had the nerve to woo her. He shook his head in disgust, knowing what a disloyal pig that Tony was.

"What?" Mylee asked, seeing him shake his head.

"Nothing, I was just thinking about how lucky I am to have you as such a good friend! You're always watching out for me!" Mylee smiled lovingly, leaned to him and kissed his forehead.

"Thank you Seth, I owe you for being my true friend. You are a good guy!" She seemed to know parts of his thoughts. "Now if I catch you working with that hand, I'm going to rip your arm off and beat you to death with it!" She smiled warmly at him again as she walked out his door.

"Hey, Abel!" Seth greeted as Abel stopped by to visit one day. Their friendship flourished beyond high school. Seth remained Abel's only trusted friend.

"What's up?" Abel inquired, seeing Seth hovering over the garbage can yanking the feathers from a pheasant that he had shot.

"Just cleaning dinner! Got tired of dipping the same old soup bone in water!" Seth joked. Abel laughed thinking, like everyone else in town, that Seth was one paycheck away from starvation. Few knew that Seth's grandfather had left him millions of dollars in gas well royalties along with the old house that he lived in. Seth had no desire for a lavish lifestyle and was satisfied living on his own earnings and being the person that he was; driving an old truck that he worked on himself and affording his own beer with his wages.

"What's up with you, pal?" Seth inquired, seeing a familiar loneliness in Abel's face. Abel glanced at the ground and lifted his face to Seth's with a humble smile.

"Nothing, just came by to say hi," Abel said. He glanced at the half-plucked bird and to the vacant wall of Seth's house. He shifted his weight to one leg and stood awkwardly.

[21]

"I have the worst luck!" Seth said, yanking Abel from his thoughts. "Shit, Abel," Seth said, recounting his trip to a concert in Sacramento the previous week. "I am driving home, kind of hungover and I have to take a crap! I see this Dairy Queen burger joint and I figure, what the hell, I can use an ice cream and they have a crapper." Abel listened intently.

"I pull in and there is an arrow on the side of the building pointing to the its rear with a sign reading 'restrooms.' I go back there, I'm about ready to crap my pants and the fucking door is locked. Some guy inside yells, 'Out in a minute!' I'm standing outside with my butt-cheeks pinched shut for about ten minutes. Finally, the door opens and out comes this homeless guy and his fucking dog. There's paper towels stacked to the ceiling on top of the garbage can and the guy looks at me and says, 'He rolled in something dead. I had to give him a bath!'

I'm about ready to shit myself and this guy is giving his fucking dog a bath in the bathroom!" Seth looks up at Abel to see him grinning.

"So I go in. It smells like a dead rat. This little bathroom is about as big as a hall closet. I wipe the toilet clean with toilet paper, as of course there are no ass-gaskets in the dispenser. By this time I am getting ready to shit my pants! I sit down and start crapping and some guy starts beating on the door and screaming, 'Hurry up!" Seth watched the elation grow in his friend.

"I finish taking a half of a crap with this guy continually beating on the door the whole time! I figure he is about to crap his pants so I hurry and wipe. I tuck my shirt in, wash my hands in the cold water, which is all they had, and I open the door. Here is some other homeless guy, who also can afford a dog. He crowds his way in with me and starts crapping before I even step out. His God damn dog growls at me!" Seth's eyes are wide with a look of shock on his face.

"So, I get out of that fuck-story and I walk inside the Dairy Queen to get an ice cream cone. I'm looking at the menu and can't decide. I saw these two older women eating something that looked killer when I walked in so I turn to ask them what they were having. It seemed like they were trying to hide their laughing! I'm thinking what the fuck?" Seth paints a look of confusion on his face to add color to his story.

"They manage to tell me what kind of ice cream cone they were having and I order the same for myself. I pay and the girl goes to make it."

"I turn around and the old women are beet red in the face, the three kids behind them are busting up and laughing at me. I check my zipper and it's okay, so I reach behind me and there it is!"

Abel is now completely engulfed in the suspense, poised to laugh.

"When that homeless asshole rushed me in that postage-stamp-sized bathroom as I tucked my shirt in, I managed to tuck the end of the toilet paper roll in with it.

I go traipsing into the restaurant with a ten-sheet tail dangling from me!"

Abel explodes into an unsympathetic roar of laughter. Seth roars in laughter with him.

Seth milked as many good feeling into his friend from his story as possible and cheered him further with some playful teasing. They joked and chatted until Abel left.

"Poor guy," Seth thought as he pondering Abel's demons. He recalled him once hinting at their roots by saying, "I hate my mother and wish she was dead! She is a fucking evil witch that only cares about her drug-addicted perverted self!" Seth found himself thinking of Abel much of the evening over his evening beers until stumbling his way to bed.

[24]

"Fuck, these bales are heavy!" Seth moaned to himself the following day. He complained to himself about how the new hay-baler on the farm he worked at compacted the bales so much more densely than the old one it replaced. "Get on there, you son of a bitch!!" he cursed to the hay bale, trying to throw it sideways so the conveyer could grab the wires that held it together and carry it to the bed of the truck so he wouldn't have to hand lift it. He stared down briefly, feeling pain in his now-healed floss-amputated finger from banging it with the hay hook. "Ugh!" he grunted, throwing another onto the chain. It too missed the hook and required that he wrestle it into place. The misses were more due to Seth's third- degree hangover than the design of the machine. "Get on there, you bastard!" he cursed, as he kicked it with his foot to roll it into position. He suddenly lost balance and began to fall.

"Shit!" he exclaimed loudly, realizing that falling was inevitable. He fell helplessly towards the chain and onto the conveyor. "Aah, OW!" he winced, as the chain's hook dug into his flesh and grabbed his belt. It drug him across the metal frame towards the top like a bale of hay as he frantically struggled to free himself. "Ugh!" he groaned as his head slammed into the conveyor's frame support, breaking his nose and blacking both of

[25]

his eyes. "Fuck!" he screamed out of frustration, knowing that no one could hear him and thinking that the conveyor was about to slam him into the truck bed before releasing him.

Instead, the chain had entangled itself on his belt so that he was jerked under the machine and slammed against the side of the truck bed, breaking several of his ribs. "Oh shit!" he screamed. He realized the machine was dragging him to near-certain death as it chugged him towards the heavy gears that powered it, where he would painfully be ground into small pieces. He grabbed for anything to help him free himself! "Uggghhh!" he grunted as he strained to wrap both arms around the metal frame of the conveyor and hold it with all his might.

The machine's smooth rhythm changed to a labored chug as it bogged down from the resistance of him holding on for his life. Black smoke billowed from the exhaust as the machine struggled to free itself from what was holding it back. "OOW!" Seth cried, feeling the machine strip his belt and Levis from him. His skin peeled from his flesh as the mechanical monster ripped mercilessly at him until finally releasing him and letting him drop several feet to the ground.

"Bwaa, bwaaa, pffft, pop," the machine groaned as it failed to digest his pants, belt, and underwear. It sounded as if it were laughing at Seth as it ground to a halt and its engine gurgled

[26]

to a silence.    Seth grunted and gasped deeply, relieved at being free and alive. The intense pain of the broken bones, and being nearly skinned alive along his hips, set in.    He laid still on the ground digesting his near-death experience.

"Whew, lucky!" he mouthed silently.    He couldn't help thinking about the Mexican worker the previous year that wasn't so lucky when he stood to pee off of the moving hay-baler and fell, ending up baled in a bale of hay with his arms and legs sticking out of it when they found him.

"Damn it," he whined as he pulled himself to his feet using the metal frame that had saved his life.    He looked down at his bleeding thighs, seeing himself naked to the tops of his work boots that had been shredded and peeled downward as his pants were ripped from him. He held his shattered ribs in place with his hands to lessen the pain from breathing.    He limped his way to the cab of the hay truck.

"Mom!" his boss's fifteen-year-old daughter screamed seeing a badly injured Seth at their door.    He stood naked from the waist down.    She called her mom again after hearing no answer and after lowering her eyes to Seth's unusually large manhood.

[27]

"Holy shit, Seth!" her mom exclaimed. She too glanced for an uncomfortable moment at Seth's privates. "What happened? Get in the car! We're going to the doctor!"

"Think I can get a towel or something to cover myself?" Seth asked, glancing down at his bloody nakedness.

"Sure, Beth, get Seth a robe!" The daughter did, stealing another prolonged look at Seth before handing it to him. Seth spent several days in the hospital, healing both his wounds and pride. Nurse Mylee admonished him daily, reminding him of her earlier warning about hurting himself with his drinking habit.

"Here to check Big Jim and the twins!" Mylee said jokingly as she cracked Seth's front door for her daily visit since he had returned home. She visited daily to check him for infection and to dress his bandages if needed. She used the phrase Big Jim and the twins since she had heard one of his friends use it when telling him how lucky he was not to have lost his penis and testicles.

"Funny!" Seth replied, wincing in pain as he sat up to let her treat him.

"Anyway, everything looks good buddy, I'll swing by tomorrow to see if you're still kicking!" Mylee said with a warm

[28]

smile after examining his wounds. "Call me if you need me." She added, smiling and disappearing through the door.

"Damn, she is so sweet." Seth thought. He drifted into thought.

# CHAPTER 3

"Mind if I sit here?" Tony had asked Mylee one day at their high school cafeteria halfway through her sophomore year. Tony had admired her pure natural beauty since she was a freshman, but only now gathered the nerve to approach her.

"Sure," Mylee replied in a sweet and friendly voice. She was flattered that the captain of the football team, a senior, who was also the most handsome man in school would take such an interest in her.

"Want to go to the dance on Friday with me?" he asked. Her perfectly kept blond bangs highlighted her blushing face as she glanced through them with an innocent smile.

"Sure, let me ask my parents. I'll call you," she said. They exchanged phone numbers and a generous amount of small talk, each flirting with the other the entire time.

"Okay, hope to hear from you!" Tony said as Mylee left to her gym class. Tony admired her smooth and lightly olive-hued skin as the sun shimmered upon it as she left, reasoning that it was from her half-Portuguese heritage. Her naturally oversized

[31]

lips and her near-perfect woman-like, rather than girlish, figure aroused him.

"You will, I promise!" she assured him. Tony smiled and puckered his lips toward her.

"They said I can go – but I have to be home by ten," she announced to Tony over the phone later. He agreed to her parents' terms and they set the details of their date. Neither slept before thinking of the other from then on.

"Just in time!" Mylee said. They arrived back at her house before the ten o'clock curfew her parents had set the night of the dance.

"Thanks for the date, Mylee," Tony said after walking her to her doorstep with his arm wrapped around her.

Mylee smiled warmly while staring into Tony's eyes. She moistened her lips with her tongue.

"You are so beautiful, Mylee," Tony cooed as his lips fell to hers. He felt her lose her breath to the moment as he slipped his tongue beyond her lips allowing each to taste the other's warm, almost sweet, young saliva – Mylee for her very first time. She moaned breathlessly. Lust bloomed within her and propelled her a step closer to womanhood. She yearned to love and be loved. Butterflies flitted within her.

[32]

"See you tomorrow," she said, half telling and half asking, as their lips parted. She heard a stirring inside near the door.

"You will!" Tony said. He kissed her smooth cheek one last time. He held her hand as if not wanting to part.

"About time!" Mylee's identical twin sister said as Mylee entered the house. Mylee realized that the stirring she had reacted to was from her sister and not her parents.

"Idiot!" she excitedly exclaimed to her. Her sister grabbed her by the hand and drug her past their smiling parents to their room to drain her of every last detail of her date.

"Couldn't wait to see you," Mylee told Tony the next day in the hallway. He leaned close to her at her locker. They shielded their emotions and conversation from the prying ears and eyes of their classmates.

"Me too, Mylee," Tony replied. "I couldn't sleep all night!"

"I'll walk you home later if it's okay?" Tony offered.

"Sure!" Mylee responded. She glowed with teen love and her face was slightly blushed. She felt her lips begging to meet

[33]

Tony's. She took her books from her locker and held them to her chest. She was unable to pry her eyes from Tony.

"See you later," she cooed as she disappeared around the hall's corner towards her classroom.

"Hi, Tony!" a flirty voice sounded in an unnaturally long tone to the side of him. He was a short distance down the hall from where he had just parted with Mylee.

"Hey Kathy, what's up?" he replied playfully as he neared her by the door to the custodian's room.

"Hopefully this!" she said nastily. She reaching down and rubbed his penis through his pants and smiled.

"Jeez! You can't get enough!" he said. He knew that she had spent half the night before with her boyfriend "studying," as she called it to her parents. Tony had just heard about her previous night of non-stop sex from her boyfriend a half an hour earlier. "Weren't you just, ahem, studying with Adam last night?"

"Well that was him, and now I'm in the mood for you," she said. What he doesn't know doesn't hurt him—and feels good to me!" "Or are you with your little sophomore girlfriend and not into sex anymore!" she teased. She and Tony had been having sex regularly for the last two and a half years.

[34]

"Not exactly, if you can keep your mouth shut -- unless my you-know-what is in it!" Tony replied. He glanced around the hallway then reached down and began massaging her crotch. She gave Tony a coy smile and a wink and gave his penis one last big teasing squeeze.

"We'll hook up, I'll call you later!" she said. She turned to walk to her class. She gave Tony one last teasing glance and smile over her shoulder as she left.

"Okay," Tony replied. His mind drifted back to his attraction to Mylee without registering a sliver of guilt over his meeting with his pal's girlfriend, Kathy.

"I think I'm in love with you, Tony," Mylee whispered to Tony after dating him for several months.

"I love you too Mylee!" Tony replied. They professed their mutual love to each other at their every meeting or phone call throughout high school. After Tony graduated and began working at his dad's shop, he would leave work nearly every day to walk her home until she too graduated. His constant affairs never stopped. Nearly all in Edgewater knew of his trysts, but none were ever willing to violate the small town's social code of silence and tell Mylee. Would she believe them anyway?

[35]

Probably not most figured. None wanted to see her hurt. All feared jeopardizing their friendships with her.

Three months after Mylee graduated from high school Tony asked Mylee to walk with him along the river's edge, a place where they had spent untold hours hugging and kissing over the past three years. Tony walked her to face an ancient willow tree where a heart that held their initials was etched deeply into its bark. Tony had carved it to forever memorialize their love just after their first date in Mylee's sophomore year.

"You are all I have ever wanted in a woman," Tony said. He took a knee in front of her. He removed the top from a small box that held a ring. "You're all I could ever ask for," Tony professed. Mylee began to tear and her body became covered with goosebumps. "Will you marry me, Mylee?" He looked to her face to see her eyes and took the ring into his fingertips.

"YES, YES, YES!" Mylee screamed. She fell to her own knees and into Tony's arms. She pushed him to the ground and rolled in joy with him. Mylee mauled him with her kisses.

Their wedding came soon and the entire town attended. Their parents, relatives, Tony's football coach and the teachers who had taught them both. All their friends attended. Several women that

[36]

Tony had cheated with over the years came, including some that he continued to do so with. All smiled and congratulated them. None took exception to their joining when asked to do so by the priest during their ceremony. Seth congratulated them both and left the reception early. Mylee glowed in her flowing white gown. It highlighted her face's flush that deepened with each glass of Champaign. Their honeymoon took them to Maui for ten days of pure love and sex. Mylee tanned on the beach during the days admiring the calm clear waters. Tony sunned himself as well, admiring the curves of the bikini clad young women as they paraded in front of him, all of it hidden by his dark sunglasses.

"Coming home for lunch?" Mylee asked her new husband a year later. Tony had taken over his father's auto parts store—the only one in town, after his father's retirement. Mylee scheduled her nursing classes so as to allow her to spend as many lunchtime rendezvous with her husband as possible.

"Can't wait!" Tony replied, knowing that his wife would be ready to please him with either lunch or sex, and often both the minute he walked through the door.

"Okay honey, see you then!" she said, smacking a loud kiss into the phone as she hung up.

"Hi, Tony," one of his customer's wives greeted minutes later as he neared her down one of the isles in his store. Tony noticed that her body was well-toned for having a 5 year old child and being a few years his senior in age. Her shoulder length hair was neatly cut to frame her attractively round face. Her makeup was applied with perfection. A light perfume's fragrance seeped through the usually stale-smelling auto parts store.

"Hi Marla," Tony replied, " just what can I do for a pretty lady like you today?" He used a flirty voice, keeping it low to avoid the ears of his employees or other customers. A sultry smile came to her face. She shifted to straighten her body in profile to Tony and penetrated him with her eyes.

"The window in my car is always hard to roll down. I think it is sticking in the rubber around it," she said. She glanced towards the cleaning and maintenance products on the shelf briefly, then turned her attention back to Tony. She scanned the room and turned to face him. She strategically placed her folded arms under her breasts and positioned her lips to look swollen. Her eyes became relaxed as she waited for his reply.

"I like to use lube," Tony said. He smiled while brushing against her while reaching to the display of rubber-revitalizing products to her side.

"I like lube too," she said, "but I was thinking something more for my car." She smiled and glanced to the ends of the aisles.

"What about this?" she asked, smearing Tony with her breasts as she feigned to reach for one of the products. She circled his elbow with her hardened nipple as if drawing a target. She leaned away from him and looked to his pants. Tony's half erectness was apparent. She smiled in approval.

"We need to hook up, girl--ASAP!" He led her hand to his crotch where she treated herself to a probing feel.

"The old man is out of town for a few days right now. The kid is in school until three every day, so whenever you want Tony. Right here and now would work for me!"

"How about an hour from now? I'll have you for lunch!" His voice was unable to cloak his arousal. Her eyes widened at Tony's statement.

"That sounds perfect." She again glanced around the room and added, "I'll be waiting. Park in the alley and come through the back. All the neighbors are at work."

"Here, this should do," he stated loudly in a businesslike manner. He handed her the rubber lubricant and directed her towards the register. "See you in an hour," he whispered under his breath. Their eyes sealed their compact.

"Hello." Mylee answered the phone an hour after she had last talked to her husband.

"Hi honey," Tony said, "something came up on one of the oil rigs and I have to get a part out there to the mechanic. I won't be able to make lunch." He spoke quietly to her from his office. His employees had taken every incoming call and none concerned one of the drilling companies.

"It's okay, honey," Mylee responded. "I'll take off to school early so I can study in the library before class this afternoon. I can use a little more time at the books."

"Okay, honey. Love you!" he said. He heard her kiss into the phone as he hung up. He gathered some paperwork from under the counter and a part off of the shelf as his employees watched. He filled his briefcase with the papers and let them know he would return after he ran some errands.

"Screech!" Mylee's tires squealed as she came to an abrupt halt in her driveway as she was leaving for her class. She gripped the steering wheel with both hands and sighed in relief. The neighbor's four-year-old had darted behind her as she backed out.

"Whew!" she said to herself. She thought of the terror that she could have caused to the neighbor by taking their only child. She sat slumped over her steering wheel imagining that losing a child could be worse than not being able to conceive one, as in her case. "You have to be careful, baby!" she softly scolded the little boy after exiting her car. His mother, who had heard the tires squeal came running towards them. She saw the mother's look of fear and thankfulness in her face when their eyes met. She saw the innocence in the child, it not realizing what had occurred. She turned to the street and drove away.

"Damn," she thought. She was reminded of how she had innocently misled Tony about their infertility being her issue rather than his. She wanted to protect him from feeling less than a whole man. She often regretted telling the little white lie, as she quashed her ability to approach the artificial insemination subject with him. She hoped to hear Tony someday bring up the subject of adoption. She wanted to hear him want a family.

[41]

"Maybe I should just tell him. But he might feel bad." She left it at that—for now.

# CHAPTER 4

"Hi Mom," Samantha said as she arrived home from school. She wore a warm smile and reeked of positivity. Her year-old neatly kept dreadlocks accentuated her natural beauty. Unlike true Rastafarian dreadlocks that were formed from time and neglect, hers were built meticulously at an expensive hair salon in the Bay Area. Her boyfriend Andy's were built there the same day. She wore little, if any, makeup most days.

"Hi Samantha, how was school?", her nineteen-sixties-era hippie mother, Joy, inquired. Sam looked to her and began to answer but her mother interrupted.

"Went to the co-op today honey, so there's food in the fridge," Her mother said. She spoke loudly from her smoking perch on the porch. She pulled another cigarette from her pack after just putting the last one out. Seeing Sam's dismay, she announced with her usual self-righteous voice, "They're all natural!" She held up the cigarette package, displaying its brand of 'NATURALS' across its front as proof.

"They're still the same poisons, Mom," she said. Her mom glared from behind her lighter. She exhaled the smoke at Sam with contempt. "Natural," Sam thought, "Whatever that means!"

"You're home early," she said to her mom. She typically spent her day until five spewing her liberal agenda while flailing her hairy-arm-pitted arms around to her clients. They were forced to sit through her tirades in order to collect the welfare benefits that she controlled. Her mother nodded and inhaled another puff, this time exhaling it to the sky--half through her mouth and half through her nose.

"Hello sweetie! How was your day?" her dad Barry inquired as she entered the house. He rose from his computer desk to give her a hug and, unlike her mother, truly wanted to know the answer. She walked to him, looking forward to his embrace.

"Good Dad! How about yours?" she inquired equally as sincere. She had grown much closer to her father than her self-absorbed mother. Her mother had once not been able to recall what grade in school she was. Her dad knew each course she studied. Sam no longer expected her mother's attention and often felt sorry for her father. She couldn't recall her mother ever kissing him, complementing him or letting him finish a conversation without interrupting. She felt guilt at times, thinking that he bore her mother's wrath and disrespect only out of his love for her. Having no siblings, her bond with her father was deep.

"Good!" he responded, "Got a job teaching online cybersecurity classes and computer programming. It's fun. There is going to be a lot of money in this cybersecurity stuff in the future honey," he added. He had a passion for computers and especially for his particular specialty of securing them from intrusion. He had become a self-taught expert at it over the years and gained more recognition as each year passed.

"Great, Dad!" she said, "You're the man!" She gave him a two thumbs up and smiled. "Hurry up and get us rich so I can retire," she said with a broad grin and laughing. Her dad smiled, as if he liked her idea.

One day her mother finally walked in and announced, "I've had enough of this shit! I'm leaving and we're getting a divorce!" Sam and her father glanced at each other, trying not to applaud.

"Wonder what 'shit' she is talking about?" Sam thought, "She's the only one around here that ever gives anybody any!" Sam saw identical confusion in her dads face.

[45]

"Do you hear me!" she exclaimed. She cocked her hands onto her hips. They looked as if they were the jaws of a bear trap ready to spring on the first person who opened their mouth. Her eyes swept side to side from Sam to her dad waiting to hear begging for her not to go. She angered at their silence. Sam sensed her anticipation for the opportunity to launch into a protracted yuppie diatribe about how people sometimes grow apart as their lives "matured into their next phase" or some other cosmic crap.

"Fuck you!" she blurted. She turned and stormed from the house. Sam and her dad shook their heads in amazement and giggling at each other, both wondering why this occasion hadn't happened earlier. Both were relieved.


"My mom left and they're getting a divorce," Sam told her boyfriend Andy over the phone that evening. She promised herself that if they ever got married that she would never be like her mother.

"You okay, Sam?" Andy asked. He was concerned but knew that she had always spoken as if her parent's divorce was inevitable. Sam had told him several times that it would be the best thing for their family, especially for her dad.

[46]

"Yeah, fine!" she answered. "Nice and quiet around here for a change!"

"You have practice tonight?" Sam inquired, referring to Andy running laps around the track in training for their next meet. Andy was average in height and build and lacked the bulk of a football player, a sport he had no interest in anyway. His legs were long and toned in firm muscle and he excelled in long runs as well as the hurdles. He tied his salon formed dreadlocks to the rear in a ponytail during his events. He and Sam developed an attraction to each other early on as freshmen. Both had a calm and sweet air about them, enjoyed participating in environmental events, and loved animals. Both were vegetarians. Andy also reminded her of her father. He excelled in math and was one in the top computer students in their school. Andy had seen Samantha struggling in their beginning algebra class and had offered to help her. From there, their romance blossomed.

"Yeah, running the 3-mile this time," he told her, "Ton of math homework tonight too." Sam admired how serious Andy was about his future. He wanted to be an engineer like his father. Sam, unlike both her father and Andy, had no interest in the digital age and studied towards a career in nutrition, organic farming, and animal care. She loved being involved with the local animal shelter.

[47]

"Okay, see you at school tomorrow, Andy," she said, adding, "Hugs and kisses!" Both signed off with this same phrase as they departed each time. The house was remarkably calm. An ease came to Sam and her father's life. Sam went to school and Barry got to be himself.

"Barry, you come here for an ounce of weed twice a month. Why don't you just take a quarter pound and sell it to your friends and earn yours for free?" Samantha's father's friend who sold him his pot counseled one day. "Hell, half the time you are here picking it up for them anyway!"

"Makes sense to me, I'll take one," Barry said after thinking about it a moment.

A month later, a friend of Barry's that was buying weed from him inquired, "Hey Barry, think you can score me a quarter?" adding "I got a couple of buddies that want some and I can make a couple of bucks."

"No prob," Barry said. Innocently enough, Barry began buying a pound at a time because his other friends liked the idea of getting theirs for free as well. One thing led to the next, and before he knew it, Barry was selling ten or twenty pounds a month and was enjoying both the smoke and a couple grand a

[48]

month in tax-free income. "Hell, it's just weed!" he rationalized to himself.

The local police chief, Captain Mike Smith, or 'Shitbag Smith' as he was known by most of the folks in town because of him being such an ass, caught wind of Barry's extracurricular marijuana activities. A particular asinine-wannabe-cop that graduated in Barry's class, and who visited him on rare occasions, spilled the beans to the police chief trying to kiss his butt. Nobody liked Captain Smith, but his family had deep roots and political connections in the community, so he got the position.

"I'd like to put that long-haired hippie son of a bitch in jail!" Shitbag Smith thought to himself as he patrolled their little town one afternoon. "It would be nice to be known as the one who finally cleaned up the drugs in this shithole town and make a name for myself!" He removed his drill-instructor-type hat and wiped his flat-topped hair with his hand to remove the sweat. The scalped sides of his head glimmered in the sun as he drove down the street.

"GET THOSE MUTTS ON A LEASH OR I'LL TAKE THEM TO THE POUND WHERE THEY BELONG!" He screamed out of his car window to a pair of old women walking their aged dogs in the local downtown park as he passed. He didn't see both old ladies give him the middle-fingered salute and mouth the word "PRICK!"

[49]

Barry passed Shitbag Smith a couple of days later while walking to his car from the local coffee shop.

"What's up with your what's-up Smitty," Barry said, knowing Smith liked to be referred to as Captain Smith. He drew further ire by lifting his chin once to greet him in a street-slangy way. Smith's face reddened in anger.

Smith mumbled, "you long haired hippie prick!" under his breath so that only Barry could hear it. Barry noticed a more-than-usual evil air about him. Smith's eyes shifted oddly and Barry sensed a determination in him. He noticed Smith's body language conveying an "I'm going to get you" air.

"Weird," Barry thought. He knew that Smith didn't like him for a plethora of reasons, the first being that he had an I.Q. about triple Smith's. "Hmmm," Barry thought, "that prick is up to something no good. Must be the pot. I don't trust that bastard!" Barry cleared the pot from his house that evening and stopped by each of his friend's houses who were also in the business.

"I think Shitbag Smith is on the prowl for us," he informed each one.

All of them responded identically, "Fucking prick!" and cleared the pot from their houses.

"I know that long-haired hippie bastard is pushing drugs!" Smith said as he sat with his old pal --the equally despised district attorney Jerry Ramsey. "All we need is a way to search that hippie fucker's house and his ass is ours, Jerry!" Smith said with an evil smirk on his face. "Wouldn't hurt either one of our careers either, you know Jerry." He looked at the D.A. with a more serious look. Both knew that recent budget cuts had the city council evaluating every department's performance and that a new city manager was being sought.

"All we have to do is tell the judge we have a confidential informant, and he won't question us," Smith told Ramsey. "The judge's daughter was in rehab twice for crank and he hates drug pushers," he added. He was unaware that the term "pusher" hadn't been used for several decades. Ramsey agreed and they drafted a search warrant for Barry's house. They claimed under oath that they had a confidential informant saying that Barry was selling large quantities of drugs from his house. As predicted, the judge granted their warrant to tap Barry's phone.

"That figures!" Barry thought to himself. His phone tap detection device began blinking during each of his calls a few days after seeing Smith at the coffee shop. "What a prick!" He drove to each of his buddies' homes and let them know that his phone, and possibly theirs, were under surveillance. He organized a meeting with them all at a local pub the following evening. At the pub, he shared a plan to embarrass Smith and leave him looking like an ass. The plan was creative and sounded like fun. They all laughed the evening away, refining their ploy while drinking their ale. They clinked their mugs in toast to their plan before leaving.

"I wish I could get my hands on about 10 kilos of the best memory enhancing shit I could get," one of Barry's friends said to him over the tapped phone line.

"I can get it for you but it's going to cost you," Barry replied. He strained to not allow a hint of the grin he sported to be revealed in his tone of voice. His other friends chimed in similarly until Barry was tasked with obtaining nearly a hundred kilos of the best "shit" he could get. He called each friend informing them, "My house, at two tomorrow afternoon!" They all agreed to meet, money in hand, for the big transaction.

"This is it!" Shitbag Smith exclaimed to Ramsey, "We've got that hippie fucker now!" Both reeled with excitement, envisioning the upcoming boost to their careers. Smith sprang into action and put together a task force for the big bust. Officers from every surrounding county were recruited. Warrants to search the houses of three of Barry's friends were obtained using both the fake confidential informant's statements and a summary of the telephone wiretap's transcripts.

As planned, at two the following after noon, Barry's buddies entered his house, all carrying empty bank-issued money bags and carrying empty satchels that Smith knew was to carry drugs back to their homes. Barry and his friends sat laughing, drinking beer, and eating pizza. Suddenly, the street came alive! Police cars, some marked and others not, skidded to a halt at various angles in front of Barry's house. Two dozen officers, all clad in camo dungarees and bulletproof vests and armed with an array of military-style weapons exploded from the vehicles.

"FREEZE!! Don't move!" one of them screamed as they kicked Barry's door open. The unlocked door slammed against its stop, surprising the officers.

"Get on the ground!" a chorus of police voices sounded as they waived their assault weapons in every direction.

"Don't shoot!" Barry screamed. He and his friends readily complied with all of the officers' demands. Smith's adrenaline was pumping; pride and satisfaction emanated from his face. He looked down at Barry who was lying face down with his hands cuffed behind him.

"You're going up the river for a long time you long-haired hippie piece of shit!" he said. The district attorney stood for a photo op with the press, who he and Smith had notified just prior to their leaving the station. The press nearly beat them to the location of the impending bust. Barry looked over his shoulder at Smith from his face-down prone position on the floor.

"What the fuck are you talking about Smitty?" he said. The casual address of Capt. Smith caused one of the officers from the next county to look perplexed, thinking the two of them were friends.

"It's Captain Smith to you, hippie scum!" Smith responded while glancing toward the officer. "Search those boxes over there," he said. He pointed to some unmarked cardboard boxes stacked in a corner of the living room. "And turn this fucking place upside down," he added. The officers scattered through the house, dislodging drawers from their pockets, dumping canisters into the sink and emptying books from their shelves.

One of the camo suited cops slung his weapon over his back and began to rip into the boxes, all marked with a number and the word "kilos" following it. He tore from one to the other, seeing nothing but metallic discs and circuit boards. Each was labeled in red permanent marker with the same number as on their box. Atop the contents of each of the boxes was an eight by twelve inch color copy of a cartoon pig wearing a pink tutu and standing on its toes in a pirouette position. Each pig was winking one of its huge eyelashes. The quote "What's up big boy!" appeared in a speech balloon over its head. Handwritten on the inside of each card was: "To Capt. Smith and District Attorney Ramsey-- How many kilos of this memory would you like to buy. It's good shit!" A hand-drawn smiley face was drawn under the writing.

"You motherfucker!" Smith screamed at Barry. His face turned in stages from blood red to purple.

"Nothing back there. Nothing anywhere," the officers each reported as they returned from searching their designated rooms. The one officer who opened the boxes and passed the drawings to Smith and the DA grinned to the others and handed them their own copies of the pig.

"I don't get it," Smith said to the district attorney under his breath. Both had huge fake smiles adorning their faces for the benefit of the news cameras. The pictures of him and the D.A.

were to be printed the following day representing the biggest fiasco ever to have occurred in their community.

"Smooth move, Ex-lax!" one of the officers from the next county taunted to Smith. He laughed in his face as he left. The sheriff's captain from the next county shook his head in disgust and ordered his men to return to their vehicles. He ripped all the search warrants up and threw them at Smith's feet.

"Fucking dipshit," one of the other cops exclaimed to Smith as he walked by on the way to his car.

"Fucking idiot!" another exclaimed, letting out an audible wince of disgust as he passed.

"Nothing here, let's go," D.A. Ramsey orated to the press. He ushered them out the door as quickly as possible. He saw each one laugh at him over their shoulder as they left. "You fucking prick!" he scowled at Smith as he left the property.

"You're going to be sorry, you motherfucker, and I mean sorry!" Smith said. "Sooner or later, you hippie fucker, your ass will be mine!" Smith jerked Barry to his feet as painfully as he could. He removed his handcuffs and stomped out the door, still purple-faced with anger.

It all made for good press in the small town and the surrounding communities. The lies on the affidavit almost cost both Smith and Ramsey their jobs had a local heroin junkie not overdosed and died the following day so they could claim he was the informant. Captain Smith seethed with anger every day.

# CHAPTER 5

"Mom, I'm in love with a boy," Layla told her mother, failing to recognize the sadness in her mother's face. Her mother laid the laundry that she was folding on the counter.

"Since when? Who are we talking about here, honey?" her mother inquired of her sophomore-in-high-school daughter. "And what makes you think that?" she added before Layla had time to respond to her last question.

"I don't know, Mom, I just feel it. He is just so sweet, and I know he loves me too!" Layla responded. Her face was flushed and butterflies flitted within her.

"Who?" her mom responded again anxiously.

"Ian." she replied, "You know, the kid whose dad has that place where Uncle Ray buys the hay for his horses out on Bird Road."

"Oh, yeah," her mom said as her mind's eye built an image of Ian, " that good- looking blond kid who always wears jeans and a white t-shirt? He's always working out there on his dad's place when we drive by?" she continued, making sure she had the right young man pegged as her daughter's first love.

"Yeah, Mom, him," she cooed.

"Hmm…" Her mom exhaled and tilted her head and eyes upward in deeper contemplation as she turned outward from the laundry room. The room's permanent smell of fabric softener followed her to the kitchen where she sat with her coffee to digest the news. Layla followed. "Good family," she said. The boy's father had a reputation as a hard-working, quiet and well-thought-of Viet Nam veteran. Everyone in town considered him a war hero.

"Seems like a nice boy," she said. Layla's eyes glowed at her mother's compliment.

"He is, Mom," Layla chimed, "He's going to be a Marine, like his dad and uncle!"

"That's nice," her mom replied, "He has that look of a Marine." She pictured his not-bulked-up but well-proportioned over-six-foot frame, his square dimpled-chinned jaw, and his closely groomed well-kept hair.

[60]

"His parents are really sweet too, Mom."

"That's what I've heard." Her mom recalled one of her friends mentioning that the wife had told her that they never argued and how she had a nearly reverent respect for her husband. "A good man," she thought, reflecting on her own husband's same qualities.

"That's good, honey." Layla was comforted by her mother's approval. She knew that her father would trust her mother's judgment and be equally accepting. Layla bounced upstairs to her room.

"Not the time," her mother thought, having planned to tell Layla that day about the dire results of her father's recent doctor's appointment. Her body filled with dread. She imagined her daughter's upcoming pain when she learned that her father was diagnosed with a fast-moving and terminal lung cancer. Layla, nor her brother had an inkling of his illness.

Layla's father returned from his final day at work as a petroleum engineer. He kissed Layla's mom, but forwent his usual chat with her. He settled alone in the living room to read the paper.

"Well, our daughter has her first love, honey!" Layla's mom informed him. He raised his head from the newspaper and glanced curiously over the top of his reading glasses. He turned an ear towards his wife and stared at her.

"It's that kid..." Layla's mom went on, describing Ian's dad's farm and who he was. She saw her husband become more relaxed at her every statement. He began to realize who she was describing. He knew the boy's family and had the highest respect for them.

"Think it's too young?" Layla's dad inquired. He listened keenly for her response.

"Probably," she answered with a joking grin on her face. Her husband smiled as well. He realized that they had met and fallen in love at the same age.

"Whatever," he replied. He went back to his paper. She kissed his greying hair and hugged him with a loving grip on the nap of his neck.

"That boy Ian is a good kid, honey," Layla's dad said at dinner. Layla beamed with pride as she thanked her mother with her eyes. "Just don't get too carried away!" he counseled in a firm voice.

"Okay, Daddy. I promise," she vowed, slightly cringing in shyness at his meaning.

"Good for you, Layla!" her six-year-older brother Scott said when she called him that evening. "You just don't get carried away, Layla!" he scolded.

"You sound just like Dad!" she scoffed kiddingly. "I won't Scott, I promise."

"Hey Layla," her brother said in closing, "pull Dad's finger for me would you!" They both laughed as they shared the thought of their dad's favorite antic. They both recalled how they used to brawl trying to be first to him for the honor of doing so when he asked. Layla laughed as her brother mimicked her mother screaming "ERIC!" each time he farted. They laughed over her acting shocked over his not-so-aromatic antics, having been married for so many years.

"Hey Scott, I almost forgot, Mom wants me to ask you to come home this weekend for a visit and a little family meeting. Can you make it?" Layla asked her brother.

"Why, what's up? Is everything okay?" he responded with concern in his voice.

"Yeah, I think so. Mom didn't say much, but I know they mentioned selling the house a while back. Probably something to do with that."

[63]

"Sure, I'll be there Saturday morning," Scott replied.

"Remember sis, you be good!"

"I will", she again promised.

"He just needs your love, kids, and to know you will never forget him," Layla's mom consoled both Layla and Scott the following Saturday afternoon. She had taken the kids to a quiet riverside park to inform them of their father's terminal condition.

"They say it will be a few months, actually very few, kids," she told them. They all sat in tears, fearing life without the anchor of their father. "He is a strong man. His only fear of dying is that he worries about you kids. Let him know you will be okay. It will help him through this." They collapsed into each other's arms, crying and searching for the perfect words to convey their love to their father. There were none.

"I love you so much, Daddy," Layla purred into her dad's ear a year later. She poured her heartbroken body into his arms as he began to fade into unconsciousness. She was angry that the cancer was taking her father so quickly and unable to be grateful that he had lived a few months longer than predicted.

[64]

"I love you too, honey, I'm sorry," he said with a weak but loving smile on his face. She wept into his chest and held him as if trying to keep him from going.

"You're the best dad in the world, Daddy, please don't be sorry for that," she begged through her tears. Her father looked at her. The light was glimmering in his tears. "I will love you every day until I die and I will think of you and pray to you every day." A weak smile grew on his pale and shrunken face. "Daddy, you have made me so strong and taught me how to love. We all love you so much." She held her face to his, imagining what it was going to be like to never again feel his whiskers abrade her cheeks. She already began to miss his fatherly scent. She had lived her entire life as if this day would never come. She swallowed her tears as she gave him a final hug. She kissed his cheek as she felt him become limp in her arms. She lifted her saddened face to her mom and brother. "He's gone." she cried in disbelief. She crawled into his bed and covered herself with his arms, pitifully wanting him to hold her.


Layla laid alone in her room and cried each night until his funeral. She was inconsolable for days after it, but knew her dad would want her to be strong and be there for her mother. She did her best. Her brother returned each weekend to lend his strength to

[65]

their family—and perhaps to gain some. Time became their friend, helping them to heal with each passing day. Weeks passed, then months, then years.

"Whoops!" Her brother insincerely exclaimed. He passed the loudest gas she had ever heard while hugging Layla a couple years later. "I meant to offer you the pleasure of pulling this finger!" He held his index finger erect into the air. Layla feigned trying to pull herself away from him, stopped herself to yank firmly on his index finger. Their eyes met and they both fell out laughing. That was the moment when everything became all right. Good memories began to flow.

"Dad is cracking up in heaven!" she said. They laughed heartily through their tears.

# CHAPTER 6

"You make sure you respect that girl, son," Ian's father counseled after Ian had professed his love for Layla to his parents at the dinner table.

"I will, dad," Ian promised.

"She's very pretty and her parents are good folks, son," his mother added. She was picturing Layla's near perfect model height and her attractive long legs. She seemed as more of a woman than a fifteen-year-old young lady to her.

"They are really good people," Ian replied, "and Layla is the prettiest girl in school!" Her picture appeared in his mind. He saw her cute and slightly-pointed-upward nose, piercing green eyes that seemed to change color with her mood, and her almost unblemished pastel-hued skin. He sighed as his mind drifted to her full and soft lips that he had kissed only hours earlier.

"Potatoes, Ian?" his mom asked as she leaned towards him from her chair with a heaping spoonful.

"Sure, Mom," he answered. His precious daydream disappeared into his meal. He completed his final evening chores, showered and went to bed. Layla's image never left him.

Their love flourished all through high school. Layla's friends, many of whom had lost their first loves to teen lust, envied her relationship. Ian's devotion to her remained unwavering. His goal of becoming a Marine never ebbed. Ian and Layla were deeply bonded from their first meeting.

"I do!" Layla enthusiastically responded to the priest. She vowed to love and cherish Ian until her death at their wedding just after she had graduated from high school. They added their own flavor to their vows, the last of it being their promise to one another to never be untruthful and to never break a promise.

"I pronounce you man and wife!" the priest declared. Layla leaped into Ian's arms and began kissing him passionately, even before being granted the priest's permission to do so. A roar of laughter erupted from the crowd, including from the priest himself.

"Congratulations, Layla!" her brother told her, still beaming from the honor of standing in for their father to "give her away".

"Thank you, Scott," Layla replied, "and you too, Lauri," she added to her brother's wife. She was a truly kind schoolteacher that he had met in college. She kissed Layla gently on the cheek.

"Welcome to the family, brother!" Scott said as he shifted his hug from Layla to Ian. Layla's mother came next. Ian's entire family found their turns with them both, as did every person in the crowd. Layla glowed and leaned inward to accept a kiss and hug from each well-wisher. Ian stood directing most of the admiration to his bride.

Their marriage was their dream—Ian's dream of being a Marine was part of it.


"I love you Ian, and I always will," Layla sobbed through her tears. Only a year later they stood on the Tarmac at Travis Air Force Base. Ian stood dressed in his sand-colored camouflaged military dungarees.

"Please be careful and come back to me Ian, I can't live without you!" she begged. For the first time Ian was leaving for deployment to a war—not a training mission like all the others. She tried to accept that within hours he would be landing in Iraq. Her stomach was in knots.

"Quit worrying, Angel!" Ian replied in a dismissive tone. He hadn't shared with Layla about being accepted into the elite Marine Recon whose assignments were some of the most dangerous. He grasped her shoulders and leaned her back so she could see into his eyes.

"Don't worry Honey, I will be back, everything will be fine." His eyes were unconvincing. She hugged her head against his chest. His uniform became drenched in her tears.

"Ian, I love you and you will be in my heart every day.

"I know Angel", Ian said as he pried her from him. "I'll call you every chance I get, I promise."


A firm military voice suddenly echoed across the tarmac, "Fall in!" They hugged once more. He turned toward the plane to board as ordered. He looked back as he reached the door of the plane, seeing tears flowing freely down her cheeks from the distance. They smiled at each other as he disappeared into the bowels of the sand-colored plane. She turned and collapsed into her mother's waiting arms.

[70]

Ian grunted as he slung his duffel bag over his shoulder after landing in Iraq. Just as his feet hit the tarmac, the sergeant that was there to greet them screamed, "Atten-hut!" They all stood erect as 15 flag-draped caskets were carried towards the plane that sat next to theirs. The Marines that held them marched in half-steps at half-time—the funeral march.

"Order arms!" the NCO screamed as the coffins passed them. Ian and his fellow Marines raised their flattened hands briskly to the brim of their hats in salute. Sadness filled Ian's heart. He stood imagining the pain of the families waiting at home for the remains of what was once their son, father, or husband. He pictured another newly arriving group of Marines standing in this same place watching his own body being loaded onto his final flight home. "I'm so sorry," he said to himself. His head bowed toward the ground and a tear fell to it.

"At ease!" the sergeant announced once the last body was loaded onto the plane. Ian relaxed his salute and rolled his sleeve across the palm of his hand to wipe the tears from the sides of his nose. He hoped that no one had noticed his crying. He looked to the sergeant who had screamed the orders and saw him doing the same, uncaring of being noticed doing so. The sergeant dried his tears and immediately motioned to Ian and the rest of the men to gather around him using sweeping arm motions.

"We're in a war zone now, boys," the sergeant said, "be prepared to fight for your life and your fellow Marines' lives at any second. From here on out, here and now, on base, or anywhere in this shithole country you can die any minute. There is your fair warning. Now stay alert and you might leave here alive! Follow me." He turned and led them towards a half-burned aircraft hanger where they were issued weapons of various sorts. Each donned an uncomfortably heavy flak jacket. They were supplied with state-of-the-art night vision equipment, and shirt-mounted communications gear.

"Whew!" Ian exhaled to a fellow Marine who had donned all the same gear as he. He saw an equal amount of perspiration pouring from his fellow Marine's face. "Shit's heavy!" He said with a strained look to his face. Two fellow Marines standing nearby nodded in agreement.

"Oh, and stay fucking hydrated Marines!" the sergeant ordered. "Half the sick calls here are from idiots that don't drink enough water. There are drinking fountains set up everywhere around here and you don't ask to use them. This ain't training anymore and if the Marine Corps wanted you to have a babysitter, they would have issued you one. Take care of yourselves." A line formed immediately at every nearby water fountain.

"Come on guys!" the sergeant yelled after allowing the Marines to hydrate. He again used sweeping arm motions after realizing that a nearby jet had drowned out his voice. He led them across the mortar-scarred tarmac to a group of armored personnel carriers there to transport them to their base.

"Keep magazines in your weapons at all times gentlemen! Don't put a shell in the chamber when you are in a vehicle or barracks, but any other time you feel like it, knock yourselves out! And goddammit, keep the fucking safety on until you go to shoot one of those bastards for Christ's sake so you don't blow somebody's fucking head off!" They all nodded in understanding.

"Check it out," one of the marines said, flicking his head towards the side of the road.

"Holy shit!" Ian exclaimed, seeing a hole from a roadside bomb the size of a three-car garage. They both began dissecting the vehicle in which they rode. The same flick of the head and same view was seen several more times on the twenty-two-mile trip from Baghdad to their base.

[73]

"Be prepared for those, driving or walking, as that's how these chicken shit mother fuckers fight," the sergeant instructed. He noticed the men in awe of the massive bomb craters. "I guess I can't blame the fuckers, it's their only chance. They don't own so much as one plane or chopper."

The ride in the armored personnel carrier was rough, slow, hotter than hell, and other than a couple of bullet-proof side windows, had only a view of the other Marines and the metallic insides of the vehicle. The air was still and stale. After about forty-five minutes of breathing diesel fumes and not being able to hear himself think, Ian arrived at his remote Marine base. The entire perimeter was lined with thick concrete blocks stacked into walls about ten feet high. Heavily fortified guard towers appeared every hundred meters or so around the perimeter. Each had two portholes on all four sides from which to shoot. Ian wondered about the ones that pointed to the interior of the camp. Small heavily fortified sandbagged bunkers were scattered throughout the inside of the base to dive into during the too-often enemy mortar attacks. Over time, Ian made use of these small shelters too many times to count, barely making it inside one in time on more than several occasions. The sleeping areas were underground bunkers, reinforced with steel and sandbags over concrete blocks.

"That ought to do!" Ian thought, examining his sleeping barracks and seeing only slightly damaged sandbags around it. "At least there's no holes like those on the road. He felt relief from knowing the enemy had no air force.

"I'm just a watcher, pretty much," Ian described to Layla about what his job was when he called her a few weeks later. He considered his not-so-white lie acceptable in order to keep her from worrying. 'Reconnaissance,' Layla surmised was, by its definition, just that. She didn't realize that Marine Recon was the equivalent of the Navy Seals or the Army Green Berets--the most specialized commandos of the armed forces. They were used for the most important and risky missions.

"We aren't here to fight," he told her. "We kind of just sneak around in four-man teams to see what the enemy is up to so the platoons can raid them and take them out." He didn't mention his second job of being a sniper, whose job was often sitting atop a building during a heavy firefight and killing the enemy one by one from his perch.

"Well just don't take any chances that you don't have to, Ian", Layla said. "I worry." Her voice trembled. They expressed their usual love and Ian relinquished the phone to another waiting Marine.

"Layla would kill me!" he thought one evening a couple months later. He'd barely made it back to base alive and was talking to her from a wheelchair. He sat recovering in the base hospital after receiving a wound that nearly severed the main artery in his left leg but had broken no bones. One of his four-man team members had perished in the same firefight. He was offered a leave to heal for a month out of the war zone, but he wanted to stay with his team. The doctors expected a full recovery in just a few weeks.

"Not much happening here right now so we are taking a little break in base camp," he explained, again telling a not-so-little white lie.

"Are you sure you're okay, Ian?"' Layla asked.

"Fine," he replied. "Quit being such a worry wart!" He monitored his own voice's tone.

"I just worry," she said.

[76]

"I know you do. I'll be home before you know it!" Ian said. He was thinking about how he was going to explain the gaping scar from the gunshot wound. "Just a 'flesh wound'," he planned to tell her. "Hey, these buttholes want me to come play cards with them, honey, I better go," he told Layla. The nurse was summoning him to his doctor's appointment.

"I love you and you be careful for me. Okay, Ian?" Layla softly admonished.

"I will Angel, I promise," he replied. He heard her kiss the phone as he took it from his ear.

Ian sat still in his chair, his arms folded in front of him, and his eyes seeming to stare through everything around him. He began reliving the firefight that led to his wound.

"Should have seen it coming!" he thought. "No locals, just dogs, way too quiet!" He pictured his team being ambushed by two dozen enemy fighters. He relived the hail of gunfire and seeing the first shot nearly sever the lower jaw of his team member, who ran for cover while firing back as if the bullet had missed him entirely. He felt his adrenaline flow as he pictured several enemy fighters crumpling into dead flesh piles after he placed their hearts into his sights and squeezed his trigger. He recalled the hollow thump of the enemy's round piercing another

[77]

of his team member's stomach, and how he fired at them madly as he dragged him to safety behind the concrete wall of a house. Only later did he realize that the bullet pierced the man's heart, killing him instantly. He had run toward the enemy, killing a half dozen of them as they exposed themselves. He reached a point where he was able to heave a grenade into their midst, killing almost every one of them. The few that were left scattered in fear for their lives. The gunfire then faded to an eerie silence – except for the moaning of the dying.

"Ready, Ian?" a white-clad nurse chimed with a cheery voice. Her voice startled him. He paled.

"Sure," he said. She grabbed the handles of his wheelchair and maneuvered him to the examining room. His color returned to him as they went.

"Thank you, sir," Ian said to the base commander upon his return from the hospital. Ian stood in freshly pressed camo dungarees as the Colonel pinned a Purple Heart medal to his chest and a Silver Star for bravery.

"Above and beyond the call of duty," Ian thought as the award was read aloud. He stood thinking more as if he deserved a beating for letting his teammate die like a dog that evening. "What the fuck do they mean by that? I just did my job."

"You deserve it, Ian," he heard from behind him as he felt a hand lay on his shoulder. "If it wasn't for you, none of us would be alive!". He turned to see the voice was from his team member that wasn't killed or wounded, and who had recounted the story to Ian's superiors that led to his being recognized for bravery. The man served proudly under Ian for the rest of their tour in Iraq. Each saved the other's life on more than one occasion. They identified themselves as brothers.


"What a thirteen months!"' Ian reflected as the jet taking them home began its taxi down the airstrip. The six team members he had lost during his tour came to his mind. "I made it alive out of this shithole!" he thought, accidentally verbalizing the statement aloud. A fellow Marine seated next to him nodded with the same sentiment. The flight home was somber. The in-flight sandwiches were stale. The acrid odor of burnt flesh seemed to be imbedded in his mind.


"I love you so much!" Layla blubbered through tears as threw herself into his arms. She cried and smothered him with kisses.

[79]

She began smearing her face against his chest like a purring kitten.

"I love you too," Ian replied. She lifted her head and grabbed him flat-handed on both sides of his face and again devoured him with kisses.

"I was so afraid for so long, Ian," she purred, "I missed you so much. I never want you to leave me ag...." She stopped mid-sentence. Ian hugged her to him.

"Don't worry now, I'm here, Layla." He said.

"Hi, honey!" Layla's mom said to Ian as they neared the car. She hugged him firmly and kissed his cheek. She left a bright red imprint of her lips on it.

"Hello, mother-in-law!" Ian greeted. His oft used term of endearment caused a warm smile to bloom across her face.

"Good to have you back, Ian", she said. "I look forward to spending some time with you as soon as I get back from visiting Scott for a couple days." Layla glanced at Ian and smiled.

"She is such a golden person," Ian thought, thinking how she and Layla shared so many good qualities.

"Guess what?" Layla chimed to Ian with a big grin on her face.

[80]

"No telling," Ian kidded with his own smile.

"Stuffed red bell peppers!" she blurted out. Ian's face lit up and his mouth began to water.

"Mmmmmmm," Ian murmured. His stomach suddenly growled like a bear. Layla laughed at him. He swept the saliva from the edges of his mouth with his tongue.

"I thought we would go out for dinner tomorrow to see all your friends. But I have plans for you tonight, Big Boy!" Layla said provocatively while leaning to him so that her lips nearly touched his. "Am I being selfish?"

"Oh, hell no!" Ian replied. He grinned widely.


"Here," Layla said. She lifted each of Ian's legs to unlace his boots as he sat on the couch after finishing dinner. He sat with his eyes closed as she massaged his feet. She was unable to remove her eyes from him.

"I've missed you so much," Ian said, smiling gently at her. He fought to not drift any further towards sleep. Layla rose to her feet and presented her hand in invitation. She grinned broadly, then suddenly jerked him forward to his feet. She drug him at race-car pace into their bedroom, giggling the entire time.

[81]

"I'd report you for rape if I had the energy!" Ian teased after their sexual session. Layla sat unclothed straddling him. She let him catch his breath for a moment and launched herself upon him again before letting him rest.

"Go to sleep baby, we have a big day tomorrow," Layla said after their encounter. She massaged him gently using only her fingertips until feeling, and then seeing, the massive scar on his left inner thigh.

"It's just a scratch," Ian said, seeing Layla's eyes locked onto the scar. "You sleep too, Layla, your day will be just as busy as mine." He moved her hand from the scar. She massaged her husband into a deep sleep.

"I hope!" Layla thought as she laid next to Ian, contemplating their mutual decision to forgo contraception during his leave. Her mind drifted as she listened to Ian's deep breaths. "Poor guy," she thought, feeling him twitch and hearing him mumble through his deep sleep. She laid her head on his arm and drifted to sleep with him. Her last thought of the evening was of becoming a mother.

"Hi Ian, it's Mom!" his mother chirped over the phone. He could tell that she was powered by too many cups of coffee. She had awoken early.

"Hey, Mom! What's for breakfast?"

"Guess!" she teased.

"Let me see, hmmm," Ian insincerely pondered, "biscuits and gravy, scrambled eggs and Linguica sausage." His mother laughed. She knew he was aware that she would make his favorite.

"We'll be there in about an hour, Mom."

"Okay, love you Honey!" she said. She hung up the phone and rushed to tell his father before hearing his 'I-love-you' reply. They dined on his favorite breakfast and stayed for both lunch and dinner. His mother followed them to the car as they left. She waved as they rounded the corner out of sight.


"Hey buddy, beer me!" Ian heard from his pal Seth over the phone as they entered their house that evening. Ian laughed. Layla saw his face glow at hearing Seth's voice.

"I will, you crazy bastard. How about four o'clock at the pub tomorrow?" Ian replied.

[83]

"You got a date, big boy!" Seth said as he laughed. He hung up the phone and alerted the rest of their mutual friends. Layla loved watching her husband being smothered with attention.

"It's going to be a fun day, honey," Layla said, smiling at Ian warmly. They enjoyed another wonderful and intimate night together.

"It's good to see it all still here," Ian said to Layla in a nearly inaudible voice the next day. The drove slowly on their way home from their meeting with Seth and his friends at the local pub.

"What do you mean?" Layla asked.

"You know, my friends, my family." His voice became contemplative. "You," he added after a long pause. Layla reached across the car's center console and took Ian's hand. She listened.

"I don't know," he continued, "It all seemed so far away when I was over there. I sometimes wondered if it would all be, you know, changed. Sometimes I wondered if I would be too different to be a part of it all again." Layla noticed moisture gathering in his eyes. She lifted his hand to her lips and kissed it. "I even wondered a couple times if I was going to make it back."

[84]

Layla was sickened with worry from his words. She again kissed his hand.

"I'm here Ian. I always will be. You never doubt that, okay?" She said, "All of us will all always be here Ian. We all love you!" She sensed a loneliness. "I promise Ian, Seth will be on that very same barstool when you get back the next time!" Ian looked up at her with a wide grin.

"I'll take that bet!" Ian said. They both laughed. Layla hid the worry that had overcome her from hearing his thoughts. The terrible wound on his leg appeared in her mind.

Ian felt his thirty-day leave flying by as if it were one of the many low flying fighter jets that buzzed him every day in Iraq. "Here one minute, gone the next," he thought as he compared the two in his mind. He savored the time he spent with his mom, doing little chores that she implied only he could do, so as to steal little bits of time with him. However, she took great care to leave him mostly to his wife.

"Fishing tomorrow?" Ian's dad asked him one night as he was leaving his parents' house after dinner. His leave from the

[85]

military was nearing its end and he'd promised his father some time together on the river.

"Sure dad," he said. His father sealed their arrangement with a nod.


As planned, at six the following morning Ian's dad showed up to his house with his boat in tow. The sun was just peeking over the top of the levee across the river to the east.

"Ready?" his dad yelled through the half-rolled-down passenger window of his truck after seeing Ian poke his body out the door to acknowledge his arrival. Ian nodded and grabbed his fishing gear that he had waiting on the porch. Layla waved "good morning" to her father-in-law from the front steps before kissing Ian goodbye.


The fishing was good—thanks to Ian's dad's many years of knowledge of the river. He knew all of the 'when's' and 'how's. They spent as many hours talking as they did fishing. They dined on the two paper-sacked lunches that Ian's mother had meticulously prepared for them the night before. They each drank two beers.

"What do you think, son, call it a day?" Ian's dad asked. The sun was melting to bed behind the rolling hills to the west.

"Why not, we've got a meal!" Ian said. He glanced over the side of the boat at the three arm's-length fish they had on the fish stringer. Ian added kiddingly, "Kicked your ass again, old man!" A broad smile grew on the face of the man that had taught him to fish. Ian pulled the fish stringer on board and laid it in the bottom of the boat. His dad began to pull the anchor. Suddenly his dad stopped and turned to Ian with deep concern carved into his face. Ian looked to see the reason for the delay.

"Son, I know they are going to send you back over there. Promise me that you will be careful. I couldn't imagine losing you." his dad said. His head tilted sadly to the bottom of the boat, then returned his look to Ian.

"I will Dad, I promise," Ian said. He saw love in his father's eyes. His dad had noticed the two medals adorning Ian's uniform when his wife had taken it to the dry cleaners. He recognized them both as being the same ones that hung on his own uniform in the attic of their home. He took Ian into his arms.

"Son, think before you do anything stupid," he said. His eyes begged, but he knew well that such awards are only given for

[87]

acting selflessly during a fierce battle and that Ian faced more of them.

"I will Dad, I swear," he again promised. His dad nodded but knew that such a promise was only good up to the point when a fellow Marine's life was on the line and reaction preceded judgment.

"I love you, son," his dad said as he hugged Ian with all his might. He kissed his head just above the temple as he did when Ian was a child.

"I love you too, Dad," Ian said. He returned the hug with an equal amount of force. His dad pulled the anchor and they sat quietly beside each other as they returned home. Ian sat staring at the shores of the islands, wondering if he would ever see them again. His time at home seemed so short.

"I love you so much, Ian!" Layla repeated over and over to Ian as they stood on the same tarmac that he had arrived on just thirty days earlier. Ian was again leaving to what Layla saw as pure terror that could take her husband away from her forever. Tears that she had tried unsuccessfully to dam within her streamed from the bottoms of her saddened eyes. "Come back to me!" she said, looking at Ian with an almost scolding look.

"I will, I promi...," he said, unwilling to finish his sentence. His mid-sentence stop frightened her. He hadn't told Layla that the war had worsened. "Hey, I will be fine", he said, while faking a look of certainty. "I love you, Layla." He handed her weakened body to the arms of her mother when called to board the plane. He waved to her briefly at the top of the stairs and disappeared from sight.

"Hi, angel!" Ian greeted Layla on the phone after being in Iraq for several weeks.

"Ian!" Layla screamed at the top of her lungs.

"What Layla, what's wrong?" Ian screamed. He became sick with worry from the tone of her voice."

"Honey!!" Layla blurted several times in repetition as if searching for words.

"What Layla? Calm down and tell me what's wrong!" Ian demanded.

"I'm pregnant!" she finally managed to utter.

"Are you kidding me!" he said. He drifted into a moment of thoughtful silence. Separated by oceans, but never feeling closer, Ian cupped the phone with both hands and pressed it to his mouth. He blubbered undiscernible words through his tears.

"I love you!" Ian finally blurted in a decipherable voice. "And tell the baby I love her too!" He paused and looked up from the phone. "Is it a her?"

Layla laughed heartily. "We don't know yet Daddy, not for a few more months!"

"Okay then," Ian corrected, "Tell it I love it!" He began to laugh. After many minutes of excitement, they ended their conversation.

"Daddy...," Ian spoke aloud as he threw his feet up on the desk. He sat in silence, his hands folded behind his head staring at the ceiling with a grin.

# Chapter 7

"There goes that crankster bitch from down the street!" Abel heard the worker at the gas station point out to his co-worker as he was putting gas into his car. "She comes down here to meet guys that she whores herself out to for drugs."

"Nasty looking bitch!" the co-worker exclaimed with a look of disgust. Abel glanced from behind the pump, seeing his mother for the first time in months. He couldn't help but agree with the workers.

"God, she is a nasty looking bitch," he thought, "hasn't changed a bit." A look of disgust overcame his face. "I'm so glad I'm out of her life!" He hid behind the gas pumps so she wouldn't see him. He reflected on how lucky he was to be living on his uncle's ranch. He slid into the driver's seat after getting gas and pulled onto the street, relieved that she hadn't seen him.

"What's up, dipshit?" Seth joked kiddingly to Abel as he pulled up in front of his house in his uncles old work truck. Abel looked at

Seth with a grin, having come to enjoy Seth's favorite endearing term.

"Not much ass-hat!" A wide grin appeared on Seth's face.

"How's it going, Abel?" Seth inquired sincerely this time. He sensed a more-than-usual loneliness in him.

"Aw, nothing. Just getting out of the house," he said. He closed his car door behind him and joined Seth on his front lawn.

"Good, then help me roll these hoses up so I can mow the lawn this evening," Seth demanded kiddingly. Abel jumped on the chore immediately.

"I saw Sandy and her friend with the red hair and freckles walking a couple blocks away," Abel mentioned.

"Yeah, they were just here," Seth answered. "They are kind of dingy and giggle a lot, but they're fun and really nice."

"I think they think I am weird," Abel said probingly to Seth.

"Why do you say that?" Seth responded. He stopped winding the hose and looked directly at Abel.

"You know," Abel said, "They always whisper and giggle into each other's ear when they see me." His eyes met Seth's.

[92]

"The girls think you're hot, dipshit! They like your looks and are intrigued by your mysterious ways!" Seth said, adding a haunting tone to the words 'mysterious ways'. Some of their boyfriends are even a little jealous of you."

"Hmm?" Abel said. His voice expressed a mixture of relief and disbelief. "You think?"

"Fucker," Seth again said jokingly, "sometimes I even get jealous of them ogling over your pretty boy ass!" Abel grinned. "And hey!" Seth added, "Remember dipshit, don't sweat the petty, pet the sweaty!" Abel shook his head and laughed. Seth sensed a relief in Abel.

"I love that poor guy. He's a good man," Seth thought to himself. He stared and pondered as Abel disappeared around the corner. Abel pried the same answer about the girls' giggling from Seth several times over the following month. He prodded, as if expecting to hear something different. He didn't.


"Hi Sandy, hi Gail!" Abel greeted the two girls as he and Seth passed them at the school one day. Seth was surprised that Abel had initiated a conversation.

"Hi Abel, hi Seth!" the two of them said in unison.

"I can't believe we are going to graduate next month!" Sandy exclaimed. Gail, the redhead, playfully adjusted the sleeve of Abel's jacket as Sandy spoke. Seth's eyes met Abel's.

"We're going to be late to class," Sandy said to her friend. Gail giggled and smiled seductively at Abel.

"Bye, Abel!" Gail said. "Oh, and bye Seth."

"Oh, I thought I was just chopped liver standing here!" Seth said. He poked Abel in the ribs with his finger as they walked away.

Abel pondered himself holding hands with a girl, kissing her, and even falling in love as he walked. He finished high school never allowing himself to become close to anyone—except Seth. He tried to join the military after graduating but was rejected for service after a heart murmur was found during his enlistment physical. He landed a job at the local Ford dealership as a mechanic and purchased a small home on the edge of town. He worked and, except for his visits with Seth, he kept to himself. His feelings of loneliness sank to deep within him. He rarely felt them.

"Good morning sweetie!" the waitress in the local coffee shop sang in her angelic waitress-like tone to Abel as he entered

[94]

the local diner. He sat in his usual booth for his equally-as-usual breakfast of sausage and eggs before going to work. The new girl did a great job and everyone seemed to like her.

"Good morning Debbie," Abel replied as she grabbed the coffee pot off of the brewer with one hand and handed him a coffee cup with the other. She inspected the cup carefully for cleanliness before pouring his brew.

"What'll it be? Or should I even ask," Debbie teased.

"Same old thing, I guess," Abel replied. He admired her warm and friendly smile and how she seemed to wear her bright red lipstick with such ease. Her lipstick's brilliance was magnified by her straight jet-black hair and green eyes. Abel was intrigued by her. She carried herself with such a positive air.

"Okay, Sweetie. I'll get that right out to you," she said as she scribbled his order on her pad. Her smile seemed to never leave her. Abel noticed that her perfectly manicured fingernails were painted with the identical bright red hue that adorned her lips. She winked at him as she left his table.

"Order," she announced to the white-hatted cook behind the chest-high counter. She clipped Abel's order onto the stainless-steel wheel and spun it around so the cook could read it. The cook squinted towards it and began gathering its ingredients.

"Twisting wrenches today?" she asked Abel. She refilled his coffee cup to its brim without spilling a drop.

"Yep," he answered. He took a careful sip of his coffee, not wanting to spill it in front of her. "I didn't see your car out front this morning."

"Wouldn't start," she explained. "It's a good car, but it's getting to that age where stuff goes wrong, I guess." Abel pictured the twelve-year-old Subaru with its oxidized paint in his mind.

"I'll take a look at it if you want," Abel offered. He knew from overhearing her conversations with her co-workers that she had been dumped by her lawyer boyfriend and was struggling to earn the money to move back to her home in Oregon.

"You sure, sweetie?" she asked sincerely. "You probably don't want to look at another car engine after you get off work every day."

"I'm sure," Abel responded with a firm tone in his voice. He liked it when she referred to him as 'sweetie'. "Actually, the shop is slow and the boss told me I can take the day off if I want. I was just going in to organize my tools, and I can do that anytime. can look at it right now if you want."

"You sure for real, sweetie?" she again inquired. Abel nodded his head in answer. She swept her purse from under the counter and tossed him her key ring. Abel thought that it most likely included the keys to her house, post office box, and the rest of her life. "It's in my driveway. You know where I live?" she asked. She figured that he did since everyone in their little town seemed to know where everyone else lived.

"Yep," Abel said, "I'll go take a look. Probably nothing serious".

"Thank you sweetie!" she sang in her sweet high-pitched voice. She left to greet the new customers who had entered the door, grabbing menus for them on the way and smiling at Abel as he left. He liked something about Debbie's unique look. He couldn't help but think of when Seth once referred to her as "Elvira."


When she got a ride home from her co-worker that afternoon, her keys were under the doormat where Abel had been instructed to leave them. Her car revved to a start when she turned the key. Debbie noticed that Abel had repaired the sun visor that had been dangling down into her face since she had bought the car. "Wow!" she thought, seeing that Abel had taken the car to the car wash and given it a much-needed bath and vacuumed it out. "How sweet."

"Hi Abel!" he heard that evening as he was engulfed in working in his garden. He jumped from being startled. Debbie laughed.

"Hi," he said after regaining his composure. The sweet black-haired waitress carried a huge platter of chocolate chip cookies to him and held them in front of her.

"Wow, this is nice," she said. "Is it organic?"

"Yeah, all raised on my own compost. I get the manure from that horse stable out on the other edge of town. It's already mixed with straw, and the guy even throws rabbit manure in it from the rabbits he raises." He was surprised that someone had taken an interest in his favorite hobby.

"Try a cookie," she said as she held platter up to him. Able lifted his palms up to look at them. Debbie noticed their filth from shoveling the compost.

"Here," she said. She sat the cookie platter on a nearby picnic table, and grabbed one of the larger cookies from it. She held it to Abel's mouth to feed it to him. Abel hesitated, somewhat taken aback by her attention. He smiled and took a generous bite of the cookie.

[98]

"MMMM," he mumbled with a full mouth. Debbie wiped some rogue chocolate from the corner of his mouth and giggled. She held the rest of the cookie up to him for another bite. She rammed the entire thing into his mouth when it opened.

"I love your garden, Abel!" she said after serving herself a more-than-ample bite from one of the cookies. Cookie crumbs rocketed from her mouth as she spoke. After swallowing her mouthful, she placed her hands on her curvy hips as if she were taking in the view of the entire Grand Canyon while surveying his garden plot. She tilted her head back and breathed deeply through her nose.

"I love that organic, earthy smell!" she said. "It's so pure. It reminds me of back home in the mountains outside of Bend, Oregon." Her unique green eyes seemed to become reflective and painted with a hazel tint.

"It smells like horse poop!" Abel said with a shy smile. Debbie grinned with a playful scorn on her face and punched Abel softly on her arm.

"You butthole!" she exclaimed. Then she laughed.

"Here, have another one?" she said. She took another cookie from the platter and fed it to him in the same way as the last. "Thanks for fixing my car Abel."

[99]

"No problem," Abel said while smiling at her. She stared lovingly into his eyes.

"Here, let me pay you," she said. She began digging into her jeans pocket feeling for money.

"No way!" Abel said firmly. "It was just a battery cable that needed to be cleaned! You don't owe me nothing!" She stopped probing her pocket.

"You sure?" she purred. She took Abel's one hand gently into the two of hers and cradled it softly like it were a newborn child. "Thank you," she added in a sincere voice, "You're so sweet!" Before he had time to react, she leaned to him and planted her bright red painted lips firmly upon his cheek. Withdrawing her lips slowly from his face, she said, "See you tomorrow at breakfast, sweetie." She pranced off as quickly and cheerily as she had appeared. Abel felt a cheeriness that he had never experienced before. He went back to spreading his compost. He couldn't take Debbie from his mind.

"You're the sweet one!" he exclaimed out loud. He wished he would have told her that to her face.

Before making dinner, he went into the bathroom to wash his hands. The mirror showed Debbie's red imprint from her lips on his cheek. He stood staring at it and thinking for nearly five

[100]

minutes. He rinsed his hands and wiped the lipstick off his face with a washcloth. He held the washcloth in both hands, as if worshiping an idol for a moment, then tossed it on the edge of the tub. He sighed a deep contemplative breath.


"Hmmm?" Abel thought to himself one day a week or so after Debbie brought him the cookies. Debbie wasn't at her job as usual.

"Where's Debbie?" he asked the other waitress.

"Oh, she'll be here. Her landlord was coming over to replace her water heater or something," she answered. She scurried from table to table refilling coffee cups and slipping the customer's bills onto their tables. Abel felt an odd relief.

Abel sat stirring his coffee and thinking. The coffee's fresh brewed aroma wafted through the diner's air. The more dominant odor of the frying bacon soon replaced it. "I wonder how this place ever managed to get its name," Abel pondered as he sat patiently. "Riverview Café... This place is nowhere near the river--even if it were built before the homes and other businesses between it and the river, the huge hill that peaked in the center of town would block the river's view! It wasn't like someone would drive up and be fooled and say, 'Oh honey look, the Riverview Café, you must be able to see the river from inside. Why not the River Town Café, or something?'" He then realized that most of the folks that ate there were locals and had long ago accepted its misleading label. The out-of-town folks probably were just hungry and saw a diner with a flashing neon light in the window saying "Good Home Cooking" and would look to count how many cars were in the parking lot to attest to this sign's honesty.

Suddenly, "DING, JINGLE, DONG, DONG!" the little string of bells that hung on the door to announce the entry or exit of a customer rang out. The thin pale-skinned, green-eyed, Elvira look-alike burst through the door with her usual smile.

"Hi everybody!" she exclaimed. She acted as if the entire place was an auditorium sitting on pins and needles awaiting her arrival. Her thought was not entirely untrue. She glanced around and greeted all her customers with her smile. Seeing Abel, her entire attention turned to him and she darted to his table. "Hi, sweetie!"

"Hi Debbie," he said. She lovingly patted the back of his hand and hurriedly made her way to where her apron hung. She began dancing from table to table, answering questions in her usual sweet tone. She scoffed at the proposals from the old farmers through her smile as she warmed their coffee, and winked flirtingly at the shyer ones. One woman, an elderly regular, shared an encouraging glance with her when she noticed her obvious attraction to Abel. Abel's heart warmed from her near-every-moment's attention. He finished his meal and left the money on the table with an over generous tip. Debbie met him at the door, coffee pot in hand to wish him a personal see-you-later.

Occasionally, during Abel's breakfast visits, Debbie would notice him in deep and faraway thought. She could see a troubled look on his face--not like he had some issue facing him that moment, but like he was trying to stomach a feeling from the past. He would rest his cheek heavily in the palm of his hand, as if he needed to support his mind. She had noticed him nearly tear up, but catch himself before he did. She often saw him shake his head as if he were trying to shake a memory from it. At these times, she would warm his coffee and try to do the same to his heart. "Everybody deserves love", seemed to be Debbie's unwritten policy. She refused to let any person in her realm go without. Young or old, black or white, human or beast—they all received it from her. Abel was especially no exception. There was something about him. Something special-- and maybe something terrible.

One morning Debbie pranced to Abel's booth and slid next to him on the bench seat. She nudged him towards the wall with her hips to make room for herself and grabbed his hand in hers. "Hey big boy, you wanna go on a date?" She asked the question and stared directly into his eyes with a "You-had-better-say-yes look." Abel could feel himself blushing. He was unsure of whether she was kidding or serious and hesitated to answer. "You like popcorn?" she said. She sat prying for an answer with her eyes.

"Uh, yes. Uh, I guess." a confused Abel answered.

"Well, do you or don't you like popcorn?" she said.

"Yeah, I like popcorn," he answered.

"Good!" she blurted, "A movie it is! I have one picked out for us. Would Friday or Saturday night be best for you?"

" Uh, Friday, I guess," Abel responded, not realizing that he had been given only the option to pick a day with no way to escape.

"Great, I'm buying! I'll pick you up in my trusty Subaru at seven thirty at your house!" She leaned and painted another set of lip marks on Abel's right cheek before he knew it. She scurried up to meet some new customers that were coming in, glancing with a smile at him over her shoulder as she did. He felt the ridges of her lipstick on his cheek with his fingertips. It's smell was the same sweet one as the last time. Abel finished his meal. His hunger seemed to have left him. He glanced to her as he swung the exit door open. Debbie launched a kiss at him using only her lips, unable to throw one with her hand without also throwing one of the breakfast orders she held. She winked and smiled as he left.

"It'll be good," Abel thought. "I can do this. She's nice. It will all go okay." He pictured Debbie and how she seemed to always know his feelings. He'd never met anyone like her. "Might be kind of fun." A smile came to his face as he again lifted his hand to his face to feel the remnants of her kiss.

"KNOCK, KNOCK, KNOCK." Abel heard rattling at the front door of his house on Friday, just as Debbie had planned. He could see Debbie's trim, but shapely, outline through the slightly yellowed curtains that hid the outside world from him through the paned-glass front door.

[105]

"Well hello, big boy!" a nineteen-forties-movie-star voice sounded. Debbie positioned herself into a similar-era-type stance as he opened the door. All she lacked was the eight-inch cigarette holder of those times dangling from her lips to fit the perfect part.

"Hi Debbie," Able said awkwardly. He stood stunned by her dressed-up-to-go-to-town beauty. He sat silent, admiring her full and flowing newly trimmed hair. It laid elegantly across her shoulders and her lipstick, now lightened to an exotic pink and having an inviting moistness, captured his view. Her fingernails were painted to match her lips. Each pinkie finger had a delicate and tiny red rose painted upon it. Abel realized that red was her favorite color and that she had to have it on her at all times.

"Uh, you look so beautiful Debbie!" He said, surprised that he said it. It just came out. He admired her fuzzy looking earthen-toned sweater. It allowed a revealing, but modest, exposure of her near-perfect figure. The sweater draped down to below her waist, bunching up just above her bottom. She wore a fuzzy cap that matched her sweater.

"Thank you, Abel," she replied in a more womanly voice than he was used to at the café. "What did you expect," she suddenly blurted out teasingly using her sweet waitress-like voice, "me in my black waitress uniform?" She laughed and stepped to

Abel and surprised him with a loving peck near his ear. Her perfume was seductive and erotic.

"Mmm." Abel reacted, inadvertently closing his eyes and inhaling a deep breath of her aroma through his nose. "You smell so good." He'd never imagined such a fragrance. She thanked him with a look.

"Let's go, babe!" she said. She grabbed Abel with one hand and placing her other around his waist as she escorted him towards her car.

"Babe???" Abel thought.

"Here, you drive," she said, handing Abel her keys. She stood still away from the passenger door. Abel hesitated, then realized the reason for her stopping.

"Sorry," Abel said, suddenly grasping at the door handle and opening it for her. She laughed as she slid onto the seat and stared for him to close it.

"I couldn't wait to see you, Abel," Debbie said. She shifted her body as close as possible to him over the center console. She took his right hand into the two of hers. Abel's face reddened.

"Up here," Debbie said. She tugged Abel by the hand to the center of the top row of seats in the mostly empty theater. "I like sitting in the back." She plopped clumsily into one of the worn cloth seats. She folded the adjoining one down and patted it with her hand while looking at Abel. She pulled him close to her as he sat and snuggled to him as if making a nest from which to view the movie.

"Sniff, sniff," Abel heard. It was Debbie inhaling in her tears as the couple that had fallen in love in the movie broke up over a simple misunderstanding.

"Sad," she whispered while using Abel's shirtsleeve to dab the tears from her face. She snuggled even closer and wrapped herself in his arm. Abel hugged her.

"That was a sweet movie," Debbie said as they were leaving the theater. Her eyes were swollen from crying during both the breakup and eventual happy reunion. "You like it, babe?" she asked.

"Yeah, it was good," Abel said, again pondering being called Babe. "It was a happy ending. Even had me tearing up a couple times!"

"I saw!" Debbie said with a teasing giggle. Abel's face reddened, and she pecked his cheek with a kiss.

[108]

"Full moon! Let's take a walk," Debbie said. She drug Abel away from the car as he aimed the key towards its door lock.

"Hi, Abel." He heard. The redheaded girl that had a crush on him in high school and her date were passing them just as Debbie turned him from the car. The girl seemed to be sizing Debbie up in comparison to herself.

"Hi Gail," he said, smiling shyly and glancing at Debbie. Debbie greeted them both with a warm and sincere smile as she encased Abel's arm in hers and drew herself close to him. "Well, see you later," he said only seconds later. Abel smiled and nodded a friendly acknowledgement to redheaded girl's date.

"Let's go to the river," Debbie said. Her pace became hurried, as if being drawn to the river by a force. She began swinging their hands between them like two school children. "I love the river. I love any water!" Abel admired the ease with which she took life. He saw happiness as he had never seen it.

"Wonder why they named this Main Street?" she joked as they walked along the only street in town with stores, restaurants, the one bank, and the theater. She laughed. The light around them faded with each step toward the river's darkness.

"Wheng, wan, qui, chang!" they heard from two Hmong men fishing under the dim light at the edge of the pier. They sounded as if they were arguing, but laughed at the end of their exchange.

"Nice out here," Debbie said. She stood looking across the half-mile wide river to the eucalyptus-lined levee on the other side. The moon's reflection was glimmering like a gigantic star dancing across the swirls formed from the tide's current. She tilted her head back and closed her eyes and took the river's cool nighttime into her nostrils. "AAAHHH..." she exclaimed calmly, "It smells so fresh."

"Smells like dead fish!" Abel joked.

"Shut up!" she said. She slapped Abel playfully on his arm. Her cotton white teeth rose from the darkness when she smiled.

"Butthole!" she said, smiling and pushing at Abel's shoulder. She wrapped his hand around her shoulders and hers around his waist and leaned them both against the railing that fenced the edge of the dock. They stood in silence until jolted into the moment by the Asian men erupting into loud foreign screaming. They watched one of them spring from his squat against the railing and yank his pole with all his might backward.

"Hhmmpfft!" Abel heard Debbie sound as she tried to contain her laughter. The fisherman, who had clearly missed his prey, and his friend burst into what could have only been their version of profanities.

"We better go," Debbie said under her breath. She fought to contain her laugh as the two fishermen quieted and scorned at them. Once out of sight of the fishermen, they both laughed heartily.

"Come 'ere," she said softly to Abel. She leaned back against a wooden picnic table aside the river and pulled him to her. She rose to her toes and placed her moist pink-hued-hued lips to Abel's.

"Mmmm," Abel murmured. She pried his lips apart with her tongue and began to probe the depths of his mouth. "Ahh," Abel again sounded breathlessly. Debbie placed her hand behind his head and pulled his lips tightly to hers. Abel felt butterflies. He felt scared. Her felt good. He didn't know what to think, but he didn't want it to stop.

Debbie removed her lips from his and caressed his ear with her tongue. "You are a beautiful man, Abel. I've wanted to kiss you since the first time we met," she said. Abel stood speechless, in full submission to the angel in front of him. She kissed him again, even more passionately than before.

"Don't say anything," Debbie told him. She continuing kissing him for several minutes and then gave him a soft peck at the tip of his nose. She let herself down from her tip-toe position in front of him and pierced him with her now-hazel-hued green eyes. Abel stood breathless.

"Come on!" she ordered playfully as she grabbed his hand again. "Let's walk some more!" She turned him forward towards the street and replaced his arm around her. This time her pace was slow, as if she had the entire night to spare.

"Have fun tonight?" Debbie inquired after arriving at Abel's house after their date.

"A lot of fun," he answered, as he helped her from the car to escort her to the driver's seat. "It really was nice." Debbie's eyes widened. She kissed him. The scent of her perfume swept her image into his mind, even though his eyes were closed. He saw beauty.

"Okay then, will our next date be Friday or Saturday?" Debbie said laughing.

"Whichever," Abel answered without hesitation.

Friday it is then," she said.

"I really did have a wonderful time with you Abel." She opened her arms to invite a parting hug. He hugged her to him and she turned towards the car's open door. She suddenly stopped mid-turn and faced him. "Kiss me," she said. She stood still and away from him, forcing Abel to bring his lips to hers. He did.

"See you tomorrow morning!" she said, smiling at him as she started her car. She waived with her cupped fingertips as she drove away. Abel stood in deep thought as the little green Subaru disappeared around the corner. A deep uneasiness left him as her car faded into the darkness. He didn't understand.

# CHAPTER 8

Ian, standing with a group of fellow Marines, listened as they were briefed by their platoon commander.

"It's gotten really bad here, men-- way worse than the last time you were here. And this place is the worst of the worst. They're desperate, their bombs are bigger, the locals fear them, and they have spread out into nearly every town!" he added. He paused and let his eyes meet each of theirs to impress upon them his seriousness. "The heavies want us to win their hearts," he said using a sarcastic tone and making quotation marks in the air with his fingers as he said it. "There's a group of insurgents planting IEDs and ambushing our troops and we have intelligence that they are hiding out in this area." His index finger circled an area on a map that included several towns. "So, when you are in these fucking villages passing out candy and kissing their asses, keep on your toes! Watch for anything weird, and if you feel it, get the fuck out of there!" he instructed firmly. "See if you can find the English speakers, especially friendly ones, and get intel from them – everything, who the local enemies are, who's making the

[115]

bombs, and, like I said, anything. And, goddamn it, don't get your fucking selves killed!" He again swept his eyes to meet each of theirs. Ian saw sincere compassion in them. Ian's four man team, which he was now the leader of, loaded into the diesel-smelling armored vehicle. The drivers and gunner on the top of it all secured the straps of their helmets. Ian and his troops did the same. Twenty minutes later they debarked from the vehicle and onto the streets of a strange village.

"Keep on your toes," Ian warned his team members. One was a kid on his first tour to Iraq. He hung on each of Ian's words. Ian yanked the breach back on his rifle and released it. It sprang shut with the hollow sound of a round entering its chamber. Ian pulled back on the handle enough to view that the round was successfully loaded and slammed it shut with the heel of his hand. His men did the same. "Remember be ready." Ian said, lifting his rifle in front of them and wiggling his thumb over the rifle's safety mechanism. They began to stroll slowly and carefully through the unpaved streets, greeting and sizing up the locals as they went.

"There," Ian said quietly as he flung his head upward and to the right. He directed his men's focus towards movement on a rooftop ahead. Their grips tightened on their rifles and they spread away from each other. A teenage girl with an armload of laundry appeared and began hanging it in the sun. Their grips relaxed and she smiled as they passed.

"This is creepy!" Ian's second in command told him. "I liked the good old days better." Ian knew that he was referring to when they had sat on rooftops to keep an eye on things or moved from place to place stealthily on their previous tour. "We're like fucking ducks in a shooting gallery!"

"Me too" Ian replied. "This is tense. But, so far so good." Their eyes swept from side to side as they moved. They kept their faked friendly smiles on their faces and nodded in greetings to everyone they passed. Ian noticed the new kid tighten the strap of his helmet and fold the bulletproof collar of his flak jacket more securely into place as they walked. They weaved their way through the packed-sand streets.

"Here you go!" Ian said to a group of kids. They had run to them from a row of drab looking block homes on one side of the street. They begged for candy. He tossed out pieces of hard red-colored candy--the only kind that managed to keep its form in the constant triple-digit heat.

"Hello," Ian yelled with a smile. He greeted two grey-bearded old men sitting on their front porch in dingy grey robes smoking from a hookah. They lifted their hands mechanically and waved back unenthusiastically and returned the mouthpieces of the pipe back to their lips without saying a word. "They probably don't understand English," he said to his second in command.

"Maybe, but I bet they know which ones of these fuckers around here that want to blow our heads off," he answered. He glanced to their roof and windows. They reached the marketplace a few blocks later.

"Two kilos," Ian said to one of the shopkeepers in the marketplace. He held his two fingers up over his rifle to clarify the quantity of oranges that he wanted.

"Two," the man replied, holding up his own two fingers. The man had a friendly smile adorning his weathered face. He was missing several teeth and a yellow hue covered the others. All appeared abnormally long from gum disease, and each was at a different stage of rot.

"Yes," Ian replied. He continued carefully scanning the area as the man weighed and bagged his order. All-the-while he kept the feigned smile on his face. He nodded to greet the other vendors who were selling bread and other items. All of them beckoned him with their cupped hands to visit their table of goods and smiled as if wanting to become best friends. Some of them chatted in shattered English and seemed happy to see Americans. Abel couldn't help but wonder which ones would slice his throat in a dark alley if given the chance.

"Check it out!" Ian's team member said, pointing a short distance to their right with the flick of his head.

"Hmm," Ian replied with a more alert than curious mumble. He noticed a younger man who travelled from village to village selling his wares that he had come to know on his last tour hurrying to pack up the cigarettes, candies, and magazines that he sold. The man had always been friendly and spoke near-perfect English. He had provided useful information before.

"Hi Ahmed," Ian greeted from a distance. Their eyes met briefly. His usual smile was replaced by a look of concern. He slammed the lid to his hard-sided black suitcase and latched it shut. The man stared briefly, but intently into Ian's eyes. He scurried from the market.

"Something's up, let's get the fuck out of this place!" Ian said to his men.

"Bravo 3, this is Knifeboy, come in," Ian spoke into the microphone pinned to the chest of his flak jacket. He was trying to summon a response from his base camp that held a battalion of Marines. He heard no response. Ian's team, still sporting their fake grins, became tense. Their fingers strummed at the safeties on their rifles. They began to edge from the bazaar and return toward their pick up point on the edge of town. The air seemed heavy. The bantering and bargaining of the vendors continued.

"Copy Bravo 3? This is Knifeboy," Ian repeated. His teammates all shifted their eyes from their surroundings to Ian's radio awaiting a response.

"Go ahead Knifeboy" came a response over the radio. The new kid sighed in relief.

"Something's getting ready to go down Bravo. Request infantry backup." Ian said. He immediately re-keyed the mic and added "ASAP!". Ian began recalling the same type of quietness that preceded the savage firefight that almost cost him his life and ended the lives of several of his fellow marines on his previous tour.

"Ten-four! They're on the way!" the base camp announced. Ian signaled for his team to advance. They scurried one by one, doorway to doorway, towards their pick up point. He checked his GPS on his vest to make sure the marines on their way could find them.

"Bam, bam, bam, bam!" they heard, as automatic gunfire erupted from the rooftops around them. Every doorway ahead seemed to explode in gunfire.

"Pfft," Ian heard, as a bullet pierced the neck of the new kid standing next to him. The smell of burning flesh, which mimicked that of burning hair but ten times as putrid, filled the air. Ian saw the young man die before hitting the ground.

"Mayday, Mayday Bravo 3! Knifeboy taking heavy fire, man down!" Ian screamed into his microphone. He grabbed the fallen Marine by the collar of his flak jacket and drug his lifeless body behind a cement wall at the front of one of the houses.

"ETA three minutes, Knifeboy!" the radio crackled. The team laid down a hail of gunfire in every direction, sending the enemies ducking for cover. Ian and one of his team members ran ahead to behind a cement wall, killing two Iraqi gunmen with automatic fire when they emerged from the doorways to shoot at them.

"You okay, Larry?" Ian asked over his radio to his team member who had taken cover in a doorway at the beginning of the ambush. The roar of helicopters nearing their position echoed through the air.

"Lay some spurt-fire down for me, Joe!" Ian said as he positioned himself behind the wall. His teammate followed orders and began to fire three or four round bursts and then would stop and let the air fall silent. Each time, one of the snipers on the rooftops would peek from his lair to try and find a target and would fall victim to Ian's expert sniper fire.

"I'm all right Ian, killed two of those motherfuckers in that doorway up there!" his team member Larry finally reported back. "I think that's all there was. I haven't heard another shot since I killed that last prick!"

The enemy's gunfire silenced. Ian heard them screaming at each other as they ran. One screamed in pain.

"Coming through, Knifeboy!" the platoon of Marines announced over the radio. The entire area came alive with heavily armed Marines in full combat gear. They resembled the robotic soldiers of the video game world, but were frighteningly real and deadly.

"Bap, bap, bap," Ian heard several times from the alleyways behind the rooftops that had contained the snipers as the Marine infantry hunted the remaining insurgents.

"Clear!" Ian heard from one of the many buildings as the Marines secured the rooftops and the homes under them. The

[122]

Marines searched the terrified civilians huddled in their corners for weapons.

"Boom!" Ian heard in the distance, recognizing the sound of one of the Apache helicopters destroying a vehicle.

Ian and his two surviving team members gathered as the armored vehicle arrived to rescue them.

"Fuck this place!" Larry said. They stared in silence as two infantrymen carried the young kid's body to the helicopter. They entered the vehicle, this time leaving the rounds in the chambers of their weapons. No one spoke as they sat in the armored vehicle on their way back to base. Ian's eyes met Larry's. Their stares were deep and oddly thankful. Larry rolled his head against the back of the seat and stared to the ceiling of the vehicle then closed his eyes. Ian stared blankly out the plexiglass window as streams of sweat-formed-mud traversed his face.

"KAABOOOM!!!!" was the last sound they all heard that day, one of them forever. A massive IED bomb detonated exactly under and to the rear of the vehicle, where the armor was its weakest. Its blast was directly under where Ian sat.

"Come on, Sweetie, wake up!" Ian heard as he began to regain consciousness. He saw the blur of a person bent over him and felt a moist rag being swiped across his forehead.

"Come on, come out of it, you can do it," he heard. He began realizing a nurse was leaning her face into his and coaxing him into consciousness. He opened his eyes to confusion. "Beep—beep-beep," the monitor beside him chirped in a broken monotone as the digital display bounced between numbers on its face.

"There you are," the nurse said, seeing him becoming aware of his surroundings, "we weren't sure you were going to make it! Leave it to you hard-headed Marines!" she added with a warm smile.

"I'm in a hospital?" Ian asked, looking from side to side around the room.

"That you are, sweetie," the white-clad nurse answered while lifting his wrist and gazing at her watch. She swiped his head with a rubber-tipped thermometer and made a notation on her clipboard.

"Why, what for?" Ian questioned, fingering and realizing that he had no hearing in his left ear.

[124]

"You don't remember the IED exploding under your armored personnel carrier after the firefight in that village, honey?" Ian recalled part of a firefight.

"Bad!" she said. She gave him some of the details, including how one of the helicopters that had responded to the firefight was still in the area and had flown back and picked him and the others up. "You would have died from loss of blood if that chopper wasn't close by."

"What others?" Ian asked. "Larry??"

"I'm sorry honey", the nurse said, as she looked toward the ground. "There wasn't much we could do."

"Joe?" he asked pitifully.

"He's fine and will be in to see you. His hearing isn't great but, other than that, he's fine." She said. "The two marines driving the vehicle are fine too. It went off in the back – unfortunately right under you." Ian stared at the ceiling in tears thinking of his buddy Larry.

"He was my brother," Ian told her. She embraced him and let him cry.

"How's your pain?" the nurse asked once he had calmed.

"A little headache," Ian replied. "But my legs are throbbing from the knees down really bad!" He saw the nurse's demeanor and expression change to one of dread.

"Honey," the nurse, who was about ten years Ian's senior, said, "your legs were severely mangled by the shrapnel. We did everything we could, but we couldn't save them."

Ian's stomach instantly turned to knots. He tried to un-hear what he had just been told.

"No, No, No!" he screamed as he scattered tears throughout the room with his shaking head. The nurse again took him into her arms.

"Honey, those are what we call phantom pains. The nerves that used to go to the parts that are missing are still intact and sensing pain that isn't where they think it is. I'm sorry sweetie," she said. She petted Ian's head lovingly. Ian stared blankly.

"Are you sure?" he kept wanting to ask, feeling the pain as if they were still there. He knew that whether they were there or not was apparent to anyone, doctor or not. He knew the nurse would never be so cruel as to lie about such a thing. "It's not like the doctor is going to jump up and scream, 'April Fools!' or something", he thought to himself. "This sucks!"

[126]

"Can I see?" he asked.

"Ian, it's going to all be okay, you have to trust me, honey," the nurse stated calmly. She tilted the top of Ian's bed upward with the button on its side. She folded back the sheet to expose the turbine-like bandages that covered the nubs of both of his legs an equal distance below the knee. His face contorted in terror.

"Honey, it's not as bad as you think." The nurse said. She saw him drift to a terrible place—a place she had seen so many never return from. He began to cry.

"Honey," the nurse continued, "you're lucky, you have plenty of bone and muscle intact below the knees and fitting prosthetics will be easy. You will be able to function almost normally in no time."

"Lucky?" Ian thought. He disappeared into himself, and eventually into a merciful medication-induced sleep.

"NO!" Layla screamed. Her body trembled. Her mother ran to her, sweeping her with her eyes to find the source of her pain.

"What is it Layla?" her mother asked thinking she had miscarried or had been hurt. Layla peered out the front window, unable to speak. "What, baby?" her mother said. She glanced to the window and saw two full-dressed Marines somberly approaching with their white hats tucked under their arms.

"Here baby," her mother said. She took Layla into her arms. Both of them began to cry. Layla stood. Her face was ghost white. Layla's mom freed one of her hands from her daughter and opened the door to the two Marines before they had a chance to knock.

"Mrs. Layla Johnson?" one of the Marine's asked.

"Yes, it's my daughter" her mother answered. She motioned downward with her head to the saddened heap in her arms.

"Ma'am, there's been an explosion." He said.

Layla sobbed loudly. Her breakfast traveled to her throat.

"Luckily," the Marine continued, "your husband is alive, awake, talking and stable—but he has been injured."

Layla replaced his words with those of her worst nightmare. Her trembles turned to violent shaking.

"Layla! Listen to me!" her mother said. She turned and stooped in front of Layla so that her daughter could see her talk under her bowed head. She took her shoulders and shook her to gain her attention.

"Ian's okay, Layla! He's alive! He's just hurt!" she said. Layla lifted her head and color began returning to her face.

"He's alive?" she asked. Her head swept between the marines and her mother.

"Yes ma'am" the Marine answered, again explaining that he was conscious and in stable condition.

"He's okay though?" Layla pried. Her relief turned again to terror as she saw their body language become uncomfortable.

"Ma'am, he has lost both legs below the knee and the hearing in one ear, but he has no brain damage or any other injuries except for a few cuts and bruises." He continued stoically, "he is lucid, fully aware of his condition and is expected to make a full recovery. We wanted you to know Ma'am."

"Is he on his way home? When can I see him? Is he here now? Where is he?" Layla probed desperately.

"He is still in the hospital recovering, ma'am." Understanding her anxiousness, but not having answers, the Marine added, "He will be the one to answer those questions when he calls. I'm sure his doctor is keeping him informed."

"I'm sorry to have had to bring you this news Ma'am," the Marine said politely. Both of them bowed their heads in sadness. "On behalf of the United States Marine Corp, we would like to

[129]

express our true respect and best wishes to you and your husband. May God bless you." The Marines turned in unison toward the door. Layla and her mother stood in silence watching the Marines pace towards their black Ford, replacing their spit-shined-brimmed white hats as they did.

"Goddamn it!" Ian exclaimed. He glanced under the sheets at his legless self for the hundredth time, wanting to look and find that his legs had returned to his body. "Not much of a man now, am I?" He pictured Layla struggling to roll him around. He saw the kids at school teasing his daughter. "I don't want that!" he thought. His head shook side to side in agreement with himself.

"Wish it was fucking me!" he exclaimed under his breath. He wished he had been the one killed in the explosion instead of Larry. "I'm not going to put them through it!"

"Why doesn't he call?" Layla asked. "He knows I can't call him over there!" She stared at her mother. "I know he loves me, Mom! Why doesn't he call? It's been a week! I know he is okay or they would call me or send those guys out here again."

"I know, Angel!" Ian said to himself as if he could hear Layla

begging for his call. He couldn't leave her without one last call to

tell her he loved her. It wouldn't be fair. He owed it to her.

"Damn it! I fucked it all up! I fucked our whole lives up!" he

screamed. "You wouldn't want me anyway if you saw me. You

deserve a real man. A whole man. Anything but this!" he thought

as he looked down to his fraction of a body. "Fuck this!"

# CHAPTER 9

Years later, after quitting his pot smoking, passing a drug test and obtaining a top secret security clearance, Barry became one of the nation's top cybersecurity experts. He was invited to attend his first high-level meeting with an array of government agents. One particular Gestapo-looking attendee who was angered that Barry showed up with long hair and wearing a tie-dyed T-shirt to their high-level meeting approached him. The other members of the CIA, FBI, NSA, and several other such agencies paused as he spoke. His face was reddened and his fists were clenched.

"Next time I see you in here, you better have that hair cut and be wearing a shirt and tie like the rest of us!" Barry looked up sporting a friendly smile. Without saying a word, he began to gather his notes and replaced his laptop into its case.

"Where do you think you are going?" the sleuth said as Barry rose from his chair.

"Home," Barry said, still sporting his grin. "I'm not your guy. I don't own any suits and ties and don't plan to!" Another of the sleuths that had been sitting quietly up to this point rose

[133]

calmly from his chair and placed his open palm on the front of the first sleuth's shoulder as if to hold him back. He smiled warmly at Barry.

"Have a chair, Barry," he said, "you are dressed just fine for our purposes here." He glanced to the first sleuth with a firm and scolding look. He was obviously the senior man in the room and understood that they needed Barry's best-in-the-world computer hacking and cyber-security talents. The subject of Barry's looks and attire never came up again after that. Even the mean one gained respect for him after seeing his talents in action. Barry became one of the country's top cyber sleuths, all under the guise of being an online college professor that worked from home.

"Bye, Daddy," Barry's now nineteen-year-old daughter Sam said. "I'll be back home tomorrow afternoon." She was headed out the door to a Ziggy Marley concert in the Napa Valley that she and her friends had been planning to attend for some time.

"Bye honey," her dad responded. "Drive carefully and make sure you girls lock the door to your room at the motel tonight!" He saw her give him that "I got this" smile as she headed out the door.

Not long before Sam's concert trip, police sergeant Smith was at the local Frosty Burger waiting in the office for the manager concerning graffiti drawn on the building the night before.

"What the fuck am I supposed to do about it, scrub the son of a bitch off!" he thought. "What a waste of time." He heard a familiar young woman's voice just outside the office door.

"Hey Courtney, I have our room set up at the Motel 6 in Vacaville for the concert next Saturday. I'll just meet you guys at about five and we can leave together from there. Not the fanciest room, but at least we won't have to leave the concert at ten and have to drive all the way back up here!" Shitbag Smith peeked around the corner of the door. It was the voice of who he had thought it was. His mind began whirling. He fixed his ear on her conversation.

"I'll fix that smart-assed hippie prick now once and for all! It's been so many years, that fucking hippie won't even see it coming!" Smith thought to himself. "I knew that sooner or later I'd have his ass!" Smith listened intently. Sam giggled and jabbered until the manager came in to discuss the graffiti. He had all the information he needed.

Some months earlier after midnight, Shitbag Smith was called to the downtown fishing pier used by the locals. It was somewhat hidden behind the old abandoned water treatment plant along the river. He met an old man who was walking his dog in the middle of the night.

"What's up?" Smith inquired with his usual impatient attitude. He looked at the old man and down at his mangy mutt wondering which one of them were older.

"I saw something suspicious that I thought you might want to know about," the old guy said. He lifted his cane to point to the back of the old water building. "I was out on the pier leaning against the railing under where that light's been out for a couple months." He interrupted himself, "When are you guys going to get that fixed anyway?"

"You called me down here at one in the morning just to bitch about a broken fucking light on a dock!"

"No," the old man snapped back. "I called you down here because I saw some guy stop and run back there and hide something. He looked around like he was up to something. I thought he was going to break into the place, but I think he just shoved something into the bushes and took off. Looked real shady!"

"Okay, I'll check it out. Thanks a lot." Smith said with his voice seasoned with an unappreciative tone. The old man waddled his way into the darkness, his cane in one hand and the mangy dog's leash in the other.

"Crazy old bastard," Smith mumbled. He began searching around the tangled array of spider-web-covered pipes that protruded from the backside of the building. "I don't see a fucking thing. The guy probably stopped to take a fucking piss. Senile old fucker!" He gave up and began to head back to his car. Just as he reached the edge of the building he brushed against the scraggly hedge. He heard a crinkling sound. He shined his light into the bush and saw an object stuffed into its half-dead branches. "Hmm," Smith thought, "Maybe that old fart wasn't crazy." He lifted a black canvas bag from the hedge. He could tell from its weight that something was inside it. He holstered his flashlight and made his way across the street to where he had met the old man and back to his police car.

"I'll be a son of a bitch!" he blurted aloud as he opened the backpack. Inside was a gallon zip-lock plastic bag filled with a white powder. It was meticulously wrapped inside another and taped shut. "A drop off!" he thought excitedly. He began to realize that he failed to notice the type or license number of the car that had abruptly u-turned in the street in front of the water plant earlier as he was searching. "Shit!" he scolded himself.

Smith re-zipped the bag with what he guessed to be over a kilo of coke in it and threw it in his trunk. He figured he would test it, log it in, and fill out the time consuming report the following day. He parked in the distance, hoping the car would return for their pickup. Before long he had fallen sound asleep. He returned to his home, realizing that the car had probably come and gone as he slept.

As tired as he was, just before he began to doze off, he sprang to a sitting position on the side of his bed. He became fully alert and his mind began plotting. "I'm going to finally get that no-good hippie scumbag!" He reached for the canvas bag at the side of his bed that contained the drugs. He tore at the zippers like a child tearing at his Christmas present. He carefully removed the outer baggie and found the edges of the second so he could unzip it to expose the powder. He sat the bag on his table after recovering a test kit from the trunk of his police cruiser. He dipped the moistened test strip into the powder.

"Coke!" he bleated with inexplicable excitement as if what he fully expected was a complete surprise. "I'm going to get that hippie fuck good," he thought. "Now I just have to figure out the plan!" He sealed the coke back up, replaced it into the canvas

[138]

bag, and stored it into the drawer of his gun safe. "Hippie fucker!" he said, just before dozing into a deep sleep.

After overhearing Barry's daughter in the burger joint, Captain Shitbag's time for revenge had blossomed. "That little hippie whore is going to take one for her dad!" he thought. His body vibrated with excitement. "That little cunt is going to prison and her dad can suffer for years! That'll teach the fucker to make an ass out of me!" "Hippie fucker!"

Smith's plan was laid. He made sure that the Saturday night that Samantha was staying at the hotel in Vacaville he was off duty. He took a car door opening tool, known as a 'slim Jim' from his patrol car's trunk and placed it into his own personal car along with some wire cutters. That Saturday night at eight o'clock he set off on the hour drive to Vacaville to surveil the motel and wait for Sam's return after the concert. Smith watched as the motel filled up with weary travelers. He watched them enter the lobby and exit with a key in hand. Before long the motel's flashing neon "Vacancy" light was changed to "No Vacancy." The manager's unit darkened at about a quarter after eleven. About midnight,

[139]

he saw Samantha and her friends drive up in her early eighties Honda Accord.

Smith, from his surveillance perch across the street, noticed that the girls seemed tired. They were quick to enter their room and turn out its lights. The motel's parking lot became still. Smith watched for about forty-five minutes, then put his evil plan in action. Smith knew the old Honda was not alarmed, as none of them were in that era. He also knew that his slim Jim was the perfect tool for that particular door lock release. He had his badge and a couple of official-looking files with him in case a fellow officer from that jurisdiction confronted him at any point. He could flash his badge and claim that he was trailing a drug seller for an investigation. Chances were slim of being confronted, as the Motel 6 was on a frontage road along a freeway outside of town in an area that had been slated for development earlier, but left undeveloped for the most part due to the prior economic downturn. It sat oddly alone. Luckily, and conveniently, the girls had returned to the motel so late that the only parking left in the lot was near the rear of the place, far from any of the rooms.

Smith exited his car with the slim Jim and wire cutters. He carried a small satchel. When he got near the car, he stowed the satchel behind the concrete wall that contained the garbage dumpsters in case there was an unplanned interruption. He walked to the driver door and slid his slim Jim downward between the rubber gasket and the window of the car. In seconds Sam's car door was open. Smith grabbed the lever between the seat and door and popped the trunk open. He went to the trunk and removed a brake light bulb assembly with a quick twist and turn. He cut the solder where the wire was attached to the bulb so that it looked like the weld had broken, disabling the brake-light. Smith retrieved the satchel and opened the glove compartment. He noticed the usual items, including the car's registration and insurance information. He placed a small bag of marijuana in a clear plastic bag next to the registration so that the weed would come into full view upon opening the glove compartment. He removed a brown paper bag that contained the plastic bag full of cocaine from his satchel. He slid it underneath the driver's seat of Sam's car. He locked her car and walked casually to his own vehicle and left--entirely unnoticed.

Smith, after purchasing gasoline and a flask of whiskey to drink on his drive home, drove back to Edgewater and to his house. He turned on the TV and made himself a stiff Black Velvet Whisky and Coke. "Fucking hippie!" he hatefully mumbled. He sipped the last of his cocktail and dozed off in the reclining chair.

The sun came through the sliding glass door and woke him at about seven thirty that morning. He knew the girls would be waking soon, as checkout time in all Motel 6 establishments was 11 A.M. He figured that, somewhere between about eleven and two in the afternoon, Sam would be rolling back into town to share her concert stories with her awaiting friends. Smith got up, made some coffee, showered and hopped in the patrol car that he kept in his driveway. He headed to the station where he met another patrolman that he had hired a couple of years earlier who was also coming on duty for the day. They exchanged the usual chitchat about what went on the previous day in the little town they policed. As usual, nothing had happened. The young patrolman always pried information about the only thing that had ever happened of consequence in Edgewater, it being the one murder of the young high school girl a few years earlier. It remained unsolved and the patrolman had fantasies of being its solver. Smith and the rest of the cops on the force at the time figured it was a local that murdered her and probably one near her own age. Other than the brutal strangulation by strong hands and the evidence of powerful blunt force trauma, indicating that it most likely was done by a male, the cops had no leads. All of the eight full-time cops who were on the force at the time, wanted to solve it and become the town hero, but none had, and their interest waned over time. Smith figured the new guy's

[142]

would too. But the city agreed to fund a five-thousand-dollar reward for a tip at the young officer's pleading, so he entertained him with the details.

"Lock and load!" Captain Smith said to the other patrolman. He was referencing that they both were to load and check their firearms for readiness, even though no cop in the town's history had ever had a call to fire one.

"Catch you on the rebound," the young cop said to Smith as they loaded into their respective cars. They knew they would pass each other at least a hundred times that day, like every day, as they patrolled the tiny town in circles. For insurance reasons, the town always had a minimum of two officers on patrol at one time. The crooked town attorney managed to finagle something so the graveyard shift only need one. Sometimes it had zero. When a car was pulled over during the day, both officers responded—mostly out of pure boredom.

"I'm making a stop, Randy," Smith radioed to his underling a couple of hours into their shift. "Got some hippie girl with a brake light out on the west end of the highway."

"On my way!" the other cop chimed back as he switched on his red lights.

"What the heck?" she thought. She pulled to the side of the road and brought her car to a stop. She watched the officer chatter into his radio through her rearview mirror. "I know I wasn't speeding." She realize it was Shitbag Smith, "Oh, that ass. It figures."

Both cops parked behind Sam. Their embarrassing red and blue lights blared to alert everyone in town to which of their neighbors was the culprit of the minute. Smith and the other cop spoke for a minute and then approached Sam's Car. Smith walked to the driver's side and the other officer approached on the passenger side. He rested his hand on his holster as he had been trained, even though he recognized Sam.

"Your brake light is broken," Smith informed her in his usual condescending voice. "I need to see your driver's license." He looked over the top of the car to the other cop and ordered, 'Get her registration and proof of insurance Randy, while I run her license." He headed back to his patrol car to call in the license on his radio.

"I need to see your registration and insurance papers please," the young cop said politely. Sam reached to her glove compartment to retrieve them as he watched. She pressed the button and the door plopped down. The baggie of marijuana rolled onto the glove compartment's door.

[144]

"Don't move!" the young cop screamed. "Keep your hands where I can see them!" He excitedly turned his head towards Smith and screamed, "She's got drugs in her car!" Smith, feigning as sincere of a surprised look on his face as he could, began to approach Sam's car. He began to internally celebrate the success of his plot. The young cop instructed Sam on how to exit the car with her hands in the air. Sam was shocked and speechless and barely able to comprehend what he was saying. She complied best she could as she stared down the barrel of his now drawn pistol. Her mind reeled in confusion.

"How did that get in there? I never let anyone have pot in my car!" she thought. She wracked her brain as to how it could have gotten there. She tried to recall the last time she had even looked into her glove compartment. She found no answers.

"Watch your head!" the young officer warned as he placed Samantha in the back of his car. Smith instructed the officer to handcuff her hands in front of her, rather than behind her, due to her petite size. Sam had never even seen the vice principal's office at school for misbehaving, let alone a jail cell.

"I swear that isn't mine and I didn't even know it was in there!" she pleaded to the young cop. Her stomach wound itself into knots. "Please just call my dad!" The officer walked back towards her car, ignoring her pleas.

[145]

"I'll check the trunk," Smith told the other officer. He reached down beside the driver's seat and popped the trunk lid with the lever. "You search the inside, and wear gloves. Watch for needles." While acting as if he were searching the trunk he heard a scream.

"Holy shit Mike, look at this!" He lifted the gallon zip lock bag full of white powder from the canvas bag and into Smith's view. The young officer's eyes grew huge. He laid the baggie of coke on the trunk of Sam's car and continued searching the inside of her car. Sam's view was blurred by the wire cage separating the front of the police car from the back, as well as from the tears welling up in her eyes. She saw something on the back of the car and the officers interacting, but she had no idea of the depth of her problems.


While the other cop was engulfed in searching the back seat of Sam's car, Smith grabbed the bag of cocaine with his plastic gloved hands, opened the patrol car door where Sam sat and tossed the bag into her hands.

"What's this, young lady?" he said as she lifted the bag from her lap to look at it. She sat confused and staring at it. Just as quickly as he had thrown it to her, he snatched it from her hands, shut the door and returned the bag to the trunk of Sam's car. The young officer saw none of it. Sam's fingerprints were now on the bag, and only hers. Smith had switched it from the original baggie to a new one, and had worn gloves when doing so, before planting it. A crowd gathered, drawn to the flashing red and blue lights and the unusual activities. The young officer stowed the evidence in the trunk of his patrol car. A tow truck was called to tow Sam's car. Smith was gloating over the success of his scheme. While the tow truck driver was getting signatures from the other cop, Smith opened the patrol car that held Sam to relay his message.

"You're fucked, you little whore!" Shitbag Smith whispered into her ear. "I told your fucking scumbag dad I was going to fuck him. You're going to rot in prison and you can tell your hippie prick drug-dealing dad to go fuck himself for me!" Smith leaned back, gave her an evil grin, and slammed the door violently.


"Local woman nabbed with huge cache of cocaine during routine traffic stop!" the local papers plastered on their front pages. "Largest cocaine seizure in over two decades." one headline read under a huge picture of the gallon-sized Zip-lock baggie of cocaine. The picture looked as if it had been altered to make the bag look larger. One picture showed Smith leaning into the back of the car talking in Sam's ear.

"I'm so scared, Daddy," Sam told her father the next evening. She'd spent a tearful and terrifying night in the county jail fifty miles from her home.

"It will be okay honey, we'll get the best attorney around and get the truth out there," Barry said. "I don't care what it costs!" He took Samantha into his arms. "I wish I could kill that no-good prick!" Barry thought after learning of the message from Smith that was sent to him via his daughter. "It will all be fine." He hugged her closer to him.

"I don't know, Barry, the evidence against her is so iron-clad," the attorney said. He was one of the best criminal attorneys in the state, but as he put it, "I wish I did, but I don't own a magic wand. With the car's brake light not working, which was verified by the tow truck driver, and the weed being clearly visible to the officer when the car registration was removed from the glove compartment, the search of the rest of the vehicle was legally permitted; it's a tough one, Barry. Then, with the over a pound of cocaine in a plastic bag under the seat having only Sam's fingerprints on it, no other passengers in the car, and it being her car, I think we need to look at a plea bargain," he added.

"Not happening, Grady!" Barry firmly insisted to the attorney. "She didn't do anything and I don't want her going to state prison or even county jail for that matter! Take it to trial if you have to and just get her off!"

"I'll do my best Barry, I promise both of you that," the attorney said, "Ninety-nine percent of the time I think my clients are guilty. This time, I truly believe in my heart of hearts that you are innocent, Sam." Sam smiled and nodded in thanks, but terror showed in her eyes. The attorney used every trick in his book. He studied each potential juror. He questioned the fact that Sam's fingerprints were the only ones on the baggie. "I find it hard to believe that not one other person had touched this bag. Surely if it were being anything other than planted, other prints would be on it." He had said before staring into each juror's eyes. He fought for Sam with his heart, even bringing her to stand directly in front of the jury box to face each juror. "Does this look like a drug dealer to you?" he asked them. Sam stood in front of them pale and shaking. He saw each juror dig to her soul with their eyes.

Six months later, Sam sat lifelessly still in her chair at the front of the courtroom beside her attorney awaiting the verdict.

"As to count one, possession of cocaine with intent to distribute, guilty!" the court clerk announced loudly. "Guilty!" again the clerk orated to the courtroom twice more, as she relayed the jury's findings on the additional drug charges. A low rumble sounded among the plethora of local news reporters and nosey citizens of Edgewater. Sam's attorney placed what he meant to be a soothing hand on her back, which had no such effect.

"It will be okay Sam," he said. Rivers of tears streamed from her eyes. Her sobs became loud and uncontrolled. Her mom started screaming insults to the jury and was removed by the bailiff. Andy sat crying, unsuccessfully attempting to dam his tears with the palms of his hands.

"Daddy, no! Daddy, please? Daddy, help me!" Sam pleaded loudly to her father. Her voice seemed miles from him. He swept the room with his eyes, pleading with each person in it with them.

"I love you, honey!" he said back using what strength he had left in his soul. "I will get you out of this pumpkin, I promise!" Two female officers lifted Sam from the chair that she had collapsed into upon the clerk's announcement of her guilt. They spun her around and handcuffed her tiny hands behind her. They turned her toward the courtroom's rear exit. Her legs again gave way to her emotions and collapsed beneath her. The jailers, one on each arm, lifted her from the floor and carried her from the room. She pled to her father with her eyes over her shoulder as she disappeared.

"It could be worse," the attorney tried to rationalize, "The judge only gave her the lower term of nine years with no parole, instead of the twenty he could have, Barry."

"Only nine!" Barry growled. His face became beet red and he clenched his teeth inches away from the attorney's face. "Nine years for something she didn't do!"

"I could see the doubt in the judge's eyes about her guilt, Barry. I could tell he could see through the evidence. I think our chances are good for an appeal," the attorney said, trying not to show his true feelings. He knew that finding grounds for an appeal would be nearly impossible. The evidence was overwhelming and every ruling by the judge was legal and proper. "The judge could see the innocence in her eyes and that she looked like a wholesome all-American young lady," the attorney

[151]

further consoled. "He's used to seeing the usual old looking pocked faces of the druggies that come before him, not some innocent looking healthy young girl like Sam, Barry! He normally throws the book at his drug defendants, but he gave Samantha the minimum allowed." Barry heaved into the garbage can beside the attorney's desk.

Barry fell into a deep depression for a month. His anger overcame every other feeling that he had, except for his deep sorrow for his daughter. He would visit Sam every Saturday and Sunday--the only visiting days allowed. Most weekends he would have to share the precious visiting time with Sam's boyfriend, as she was allowed only two hours per day regardless of the number of visitors that she had.

"Trust me, honey, I will get you out of this place!" Sam's dad reassured her on each visit.

"I know you will, Daddy," Sam responded each time, her hope of it happening ebbing as each week passed. Weeks passed and then months.

"Uh, hi Daddy, what's up?" Sam said curiously, noticing an unusual positive aura being emitted from him one Saturday.

"Hi, honey! You know how much I love you, right?" Barry said as he winked at her with a smile. "Honey, the truth shall set you free!" Sam was perplexed but liked the sound of the word 'free'. The conversation then shifted to the usual mundane— Sam's father's excitement did not.

"Sam, I am going to get you out of this place soon. I promise!"

Sam sensed something different...very different.

# CHAPTER 10

"Oh shit!" Tony exclaimed, "I left my fishing license at the store. I'll run and get it." He and his buddies were leaving in minutes for a combo fishing and L.A. Lakers basketball game in minutes.

"Hey, it's Tony," he said over his cell to his buddy's voicemail, "I left my fishing license at the shop. If you guys get here, I'll be right back." He hung up the cell and set it next to him on the couch, and began searching for his car keys. "Damn, I'm going to be late!"

"Here, Tony," Mylee said with the keys dangling in her hands.

"Thanks, honey, if the guys show up, tell them I'll be right back." He darted off.

"Oops, he's going to need this," Mylee said. She noticed that his cell phone had fallen between the cushions of the couch in his haste. She picked it up to place it on the table next to his bag and inadvertently pressed a button, bringing its screen to life.

It was unlocked from his recent call.  She laid it on his bag and a small red heart caught her eye.

"Hurry back!  He's out of town until next Thursday.  I'll keep it shaved and hot for you! LOL," the text read.  It had a cute emoji at its end of a girl kissing a heart.  "G.A." the contact name read.

"No, please no!" Mylee thought.  Her body began shaking and she felt as though every cell in her body was going to vomit.  She began scrolling through his text messages, searching her mind for an explanation.  "Oh God no!" she again gasped, seeing an array of similar messages with varying initials attached to them.

"Honk, honk!" a car horn sounded as her husband's friend screamed, "Hurry up Tony, we're going to be late!"

Her husband flew through the door, failing to notice Mylee standing in shock in his haste. He grabbed his bag and phone, which she had replaced on the table out of panic when she heard the car horn.

"Bye honey, love you!" he said.  He rushed by her to the front door, slowing to kiss her un-puckered lips as he passed. He disappeared before Mylee could compose herself enough to utter a word.

"How could he!" she thought. She sobbed sadly with her shoulders slumped to her sides as if her elbows were sewn to her ribs. "He was supposed to love me!" she wailed aloud. Her legs weakened and her body crumbled into a helpless heap on the floor, appearing as if her every bone had been removed. Grasping her sickened torso with both hands to try and relieve the pain, she curled into a fetal position and bawled for hours.

"What's the matter, Mylee?" Seth asked anxiously after finding Mylee at his doorstep. Her face was swollen and she stared at toward him through her reddened eyes. Tears streamed down her cheeks. She had no idea how she had come to him. Unable to speak, she sobbed and tried to fall to his arms..

"What's wrong?" Seth begged. He placed one hand on each of her shoulders. He kept her at arm's length trying to see the source of her pain. She continued to sob. "Come in, Mylee," he said. He stepped to her side and guided her to his couch. She tried to speak but kept falling into tears.

"Let me get you a glass of wine," he said. He returned with it as she began to regain her composure. She killed the entire glass in one gulp.

"Easy, girlfriend," he said. He retrieved the entire bottle and refilled her glass. It disappeared nearly as quickly as the first. She began to relax.

"Tony's been having affairs!" Mylee confided. She again refilled her glass, this time only sipping at it. "I think he's been screwing a bunch of women!" Her chin became pressed into a double one as she looked downward. Her tears poured onto her hands that fidgeted on her lap.

"It's okay Mylee, I'm here," Seth said. He placed his hand on her knee. "It'll all be okay." He lifted his arm to around her. He felt her press her body to him.

"What happened, Mylee?" Seth asked, already knowing the obvious. He felt pangs of guilt for not sharing what an ass Tony was with her long ago to save her this inevitable grief. He sat silent and listened.

"I think Tony has been screwing Gina Andrews, Seth. -- and a bunch of other women too!" Seth saw anger replacing her shock and pain.

"Maybe not. Maybe it's just a misunderstanding," Seth said, searching for a way to ease her pain. His anger boiled within him.

"I found a text on his phone," she said. She told the entire story to him. Seth listened patiently, filling her glass when coaxed. "That fucker!" she screamed. Her head tilted back towards the ceiling. She blinked between her tears, as if praying for her thoughts to disappear. Seth drew her tighter to him. "I feel so worthless and alone, Seth." She laid her head on his chest and looked up at his face.

"Don't ever think that Mylee, you are the most decent and beautiful person I have known my entire life!" he said. He looked down at her. "That prick Tony!" he thought, hiding his anger from Mylee. He kissed her forehead and smiled. "Mylee, I've always cherished everything about you. Please never think anything like that again," he reiterated softly. Mylee squirmed upwards to rest her head in the crotch of his neck.

"I don't know what to do, Seth." She brought his hand to her bosom and caressed it.

"Just rest, for now girl--just rest and let it settle in." She sat in silence a moment.

"You are my pal Seth," she cooed into his ear. Her face blushed from both the wine and her thoughts. "I'm so glad I have you." She began kissing Seth's ear, and then his neck. Seth sat still.  His eyes were wide.  He gave way to her kisses.  Each one became longer lasting and took more of him into her mouth.

"Mmm..," Seth moaned as he tilted his head aside to expose more of his neck to her.  Her kisses smacked softly as the vacuum gave way to the air around her lips between each one.  Mylee savored Seth's manly aroma and her arousal intensified with each taste of him.

"Feels good," he voiced breathlessly.

"Kiss me, Seth!"  She put her hand behind his neck and pulled his face to hers.  She felt her lips throbbing.  "It's okay, Seth," she said after seeing him pause to let her see that it was he and not her husband that she was inviting to her.  She assured him with her loving eyes.  She moaned as Seth's rugged sun-dried lips met her delicate ones.  His instantly absorbed the moistness of hers.  Hers willfully shared it.  She remoistened them with her tongue.  She tasted him.  He tasted her.  She tasted pure and sweet to Seth-- just as he had always thought it she would.  His tongue found hers.  His breath disappeared and he gasped for his next.  Mylee fought for her next as well.  She lifted her top and ripped her bra to the top of her breasts in one motion.  A high-pitched moan left her as she felt his calloused hands come into contact with her swollen nipples.  She thrust them to him and again gasped for a much-needed breath.

[160]

She began to caress Seth's inner thighs with the tips of her fingers, gently exploring his manhood with the back of her hand each time she neared it.  Seth gasped, emptying Mylee's lungs from the force as they kissed.  She caressed his stomach under his shirt and found his hardened manhood at his navel.  She unbuttoned his pants and lowered his zipper.

"Mmmm!" she moaned, as she slid her hand over him.  It was double in size as her husband's--in both length and girth.  "Feel good?" she whispered after exposing him from his underwear and stroking him.  He replied with another moan.  She began to feel her body preparing itself.

"You're so beautiful, Mylee," Seth whispered, breaking his kiss only long enough to say it.  He found her moistened crotch and pushed her legs apart.  Mylee shifted her body and slid her skirt upward to free her legs.  Seth slid his hand under her panties.  He ignored the sound of the elastic ripping at the leg opening as he did.  His flat open hand found her hairless mound.

"OOHH," she moaned as he stroked her. The heel of his palm had captured her button.  Each circular motion caused pleasure.  Seth found her rhythm.  Mylee struggled and splayed her legs wider.  Every cell of her body craved him.

"Let's go to your room, Seth," she said, "I want you inside me!" She rose to her feet, uncaring that her blouse and bra were crumpled above her fully exposed breasts. She lifted him from the couch and led him.

"You sure, Mylee?" Seth questioned after stopping her at two steps towards the bedroom.

"I'm sure, Seth, I want you, I should have married you," she said. His mind wandered. He had lived with this thought since seeing her innocent beauty as she slept the night he rescued her from the near-rape as a freshman. He realized that he had sentenced himself to a willful life of loneliness long ago, unable to settle for less than Mylee's perfection.

"I should lock the door, Mylee," Seth offered as they passed it.

"Don't bother Seth!" she exclaimed, "I could care less about anyone knowing about us after what Tony has done to me!" Seth locked the door as they passed it. "I am so glad I'm here," she said. She ripped her top and bra over her head at the foot of his bed. She pried her shoes from her feet with her toes and removed her pants and panties in one motion. She stood bare and still and faced him. He stood speechless in awe. She held her hand towards him and smiled.

[162]

"Are you sure about this, Mylee? I don't want to....."
Mylee interrupted him by filling his mouth with her tongue.

"I'm sure," She said after freeing her lips from his. She sprawled onto the bed and pulled him on top of her. She felt no resistance. She kissed him passionately and reached to stroke him, removing any doubt of her intentions. Excitement overcame her as she thought of having someone foreign within her, especially of a size foreign to most women.

"I've wanted you for so long!" he said. He lowered his body onto hers, supporting his weight on his limbs. She disappeared under him. She felt her body again preparing for him.

"You are so beautiful," he whispered. He kissed his way down her neck and to her swollen nipples. She rolled onto her shoulder blade to lift herself and feed him. He sucked every part of her breasts, giving each equal attention. Mylee felt her blood being vacuumed to the surface of her skin in places, sure to leave loving bruises. She pressed herself into him, to help them darken.

"A little harder..." she said—she wanted to be bruised. His wet kisses drifted steadily downward, across her clean shaven mound, and finally reaching the top of her crevasse. His gentle tongue kept Mylee's rhythm. He followed it. She held the back of his head and drew herself into him at each pulse. He felt her body stiffen and she began to moan. He saw her strained face appear between her breasts as she pulled his mouth to her. Her torso began to spasm and she exploded into uncontrolled cries of delight. Seth kept her warm within his mouth but his tongue sat still.

"Felt so good," she said breathlessly. She breathed deeply again and again. Her body relaxed and her breathing shallowed. Seth gently tested her body again with soft kisses and took her to the same height of ecstasy a second time when her body allowed it.

"You okay, love?" Seth asked softly as he remounted atop her to kiss her.

"Oh, yeah!" Mylee breathed. She wrapped her arms around him and kissed any part of him that came close to her lips. "Felt so good!" She smiled warmly. Her face was flushed and moist with perspiration. She shifted herself to anxiously guide him to within her. She felt him find her warm moistness. "Make love to me Seth," she begged. She felt him lower himself. Her body allowed him within her with surprising ease. She wrapped her arms under and around him and grasped the tops of his shoulders.

[164]

"You feel so good Mylee," Seth whispered. He slid his hand to her lower back and pulled her to him. She nearly bit her lip through. She shifted her grip at each of his thrusts, never allowing him to slip from her. The pace of his strokes became more rapid with each thrust. An animal-like instinct emerged in him. He pounded harder and harder. Sweat poured from him. Mylee held her legs to their widest and into the air. The air filled with the slaps of their pelvises pounding together. She felt herself begin to tremble.

"OOOOHH, I'm going to cum!!" Seth screamed. Mylee savagely gripped his buttocks and held him to her depths.

"Cum in me!" she screamed as she began to explode in orgasm. She felt what seemed like gallons of liquid spray into her. They collapsed into each other.

"Thank you, Seth," Mylee said lovingly, nuzzling close to him. Her breath and kisses warmed the side of his neck.

"For what?" Seth replied.

"You know, being my friend, always there to rescue me-- for loving me." She moistened her lips and kissed him while forcing her hands between he and the bed to hold him as if she were never going to let go.

[165]

"I'll always love you, no matter what," Seth said. He kissed the top of her head as it rested on his chest. "That's what I do Mylee." His mind drifted through a sea of possibilities. Exhaustion took them and each fell to deep sleep in the other's arms. Seth awoke hours later to a dandelion flower on the pillow next to him in Mylee's place. He laid there, hands behind his head.

# CHAPTER 11

"That game was great!" Tony said to his buddies. They all were hoarse from their testosterone-fueled screaming at the refs and the players of the opposing team. "Let's go get a beer somewhere close to the motel!"

"Sounds good! Let's do it!", one of Tony's friends seconded as he hailed a cab to take them to their yet-to-be-discovered watering hole.

"Looks good to me," Tony's friend who had hailed the cab declared. They were eyeing a nondescript friendly-looking bar that the cab driver had taken them to.

"Live Music Tonight," said a sign written on white butcher paper, the letters of which were colored in with scribbles from a permanent marker. It was stapled clumsily to the barn-wood siding on the front of the building.

"Hold on!" Tony said. He held his hand flat and into the air like a guard at a border crossing. "This is a country bar and

Mikey prefers rap music!" he teased, knowing that their friend
Mike despised rap music and that country was nearly all he
listened to.

"Fuck you, dick breath!" his friend Mike said. They
erupted into laughter as Tony pulled the bar door open towards
them.

"Friendly little place," Tony commented under his breath
when an uncomfortable quietness overcame the bar as they
entered. Nearly every patron turned to look at them. The normal
roar of barroom chatter resumed once the locals failed to
recognize anyone in their group.

"Let's sit here," Mike said, pulling a chair next to the
vacant dance area near the stage. Idle instruments sat leaned
against their amps in wait for their owner's return from break.
The other patrons seated around the stage gave them welcoming
nods.

"What'll ya have?" a busty, aged-beyond-her-years
cocktail waitress chimed with a flirty country twang. She seemed
to have come from nowhere. She wore cutoff jean shorts a size
smaller than herself. Her already considerable cleavage was
needlessly enhanced by a pushup bra.

"Pitcher of Bud," Tony ordered, adding, "May as well make that two."

"You got it!" she said. She disappeared and returned in less time than was expected, obviously knowing how to earn her tips. She spread their mugs around the table and set the one pitcher in the center. She returned with the other seconds later. She sat a large bucket of peanuts in front of them, the shells of which coated nearly every inch of the bar's floor.

"Might be good," Tony said while noticing the cowboy-hatted band taking their places. The jukebox became silent mid-song.

"Maybe," Tony's friend agreed. The band members were all nearly twenty years their senior, handled their instruments with ease, and had no fear of the well-worn one-step-higher-than-the-floor stage from which they performed.

"Not bad," Tony's friend Mike commented after the band had played a few songs. The others in the group nodded in approval. The band played a mix of country, older rock and roll, and blues.

"That's nice!" Tony whispered to his friends. He pointed with his head and eyes in the direction of a  pretty, perfectly proportioned, long-blond-haired cowgirl on the other side of the

[169]

dance floor. Tony guessed her to be in her late twenties and noticed that she danced nearly every dance. Catching Tony checking out her butt, which looked like it had been poured into her jeans, she smiled invitingly. She gave him an 'I know what you're looking at, and I'm glad you like it!' look over her shoulder.

"Hi," Tony mouthed to her as she danced a slow dance with a slightly greying man who obviously had more of an interest in her than she did him. She smiled back and nodded.

"Wanna dance?" Tony heard from behind him as the next song began. He turned to see the cute little blonde standing with her hand presented to him.

"Jenny," she said as he rose from the table, having taken her hand in acceptance. She turned her ear to Tony, expecting his name in reply.

"Tony," he replied. He already imagined himself in her loins.

"New around here?" Jenny asked. He saw her take note of his wedding band.

"Just visiting from up north for a Lakers game and a little fishing tomorrow with the boys," he said. He undressed her with his eyes as he spoke. She didn't mind him doing so.

[170]

"Good!" she said in a slightly intoxicated and bubbly voice. "Don't want a pretty boy like you being lonely! I'll keep you company!" Tony smiled, stared into her eyes, and kissed her hand with a longer-than-greeting kiss.

"Want to go have a cocktail at my place?" the little blonde whispered in Tony's ear as she nibbled it sensuously during one of the many slow country songs they had danced to. She leaned back with a seductive smile awaiting his answer.

"Sounds good to me, let me give my buddies a heads-up. I'll be right back," he said. She left to gather her purse from her table. Tony strutted to the table where his friends sat, all of whom knew what was coming.

"Fuck, she's hot, huh!" Tony said to his friends. He made sure they all noticed the features of his latest conquest. "She wants to take me home with her!" He paused and looked in each of their eyes. "I mean, can you blame her!" he added. He pointed to himself with all the fingers on both cupped hands and swept them up and down from head to toe as if presenting himself as a prize. He glanced to ensure the little blonde wasn't watching him.

"I'm going to take off, doubt I'll make it fishing," he said. "Go easy on the pictures for me guys, I don't want Mylee knowing I wasn't there!"

"Ahh, come on Tony, let's just go fishing!" Mike begged. Tony was oblivious to his friends' unanimous disgust.

"Fuck that! I can fish anytime, I'm getting some of that," Tony said. He saw the blonde leaning over a table to tell her friend something. Tony smiled at the view and batted his eyebrows at his friends. "Catch you guys tomorrow," he said. He rushed to her like a dog in heat after being teased by her backward stance. Tony disappeared for the night and met his friends at the bar near the dock after they had returned from fishing the next day. They took pictures of themselves with their fish at the dock. Tony held one of the larger ones as well as a fishing pole in most. They returned to the airport that afternoon. Tony slept the entire flight home.


"I'm back in town, we'll hook up. I have to take care of some stuff tomorrow morning but am free tomorrow afternoon," Tony texted to the person in his contact list labeled "G.A." as he rode back to his home from the airport.

"Yummy," with three hearts, came an immediate reply. "He's gone until Thursday!"

Tony texted a smiley face back, then texted two others in his harem with similar messages and received similar replies.


"Hi honey, I'm back!" Tony announced as he traipsed through his front door. He tossed his bag to the side of the couch. He grabbed a beer from the refrigerator and plopped onto the couch.

"Mylee, you here?" he again inquired. He fingered the remote and brought up the sports channel. He thought Mylee was in the back room making herself pretty for his return, having seen her car in the driveway. "Come see me, baby," Tony summoned, knowing how she loved for him to be anxious for her.

"Hmf,hmf, hmf," Mylee sniffled, hearing Tony beckoning her. She rose from the edge of their bed still composing her last minute thoughts. She was anxious. She had spent two full days avoiding people and searching for answers. The idea of leaving her only known life was frightening. The thoughts of facing her parents, the gossipy town, and herself, with the failure of her marriage was unbearable. She was driven to glue the pieces of her marriage back together. She doubted, even blamed, herself.

She may not have been an attentive enough wife. "There must be a reason!" she thought. She couldn't understand.

"Hoooo!" she exhaled slowly. She braced herself, unsure of what she was about to say and aimed herself deliberately towards the next room.

"Hi, honey!" Tony said cheerily while rising to his feet. He glanced to the television as he stood, watching to see if the player had made his free throw. "Missed you." He held his open arms to her. Mylee's stomach turned, she began to cry and turned from him.

"What's wrong, Mylee?" he said. His face changed to one of concern as he sprung to in front of her. She looked up at him. Her two-day-ago-applied makeup was washed to her chin by tears. Her eyes were red and swollen.

"What's wrong?" he screamed. He reached his hands to her shoulders and lifted her to face him.

"You're supposed to love me!" Mylee screamed. She swept Tony's hands from her shoulders and raised her arms to above her head in one motion. "How could you!" she screamed. She began pounding Tony's shoulders and chest with the balls of both her fists in unison. Her tears scattered from her eyes with each impact.

"Mylee, please tell me!" Tony screamed after gaining control of her flailing arms.

"Why? Why? Why?" Mylee screamed.

"Why?" she repeated again with a weakened voice. Her eyes pitifully found his. She collapsed into wails, then sobs, and fell to her knees. She became a crumpled heap on the floor, hiding her face from the world with her open hands.

"Please don't do this, Mylee," Tony begged. He fell to his knees and wrapped himself around her. He folded his fully extended arms over her. He laid atop her, as if shielding her from the world.

"I love you, I love you, I love you!" he repeated, trying to beat it into her head. He frantically paged through the endless possibilities of his indiscretions that might be at the root of Mylee's pain.

"I bet one of those fuckers told their wives and she called Mylee," he thought. "Almost nobody knows about Jennifer. I haven't even told anyone about Gina!" His mind raced.

"Mylee, you know I only love you! You know that!" he told her with conviction. "You are all I have ever loved. I could never love anyone else!" He paused and stared blankly. He begar

[175]

to realize the truth in his own statement and the immeasurable destruction that he may have caused.

"Then why?" Mylee said as she lifted her head from the heap of her body parts. Tears blackened from mascara poured down her face.

"Talk to me, Mylee. What are you talking about?" His harem roster scrolled through his head.

"Gina Andrews! And all the other whores talking nasty to you on your phone!" she screamed. Her tears scattered across him. "I saw them all before you left when you dropped your phone! You fucker!" she screamed. She retreated to her pitiful heap. Tony's face paled his eyes darkened and his pupils widened. He felt something fall within him. He felt its weight trying to turn him inside out. His harem's roster scrolled non-stop in his mind. He looked at his wife sprawled in pain before him.

"Baby please, I'm sorry, I fucked up! I'll never hurt you again! Please, Mylee, I love you and I can't live without you! I promise I'll never do anything to hurt you again," he pleaded. "I'm so fucking sorry!" "Please forgive me, I was a stupid fucking idiot, I love you more than you will ever know!" he begged. Mylee let him take her into to his arms.

[176]

"I love you, Mylee," he whispered as he lifted her and carried her to their bed. He sat stroking her hair and let her exhausted body drift to sleep. He held her in his arms, kissing her every second throughout the night. He laid awake until the morning, his stomach churning bile the entire time.

"It's all over with. I love my wife and she is all I want from now on. I hope you understand." Tony texted G.A. and all the other initials on his phone the next day. He deleted each one from his contact list.

"What a dick!" he said aloud. He shook his head in disgust at himself after deleting the final woman from his phone.

"I love you Mylee. I will make it all up to you by loving you with all my soul for the rest of our lives. I am so very sorry, Mylee. You are all I want," he texted, having left her sound asleep that morning as he went to work. He texted the same several times during the day. He got no reply. He sat in his scheduled lunchtime meeting, yearning to be home with his wife. He let his workers close that evening and left an hour early.

"Hi, Mylee," Tony said, as he approached her from the rear as she stood at the kitchen sink that evening. He embraced her and kissed the back of her neck. She leaned into his lips. "It's over, Mylee. It's all ended, never again, I promise. I texted them all and put an end to it for good." Mylee stared ahead, hearing his every word.

"Sit down, I'll make you a plate," Mylee said. She turned and faced him with a broken smile. Mylee locked herself in the bathroom and soaked in the tub for over an hour after doing the dishes. She heard Tony enter their bedroom and saw the room darken through the crack at the bottom of the door. She waited, dressed herself in her pajamas, and joined him in bed. They shared no words—he rolled to her and put his arm around her.


"See you after work, honey," Tony told Mylee after awakening her in bed the following morning. She let him kiss her on her lips.

"Have a good day, Tony," she said, again only able to form a fractured smile. She laid thinking. She again doubted herself.

"Thanks, Mylee," he said. "I'll come home early and we'll take a walk around town. Okay?"

"Okay, Tony," she replied with a warm, but pained, smile.

"Oh, and honey, call me anytime, I don't care where I am, what I am doing, or how busy I am, I promise I will answer every time," Tony said, adding, "I unlocked my phone and I am going to leave it on the table every time I come home, take a shower, or anything. You pick it up and look at it any time you want! You deserve it! You are worth it! I love you!" Mylee cried, thanking him with a less-broken smile and a single nod.


"Shit," Mylee thought to herself two months after Tony had returned from his trip. She realized that she was several weeks late for her period.

"Damn it!" she said the next day after sneaking one of the pregnancy tests from the doctor's office where she worked. The last thing she wanted was to buy one at the local drug store and alert everyone in the town of her possible pregnancy. "Oh shit!" she screamed in a muffled voice.

"It's Seth's!" Her face paled and her eyes widened. She pointlessly rechecked the pregnancy test device a dozen times. "Shit! What the hell do I do?" she asked to the ceiling. Her mind flashed to being a mother. "I can't," she thought, "I've got to get an abortion! My mom and the priest would kill me! It's a baby... it's my baby!" Her stomach emptied into the toilet. She sat at the side of the bed and thumbed through the phone book to find a clinic. She threw the book to the floor and slumped into her own hands and cried. She drove her reality from herself. She needed time to think. Her job allowed just that.


"See you when I get back, Tony." She said, kissing him on the lips. She was leaving for a two-day continuing education seminar a few hours from their home. She'd made no progress on her decision or predicament over the past several days since learning of it.

"Bye, honey," Tony said, hugging her dearly. "Drive careful, I love you! Oh, and remember, call me anytime. Call me a lot, I love hearing your voice."

"I will. Love you too," Mylee said. She blew him a kiss and forced a smile to her face as she backed from their driveway.

"I can't do it!" she screamed to herself the minute she left. "But I have to. I have no choice. What would I tell him?" Her thoughts rambled in her head for the entire drive. She attended the seminar, forcing her mind to its content. She drank an entire bottle of wine that evening to numb herself into sleep. She awoke the following morning and repeated the same procedure, except only allowing herself two glasses of wine. She rested on her thoughts and awoke the following day to her drive home. She felt a comfort. She knew what was right.

"I won't do it. I have to tell Tony something. Damn!" She drove an hour thinking. "It makes no difference, I am not killing my child. This is my problem, not the baby's." Another hour passed and her thoughts began to gather. She felt a warm excitement.

"Hi sexy," Mylee said to Tony. She pranced through the door as she returned from her trip with an unusually large grin on her face. She kissed him more passionately than she had in months. She took his hand, yanked him up from the couch, and drug him to their bedroom.

"What the hell is up with you?" Tony said, infected by her smile. He stood with one of his own as Mylee ripped herself from her clothes. She sprawled wantonly across their bed.

"What the hell?" Tony said as he ripped the clothes from his own body. "Whatever!" he exclaimed as he pounced on her.

"Hah!" Mylee laughed. She clasped her body around his and rolled him beneath her. She mounted him and raped him wildly. Her almost insane lust brought Tony to a lightning finish.

[181]

"What the hell's up with you?" Tony asked with his face contorted with a look of confusion. "You wreck into a truckload of Spanish fly or something!"

"Guess who's pregnant!!" Mylee blurted. Her entire body glowed a healthy rose color. Tony's brow formed lines of confusion. "Guess!" she screamed through her broad smile.

"Who?" Tony asked. He thought of her unmarried sister. Then her unwed best friend.

"ME!" Mylee screamed. She pounced atop him again and devoured his lips with her own. Goosebumps covered every inch of his body. He tore himself from her grip and scowered her face with his widened eyes.

"You have got to be shitting me!" He said. He felt a flittering in his guts.

"I'm pregnant, Tony!" she screamed. She began to cry. He took her in his arms as tears of happiness poured from his own. He held her tighter than ever before. Their glee grew with each month. Mylee celebrated her morning sickness. The baby's pink powder flew into the wind from the black balloons, announcing its sex to all at once at the reveal party. Everyone embraced. Tony and Mylee cried in one another's arms. Their

[182]

families and friends showered them with gifts just before her birth.  Their dream came true.

"Here's your daughter, Dad!" the nurse said.  He handed Tony a bundled blanket that held his daughter.  He folded the cover back and melted to her beauty.

"I can't believe it!" Tony cooed to Mylee.  He was unable to pry his eyes from their daughter.  "She's perfect."  Mylee smiled.  "You did good, Sweetie.  She's so beautiful.  She looks just like you," he said.  He looked at her and then to the baby again.  He lifted the bundle to his face and kissed it.

# CHAPTER 12

"It's already been a year and a half," Samantha's mother announced as if to say, "Oh my, how time flies!" Sam amazed at her mother's insensitivity. Facing another seven and a half years in prison for the crime she didn't commit was not going to "fly by"!

"You need to look at this as an opportunity to bond with the universe and grow as a person." Her mom said. Sam sat in awe of her stupidity. "Well, I better give your dad his turn."

"Okay Mom, love you!" Sam said. She was grateful that her mother's craving for a cigarette was driving her from the room before she was compelled to verbally do so. "Hope nobody tells her about Copenhagen chew—I'd have to put up with her forever!" Sam thought sarcastically. "What a dingbat."

"Hey, honey!" Sam's dad said. The unusual positivity again presented itself in his voice.

"Hi, Daddy," Sam replied curiously. "You look happy!" she added. Her dad winked.

"You know I love you and think of you every minute of every day, right honey?" Sam's dad asked as their visiting time neared its end.

"I know Daddy," she replied. Her face displayed confusion.

"I'm going to get you out of this place, honey," he stated matter-of-factly. "Trust me, it won't be long." He winked again while glancing over his shoulder as he was leaving.

"Hmmm??" Sam thought, "he's up to something…"

"This is a good one," Samantha's dad thought while sorting through boxes of old pictures of Sam's childhood. He separated one from a large stack and added it to a small pile to the side.

"That fucker!" he said aloud. He expressed his hate for Captain Shitbag Smith again, as he did a thousand times a day. "I'll fix that fucker! Two can play at this game." He began focusing incessantly. He continued revising and fine-tuning his plan.

"Oh god!" he said in disgust. He found a picture of himself with Samantha's mom at a concert the day they met. "Crazy bitch! What the hell was I thinking?" He let out a long sigh.

[186]

"At least I got Sam out of the deal." He stared across the room and smiled reflectively.

"She was so cute," he thought as he sorted through his daughter's pictorial life year by year. He sighed nostalgically. He leafed through each year's pictures of Sam on Santa's lap. He viewed her leaning over each year's birthday cake, ready to bring the ever-growing array of candles to their demise.

"Ah, a good one!" he exclaimed, adding another select picture to the small pile. He re-sorted through the small pile and narrowed his selections further to only a half dozen.

"Hmm, these are good ones," he thought. He replaced all but the six into the worn black suitcase from which they had come. He returned the suitcase to the upper shelf of the closet where it resided for decades. The selected six pictures he placed into a manila envelope and stowed it in his desk drawer. He sighed deeply, crossed his feet on his desk, and disappeared into thought.

"Hello, I'm interested in your laptop. Is it still for sale?" Barry inquired. He spoke using a throw away phone the following day. He found the ad on a popular online garage sale site where people sell their personal items. Barry, being the computer expert as he was, never surfed the internet through anything other than an encrypted system called "Tor," an acronym for "The Onion Network." Its name reflected its many untraceable layers-- like an onion. It was developed by the military and became, to their chagrin, available to the general public. Used properly, its users were virtually invisible and untraceable.

"Yes, it is," the reply came back from the seller. According to his ad, he was selling his belongings to move across the country to care for his elderly mother.

"I can meet you in an hour if you will hold it for me? I have cash and won't bicker the price," Barry said. The seller agreed to hold it for him at his home in Sacramento, a place far enough away to obscure the computer's origination—"just in case", Barry reasoned.

"See you in an hour," Barry said. He drove to the man's location, paid cash for the computer, and returned to his car that he had secreted around the corner from the seller's apartment complex. Barry stopped on the levee road, removed the sim card from the throwaway phone that he had called the man from, and threw both it and the phone into the river.

"Idiots!" Barry thought after seeing the childish and ridiculously inadequate cybersecurity system employed by City of Edgewater. He easily hacked into their computer system from the vacant patio of a coffee shop, using its open and free WiFi. He took care to assure himself there were no security cameras nearby and selected the coffee shop in a large community thirty miles from Edgewater. He used the new laptop—after installing the TOR browser on it.

"Figures!" he thought. He shook his head in disgust when recognized the name of the security "expert" that designed their system's intrusion protection as a relative of the city manager. "What the hell?" Barry exclaimed. He realized that anyone with basic computer knowledge could drive the equivalent of a digital eighteen-wheeled truck through their firewall.

"Geez," he thought while shaking his head in disgust. He sat in wonder that some hacker from India or teenager from Detroit hadn't already transferred all the money in the city's accounts into their own. He almost felt embarrassed for them.

"Here we go," he said to himself calmly. He entered the police portion of the town's computer system. He gleaned work schedules, evidence storing information, e-mail communications, and any other data that he might find useful. Most importantly he found the Internet Protocol Address of Shitbag Smith's home computer.

"See you later," Barry mumbled to himself as he exited the police computer. He erased every trace of his intrusion.

"Okay Shitbag, let's see what you are up to!" he thought. He sipped a taste of his latte. He glanced to his rear, even though he sat at the outside edge of the patio against the wooded creek, to assure there were no prying eyes.

"Figures", Barry thought, seeing Smith's home computer had absolutely zero security.

"Let's see...You should be at work, dickhead," he opined. Having seen Smith's work schedule on the police computer system he knew the home should empty. He turned on Smith's computer's built-in camera and microphone to make sure. Nothing stirred.

"Quickdraw!" Barry thought as he laughed to himself. It was the nickname Smith used on the many Texas Holdem' poker sites he frequented. Barry perused Smith's entire system. He examined each of his web visits, his personal letters and documents, and the rest of his personal life. He gleaned his bank account usernames and passwords. He did the same for his credit card accounts.

"Quickdraw McGraw," Barry said. He again laughed as he pictured the old cartoon character by that name blowing the smoke from his six-shooters while sporting Smith's equally ignorant looking face. Barry imagined Shitbag sitting in front of a mirror actually practicing quick-draw with his police-issued pistol. "I'm surprised the son-of-a-bitch hasn't shot himself in the foot!" he thought.

"Who the fuck would want to date you, you fucking doofus-assed dickhead!" Barry thought, seeing that Smith had signed up on a couple of dating sites. He had quit them after getting zero responses to his online profile, even though he had used a picture from ten years earlier. "What a dipshit."

"Okay, here's a little present for you, Shitbag," Barry mused. He installed an extremely sophisticated computer program that he had written himself into the deepest bowels of Smith's computer's operating system. Even the most sophisticated programmer wouldn't recognize the program as suspicious. It was disguised as something familiar put where no one would look. The program gave Barry complete control of Smith's system and was designed to destroy itself if ever discovered and tampered with. He tested it and exited Smith's computer. "All righty!" Barry celebrated. He stowed the computer into its case and turned to the creek to peacefully sip the remainder of his latte.

"He's fucked..." Barry thought.

# CHAPTER 13

"Lights out," the guard sounded. Samantha heard the same abrupt notification every night. The loud metallic clanks of the oversized light switches being thrown soon followed, darkening entire sections of the prison at once. Personal hand-held reading lamps flickered to life in nearly every cell. The roar of voices maintained their previous levels, dying out one by one as the hours passed, but never fully silencing. The muffled moans and groans of women pleasuring themselves, or being pleased by their cellmates more often, seeped from the walls.

"Headcount," the guards would order each morning as the switches slammed to their on positions. The guards, freshly arrived for their morning shifts seemed to take pleasure in rousting their wards. The ones who patrolled each hour during the night to peer into each cell for their own count often strummed the cell bars as they walked by. Their keys rattled at their sides. Samantha rarely slept.

"I hate this place!" Sam thought, rising to start her day. She lived the same routine day after day, then month after month, and becoming year after year. The reek of overcooked fake eggs, burnt white bread, and of a sickening ground-meat-like substance they labeled as "bacon" filled the air. Dinner was no different.

"God, I hope Dad is onto something!" she thought, thinking of her dad's oddly positive demeanor at their last visit. She brushed her teeth in the reflection of the polished steel supposed-to-be-mirror in her cell. She turned sideways to it to gauge how much more weight she had lost from not being able to stomach the so-called food.

"Should we head to the dining hall?" she asked her new cellmate. The girl was about her same age. She was serving time for growing marijuana with her boyfriend on their five acres in the foothills after he had sold several pounds to an undercover policeman. Sam was grateful that the girl had replaced her previous cellmate, who was a manly looking, angry-at-the-world, large and mean woman who had spent most of her adult life in prison. Luckily, she had been transferred to a maximum security facility after attacking a guard.

"Let's," Trish, the young cellmate replied. She jokingly held her folded arm out to present her elbow as if ready to escort Sam to the prom. She rolled her eyes in dread of the meal. She was also a vegetarian like Sam.

"We shall," Sam replied. She took her arm and held it as far as the door of their cell. They walked solemnly side by side down the hallway to the source of the putrid odors. They gagged enough nutrition down to sustain their lives and dumped the disgusting remains into the garbage receptacle where they both knew it belonged. They placed the empty trays on top of the stack of others and headed towards the outdoor yard.

"Hey, baby girls! Which one of you wants a turn with Mama?" A heavy-set ten-year-their-senior masculine looking girl teased them as they walked. She obviously was the honcho of the group of similar looking women that stood laughing and making catcalls to them. One lashed her tongue at them in a crass sexual manner.

"They never stop," Sam commented quietly. They passed them without acknowledgment. They continued to the caged-in outdoor yard for their allotted hour-per-day in the open air. Drab as it was, it was a welcome break from the grey cells in which they resided.

[195]

"Let's go finish our book," Sam said as they exited the outdoor cage. She looked forward to immersing herself in the book's fantasy world--far away from her reality.

"Sounds good," Trish responded. She had a sound of anticipated relief of her own in her voice. They took turns reading aloud and getting lost together in the make-believe world. It had become their only escape and a way to make the days end sooner.

"Should we go suffer the perv?" Sam asked Trish. She was referring to the male guard who spent most of his shifts watching the female inmates shower, often masturbating as he did. He never missed the opportunity to watch Samantha or Trish shower, they being two of the youngest and prettiest women in the prison.

"May as well. Damn, I hate that sick bastard!" Trish commented. Their eyes met in dread.

"I sure am glad you're here!" Sam said. Her face showed absolute disgust as she recalled how he used to come so close he would nearly spurt his semen on her before Trish came into the picture.

"I hate this place!" Sam blurted through clenched teeth. The guard again was there to watch them and again they had to

[196]

be the subject of his sexual satisfaction. "This sucks!" she screamed as she dried herself. She turned her head to the ceiling and pinched her eyes shut.

"We'll make it, Sammy," Trish encouraged. She hugged Sam's towel wrapped body with her own as they walked in silence to their cell. They again had to ignore the catcalls. Days passed—all the same.

"How was it?" Trish asked. She inquired about the visits from Sam's father and boyfriend the following weekend. Trish noticed that her eyes weren't puffy from crying like usual.

"Andy sure misses me. I kind of thought he would have found somebody and moved on by now!" Sam said, adding, "He is a good guy." She smiled gratefully. Trish returned the smile.

"I doubt that asshole boyfriend of mine would come see me if he could!" Trish said. Sam knew that he was locked up for the same charges as Trish. "I was getting ready to leave him after I got some money together. Naturally, this has to happen. My luck!" Trish reflected. Sam listened patiently.

"How's the Pops?" Trish asked, referring to Sam's father.

[197]

"Good!" she said. She briefly disappeared into deep thought, having seen the unusual air of positivity and confidence in him again.

"It tears both of them up that I am in here. Especially my dad," Sam said. "He blames himself." A sad look appeared on her face. "He feels so guilty. It wasn't his fault. He swears he is going to get me out of here. Lately I'm starting to believe him. I can tell he's up to something." Her mind drifted again. "I know one thing, he will never quit trying."

"He'll do it Sam!" Trish encouraged with a smile. It turned to a frown as she reflected on how her own father had left their family and started a new one across the country when she was young.

"I haven't even heard from my bastard dad in over ten years! He used to call on my birthday but even that ended after three or four years." Trish said. "It's okay though, we got by without his worthless ass just fine!" She forced an unhurt look to her face. Sam gave her an understanding smile. "Glad I don't look anything like him! I look just like my mom." Trish declared as she stuck a half-profile and upright pose to allow Sam to imagine her mother's looks.

Sam admired her thick and curly shoulder-length brown hair. It perfectly framed her smooth olive-skinned face and deep brown eyes. Her petite and curvy well-toned body made Sam think that Trish could be a glamorous model if given the chance. She pictured Trish's mother as just as beautiful.

"You are beautiful, and I bet your mom is too," Sam said. "I'm sure grateful that I have you as my friend. I'd be lost in this hell-hole without you!" Sam sat beside Trish on the lower bunk and kissed her cheek. They began reading their book.


"You okay Trish?" Sam inquired, hearing her crying in her overhead bunk one night. Hearing no reply, Sam stood from her bunk, seeing Trish's face covered in sadness. Her bottom lip quivered as she strained to keep her emotions to herself.

"Come lie with me Trish," she whispered as she placed a comforting hand on her shoulder. Trish lowered herself to the floor. She cuddled beside Sam in her made-for-one sized bed.

"It's okay," Sam whispered soothingly as she combed Trish's hair with the fingers of one hand. She held Trish close to her with her other hand to keep her from falling from the tiny lower bunk.

"It's okay," Sam again repeated. She kissed her gently on her cheek several times between her pets. Trish's sobbing eased with each kiss. Trish squirmed against her.

"I love you, Trish," Sam whispered. Trish lifted her face to Sam's and kissed her on her lips. Their lips were unable to part. Sam's deep and lustful gasp robbed Trish of her breath.

"I want you to love me, Sam," Trish said. Sam felt a deep emptiness in her friend.

"I do love you, Trish!" Sam felt the heat from Trish's naked body warming her. "You're such a beautiful person." Trish drew to her again and kissed her passionately. Their tongues met. Sam lifted herself over Trish and fed one of her breasts to Trish's mouth.

"Ooh," Sam gasped. "It feels so good. I've never been with another woman." Sam began spilling her juices onto Trish's pelvis. She took her breast from Trish and took Trishes into her own mouth. "Its so soft," she cooed as she swirled her tongue around her swollen nipple. Trish reached and cupped them into her hands, feeding one to Sam and then the other. She moaned in ecstasy as Sam's mouth drifted between them.

"Ooh God," Trish exclaimed, feeling Sam's mouth sliding through the pool on her pelvis and finding her clitoris. Sam's

[200]

tongue swirled around it while she vacuumed it to her mouth. Trish moaned passionately and began tugging at Sam's legs. She pulled Sam to her and took her into her mouth as well. The sounds of them feeding on each other filled the air. The entire cellblock was silent except for their moans. Their fellow inmates devoured the audible scene and lived it through their imaginations. The final moans and screams of their simultaneous orgasms brought a hundred person gasp of ecstasy through the air.

"So what!" Trish said. They laid together laughing, hugging, and kissing, while listening to the entire cell block break into applause. Their naked bodies laid pressed together that night, and every night, from then on.

"How's Andy?" Trish inquired when Sam returned from her weekly visit with him.

"Good!" Sam replied, adding, "He really is a good guy." Trish smiled.

"I hope I can find somebody like that when I get out of here. I always seem to stick myself with buttholes!" Trish said. She rolled her eyes in self-disgust.

"You will Trish! Jesus, you're a beautiful person inside and out. Any guy would be lucky to have you!" Sam said. "Just don't get in a hurry." Trish nodded.

"He's going to make a good husband, Sam," Trish said while glancing at the picture of Andy above Sam's bunk. "Great job, honest, kind, loyal—hot looking. The perfect boy scout! What more can you ask?" Trish laughed. "You deserve a good man and a good life and I'm glad you have him," she added. Sam smiled back.


"How're things, honey?" Barry asked Samantha a few weeks later. His demeanor continued to become more positive at each visit.

"Good, Daddy," Sam responded. She noticed her father's eyes rolling downward as if he wanted her to look at the table. She saw a handwritten note pressed against the bottom of the glass barrier. "Arranging meeting with a new attorney just so we can be together. I will share a secret plan with you. Pay very close attention when I hug you! Do not say a word to anyone! We will only have a minute together. You are getting out!" the note read. The last word was, "UNDERSTAND???"

Sam looked at her father and nodded. Her father glanced over the room. He placed the note into his mouth when he saw no one looking. He chewed and swallowed it in one quick motion.

"Okay, honey looks like our time is up," her dad said. He stood and smiled at her as the guard passed and directed him towards the door. "I'll see you soon!" Barry mouthed. He wink as he stood. Sam responded with a perplexed smile.

"Your chicken-shit attorney is here and wants to see you," the gruff-and-manly woman guard announced to Sam as she unlocked her cell door. Sam backed to the cell's bars to allow herself to be handcuffed. The guard escorted her to the attorney visiting room. It was two weeks since her dad had let her read his note. After thoroughly strip-searching Sam, including her usual inappropriate fondling, she led her to the attorney/client meeting room. "We'll be watching just outside, don't be fucking up," the guard warned.

"Hi, Daddy!" Sam said. She was able to hug her father for the first time in nearly two years. The guard rapped firmly with her knuckles on the glass and gave them both a scolding finger for touching each other. Sam seated herself at the wooden table across from her father. He introduced the attorney, who began doodling on a legal yellow tablet as if he were taking important notes. Sam and her dad chatted as he did. Barry, unapologetically and in front of the lawyer, informed Sam that the attorney was aware that the meeting was a ruse so that they could spend time together. The attorney's demeanor never shifted, nor did he express any interest in their conversation.

Barry saw the guards engulfed in conversation and no longer scrutinizing their actions in the soundproof lawyer/client meeting room.

"Here honey, give me a hug," Barry said. He stood and stepped away from the table. Sam followed him. The attorney began shuffling papers in his briefcase.

"Sam, listen carefully!" her father whispered so that not even the attorney realized that he was speaking. He exposed his entire devious plan to Sam in brief summary. The plan was to allege that Smith molested her several times throughout her younger years, promising to put her away if she ever threatened to say anything. She was to claim that just before her arrest, she had threatened to do so. Barry explained to Sam about the picture of her in the back of the police car that appeared in the paper. She was to allege that Smith was telling her that he was putting her away before she could report him to destroy her credibility. She was to claim that he even fondled her then as she

[204]

sat handcuffed in the police car. Barry summarized his entire plan in under two minutes of hugging.

"I love you. You do understand now, don't you?" Barry asked. He stepped back from her. His eyes demanded an answer.

"Oh, I understand perfectly!" she said with a sly look on her face. She nodded to further affirm her understanding. She smiled and announced in a normal voice, "Thanks for loving me, Daddy! Thank you for doing this and letting me hug you."

"And thank you too, Sir," Sam said as the attorney looked up. The attorney nodded in dry acknowledgment, seeming entirely uninterested in anything but receiving his check for his time. He shuffled papers into his briefcase. They rose from their chairs.

A guard saw them standing, and after finishing her conversation with the other guard, led Barry and the lawyer to the prison's exit. The other handcuffed and escorted Samantha back to her cell.

# CHAPTER 14

"Here you go, Ian," the nurse said as she positioning Ian's wheelchair at a table. He sat in a small sterile looking room. The table was bare except for a worn rotary-dial telephone. Another small desk with its lightly padded vinyl covered chair was pushed awkwardly into the corner of the room.

"Just relax, Ian," the nurse said. She placed her hand on his back, knowing that he hadn't called his wife since his injury. "You have to trust me, Ian," she added, "Your wife knows all about your legs, she loves you, and all she wants is to hear your voice more than anything in the world." She patted his back lovingly and walked from the room. She closed the door behind her. Ian sat alone, staring at the phone.

"Hello," Ian heard Layla answer anxiously after just two rings. Ian sat still.

"Hello?" Layla asked curiously. She could hear breathing through the phone. Ian sat searching for words.

[207]

"Angel, it's me," he said. He immediately began to pitifully bawl. Layla did the same.

"I have been so wanting to hear your voice! I love you so much! I want you to come home to me!" Layla blurted through her tears. She heard the pitiful sobs from her husband become louder.

"Ian, I don't care about anything other than having you here with me and the baby for the rest of our lives! That's all I care about! Nothing else!" she told him. She wanted to claw her way to him through the phone lines.

"I love you, Angel," Ian said. "I'm sorry," he cried, "I'm so sorry!" He broke into uncontrolled sobs. "Everything is so messed up! I am so very sorry for what I have done to you! I'm so sorry for what I've done to the baby. Please find a way to forgive me!"

"Ian, you listen to me! If you have ever loved me, you listen to me!" Layla ordered.

"Do you love me, Ian?" she asked. She heard silence except for sobbing.

"Ian, you don't love me anymore?" she questioned. "You don't love our baby?",

"Yeah," he said through his tears.

"Do you believe I love you?" she said, again hearing silence. "You don't think I love you, Ian?" She sat still, finally hearing Ian's broken voice respond, "Yeah."

"You don't want me anymore?" Layla asked.

"You're all I've ever wanted Layla," he cried.

"Do you remember our vows, Ian?" She asked softly. "Do you remember we promised each other that we would love each other for better or for worse?" "What else did we promise at the very end before you kissed me, Ian? Do you remember?" she said, not allowing time between the questions for him to drift from her. "Remember you promised me and I promised you that we would never lie to each other? Do you remember that Ian?" She waited in silence.

"Yeah" she again heard him blubber.

"Promise me now that you will come home to me Ian. Promise me now." She heard pitiful bawling, then silence.

"Promise me now Ian, God Damn it!" She stood and screamed into the phone. "You promise me now!"

"I promise" she heard. She sluffed into her chair and tears gushed from her. She heard her husband bellowing into the air. She let him cry for minutes and let him calm.

[209]

"Promise me again!" she whispered.

"I promise" an exhausted voice whimpered again.

"Will you call me tomorrow sweetie?" Layla whispered.

"Yes," Ian said.

"You Promise?" she asked. She heard him do so.

"Now you go lie down and rest. Okay, Sweetie?"

"Okay," Ian responded, adding "I love you, Angel."

"I love you too Ian," she said softly. "Go rest baby", she said. She hung the phone up and turned to her mother. Tears streamed from her mother's eyes as she gave her daughter a look of proud approval.


"Layla, it's me," Ian said, calling the next day as he promised. Layla heard a welcome strengthening in his voice, but it still sounded tired.

"Hi Ian, how'd you sleep?" Layla asked, listening carefully.

"Better than a long time," he answered.

"Good, you needed some rest!" Layla said, her voice purposely being of normal tone.

"Wait until you see how big I am! I'm so fat I need a Santa Claus suit!" She laughed at herself as she said it. She heard a small chuckle from Ian.

"You're not fat," Ian said with stout conviction, "You're just perfect." Layla smiled.

"I'm going to put a pudgy little daughter, just like Mommy, in your arms real soon, Daddy!" she said, lovingly coaxing her husband further from the dark chasm in which he had been drifting.

"She won't be pudgy," Ian replied, already placing her unborn little body on a pedestal.

"Hey, Abel has a girlfriend," Layla said, feeding him mundane pieces of reality. "You remember that pretty waitress at the Riverview, the one with the dark hair that looks like that old singer Elvira? It's her."

"Oh yeah," Ian said, picturing the waitress with the bright red lipstick. "That's great, he deserves it." Adding, "He really needs someone who cares about him in his life."

He sat, listening intently to Layla as she filled him in about the new pizza joint that opened, along with a little of the town's juicy gossip.

"They're working on my legs," Ian said.

"What's wrong Ian?  Are they infected?  Are you okay?"
Layla said.  Ian heard the panic in her voice.

"No, no, no, they're building my new ones!  They came by
and made molds of what I have left and they are going to start
building them when they get to them!"

"Oh, that's good!  Why didn't you say so," she chided.

"I did!" Ian said, chuckling at her.

"How are your arms and hands Ian?" Layla inquired.

"Fine," Ian replied curiously, thinking she knew that they
were.

"That's what I thought," she barked, "I have some chores
for you when you get home and I don't want to hear any excuses
or sissy whining!"  Ian laughed with her this time.

"It figures, already slave driving!" Ian kidded.  He briefly
imagined the items on her list.

"Okay Ian, I love you, call me tomorrow!" Layla said at the
end of their near hour-long conversation.  She threw him an
audible kiss through the phone and heard the same back.
Layla melted in relief.

"Ahh," Ian sighed contently.  He leaned back in his wheelchair and stared at the wall.  He looked to where his legs once were—for the first time feeling hope.

"So sad, Mom," Layla tearfully said to her mother a month after talking to Ian the first time after his injury.  They stood on the tarmac waiting for Ian to disembark from the sand-colored aircraft watching a dozen soldiers, who were all clinging to their lives, being carried from its rear gangplank.

"It is," her mom agreed.  They watched as heartbroken wives, mothers, and fathers somberly approached the gurneys that carried their loved ones, many of which resembled mummies from extensive bandaging.

"There she is!  Geeze!" Ian said with his face reddening to the medic rolling him from the plane.  Layla jumped up and down and flailed wildly with both arms.

"Looks a little glad to see you, Marine!" the medic replied, snickering with Ian.

"That's my wife.  She's pregnant with our daughter!" Ian said as a second medic took the bottom of his wheelchair to help carry him down the stairs.  They rolled him towards Layla, who had ceased her manic greeting and was sprinting towards them.

[213]

"Hi, baby!" Layla said, falling onto Ian and kissing every inch of his face.

"I love you, I love you, I love you!" she half-shouted through a torrent of tears. The medics both grinned.

"Where's your vehicle ma'am?" one of the medics asked, after glancing and seeing a line of wheelchairs forming behind them. "We'll get him loaded up for you."

"We're fine, he's mine!" Layla said, nudging the medic that held the handles of Ian's wheelchair to the side with her hips, commandeering the chair and rolling it towards their car.

"Hello, son-in-law!" Layla's mom greeted with a gigantic smile.

"Hello, mother-in-law!" Ian replied, his grin equaling hers. She kissed his cheek.

"I'll drive, Mom, You can ride in the back." she ordered while rolling Ian to the front passenger door. "Get in baby, we're going home!"

Ian, his eyes tearing, looked up at her. She stood still near him. Her eyes instructed him. He placed one hand on the door, the other on the car's seat, and lifted himself into place. Layla rewarded him with her smile, closed the door behind him and secured his wheelchair into the trunk.

"Okay Mom, we'll see you later," Layla said, dropping her off at the front of her house.

"Where're we going?" Ian inquired.

"Oh, I have a little surprise for you," she said, grinning broadly.

"What?" he asked, his face expressing the same.

"You'll see!" she said.

She rounded one corner of Edgewater after another, finally reaching a familiar cul-de-sac that one of Ian's friends grew up on. She parked in the driveway of one of the forty-year-old homes. Its lawn was meticulously maintained. The roof was new and the paint was fresh. Ian realized that a fellow handicapped person resided there, seeing a sturdy wheelchair ramp at its entrance.

"How do you like our new home?" Layla exploded to her husband. "I got it for payments cheaper than rent and the military gave me the money to fix it up!" Her eyes were wide. "Seth and Abel and a bunch of other guys came over on the weekends and helped fix it all up for when you got home! It's our very own home!" she said. She flew to Ian's side of the car, extracting his wheelchair on the way. She flung his door open and waited..

"Come on! Let's go inside!" she said. She locked the wheels of the wheelchair and braced it with her body. Ian sat gazing at the home with a look of disbelief.

"It's nice," Ian said. He lifted his head to examine the size of the huge shade trees that shielded the manicured yard from the heat. He scanned towards the many same-aged ones doing the same for every other home on the street. He sat for a moment in awe.

"C'mon!" Layla said, jolting him to action and steering him towards the ramp the minute his butt landed in his wheelchair.

"Here we are!" Layla's chipper voice announced as she rolled him through the front door. "Home sweet home!"

Ian swept its interior from side to side. Its paint was as fresh as the exterior's. Widened wheelchair-accommodating doorways had been installed. He saw Layla had decorated it with used, but near new looking, retro-style furnishings. Their wedding pictures adorned the walls.

"Nice, Angel! Real nice!" Ian said with a look of disbelief still on his face. His head continued sweeping from side to side.

"I'm saving this wall for the baby's pictures," Layla said. He stood facing a bare wall across from the entry. She turned

[216]

and stood with her hands on her hips and carefully surveyed the room.  She suddenly again came alive.

"Look in here," she said.  She grabbed the handles of Ian's chair and rolled him into their bedroom.  The king-sized bed filled much of it, but it could accommodate Ian's chair on either side. Ian glanced at the bath, seeing stainless steel bars at both the toilet and tub.  He felt relief from them.

"Look, honey," she said.  She yanked the cord at the side of the sliding glass door to expose a view of the home's backyard. The light from the door brought a cheeriness to the room.

"Nice!" he said. He wheeled himself to the sliding door and stared in awe.  Concrete paths led to a child's play area and to a newly built raised bed garden beyond.

"We even have a hot tub!"  Layla said, pointing to the edge of the deck.  "Its got an electric cover that removes and replaces itself." "Oh, and I have plans for you in there, big boy!" she added.  Her voice suddenly quieted and she stared at the floor.

"I'm not scared!" Ian quickly replied.  He flicked his eyebrows twice and smiled at her.

"Who built the garden beds?  They're really nice," Ian said to move the conversation forward.

"Oh, that was Seth and Abel. Those guys are handy!" she answered. "Boy, they like teasing each other!" Ian smiled and nodded.

"We and our baby are eating all organic from now on and you are going to raise all of our vegetables there for us and that is final!" she said, pointing a firm index finger at him.

"You got it ma'am!" he said, giving her a rigid military-style salute.

"See the chicken coop back in the corner?" she said. She motioned to a small structure in the very back corner of the yard. "I checked, we are allowed 4 chickens but no roosters," Layla said.

"Discrimination!" Ian blurted with a laugh. "But I guess it will save me the trouble of having to get up and ring some poor bird's neck for waking me up too damned early!" Layla rolled her eyes.

"The baby's room," Layla said, after rolling Ian to the adjoining bedroom. Layla had decorated it with pink curtains and a matching pink band at the top of all four walls. Dark colored pink teddy bears holding hands were inlaid into the band at even intervals. Ian nodded in approval.

"It's happening fast!" Ian said, glancing at Layla.

"Not soon enough," Layla chimed. She began rubbing her baby-bloated belly with circular motions. She leaned and kissed his cheek.

"Come on! Let's have lunch!" Layla said, leaving Ian on his own to follow her. One end of the table was open to accept Ian's chair.

"You are amazing! I can't believe you did all this!" he said. "Thank you, Layla. Thank you for everything." He clutched her arm as she walked by the table and pulled her to him and kissed her.

"I love you, Ian and I always will," Layla told him as she served him lunch. She teared in a happy disbelief as she stood behind him.

That evening she laid close to him, letting him feel the warmth of her body. He drifted into a deep well-earned sleep. Layla laid quietly, trying to imagine what her poor husband had been through, kissing him throughout the night.


"How's it feel to be home and in my arms, husband of mine?" Layla asked a week later. They were lying in bed letting the sun rise into their room.

[219]

"Feels really good. Sometimes I thought I would never be here again," Ian said. He disappeared into contemplative thought for a few seconds. He snapped from it as Layla nuzzled her body next to his.

"I so wanted you to come back to me. I would have been lost without you," Layla said. She gently rubbed Ian's stomach as he laid on his back. His hands laid folded behind his head. "I was so worried and lonely for you Ian," she said, "I cried myself to sleep almost every night."

"Well I'm here now, and you're just going to have to put up with me!" Ian said. He lean towards her and kissed her forehead. He slid Layla's hand that was rubbing his stomach towards his groin with his own and smiled.

"Well, well, what do we have here?" Layla said, grinning and looking playfully at him. She dropped below the blankets and took him into her mouth.

"Kinda thought you were wondering," Ian said as he placed his hand on the back of her head.

"Umm, huhm," Layla answered awkwardly. They enjoyed a wonderful sexual session. They slept sound in each other's arms.

"I have to go to work, Ian," Layla said after retrieving their morning coffee. "Things sure are well in the old engine room!" she kidded as she arose to shower.

"No bomb big enough to blow that off!" Ian replied with a grin.

"Oh god!", Layla replied while rolling her eyes. "Well get up and come have breakfast with me, if you are able after what I did to you," she teased back. He smiled and rolled his eyes.

Weeks passed, each happier than the one before. Then months and then the baby. And then life tolls.

# CHAPTER 15

"Mylee doesn't deserve to be with an idiot like that!" Seth thought. He sat dangling his feet into the water from the ancient half sunken dock that acted as his second home. "She's the most beautiful person, inside and out." He pictured her lying naked on his bed and how she had looked so pure. "Damn, she's just like an angel."

"She would have had to fall for that asshole Tony!" he lamented while thinking of how she had fallen to Tony's ruse as a nice guy in high school. "Big man football stud – the lying piece of shit!"

"What a dick!" he thought. He sat recalling all the women that Tony had sexually conquered and blabbed to everyone about, most of them being his friend's wives. The memory of how Tony had bragged about screwing their classmate that was murdered, before her body had even cooled, sickened him. "What a low-rent pile of crap," Seth thought, shaking his head in disgust, "I wish I would have just told Mylee!" He kicked the water with the top of his foot and watched the rings grow in front of it.

"Aah, she wouldn't have listened to me anyway, probably. At least were friends still." He wiggled a rusty nail protruding from the dock back and forth until it freed from its decades-old seat and tossed it into the water. It faded from view as it sank in the murk. He rose to his feet and walked the short distance home, thinking of Mylee the entire way.

"Catching anything?" Seth heard an angelic voice that he recognized sound from the shore behind him as he sat on the sunken dock a week later. He turned to see Mylee sporting a big smile, clad in cutoff jean shorts and a revealing halter top. She stood at the head of the dock's rickety gangplank.

"Only a buzz, girlfriend," Seth answered, holding up his beer bottle in evidence and smiling back at her. "Be careful! Frikkin nails sticking up everywhere on that thing! They'll rip your feet wide open! You want some help?" He began to rise to help her across the fifteen-foot span of the shaky makeshift walkway.

"I got it," Mylee said. She leaned down and removed her flip-flop sandals and began her trek. Seth met her halfway with his extended hand.

"Watch these nails sticking up everywhere on this fucked-up old dock too! I've been meaning to bring a hammer and either pull them out or drive them in, but I always forget," Seth said. "Of course I've been saying that for five years!"

"Why bother! It looks like it's on its last legs anyway," she said. She scanned the old dock, seeing it rotting at its every edge. The old barrels that once buoyed it had rusted completely through. She realized that it only survived as a dock because its bottom was lodged in the mud of the shallow river-bottom.

"I'm going to miss the old girl when she goes," Seth said nostalgically while glancing over the dock as one would an old friend. Mylee smiled, knowing that Seth spent most days off work on the dock, and had done so for many years.

"No fish?" Mylee again asked as she took a seat next to Seth at the front edge of the dock. She soaked her bare feet in the cool river water next to Seth's. She leaned backward and laid on the dock with her head rested on her interwoven fingers behind her. She closed her eyes and let the sun soak into her face.

"Damn you are a gorgeous girl!" Seth said, not meaning to do so. He sat in awe seeing her breasts and nipples nearly fully exposed through her tight tank-top shirt.

"Thanks, sweetie," she replied with a warm smile. She didn't move a muscle or open her eyes. She sensed her nipples had hardened.

"Anyway, I caught two undersized striped-bass and threw them back. That's it," he finally answered. He turned his gaze from Mylee to quell his arousal.

"At least it's a nice day," she said. She opened her eyes and leaned forward to rinse her hands in the water just below the dock's surface. Seth savored her every move.

"How are you feeling, mom-to-be?" Seth inquired. He turned his head to the tip of his fishing pole.

"Good!" she said. "The baby is growing normally and I couldn't feel better." Seth glanced at her, seeing her healthy glow.

"Tony and you doing okay and all?" he inquired. He shifted uncomfortably after saying it.

"You know Seth, it's better than it has been in a long time. I think, with the baby coming and all, we worked that thing pretty much out--but I really do appreciate you caring enough to ask." Seth smiled at her.

"Tony is really looking forward to the baby. He seems to be a completely changed person. Maybe it was all for the good, you know what I mean?" She said. She look at Seth with a half-questioning look. He turned his head back to his pole.

"Probably was, Mylee. I'm glad to see it all working out. I just want to see you happy." Seth replied. He turned back to her. "That little brat is the luckiest little brat in the world having you for a mom! I know you will be the best mom ever."

"It better not be a brat! I'll spank its butt raw every day!" Mylee said, fighting to keep a straight face.

"Yeah right!" Seth said while giving her a sarcastic look. They both laughed.

"Well, I better run," Mylee said. She lifted her feet from the water and stood.

"Hang on," Seth said. He picked up the sweatshirt that he had taken off earlier and dried each of her feet. Mylee balanced herself using his shoulder.

"Here, wear these so you don't get a nail or a sliver," he said. He held each of her ankles and placed a foot into each sandal. He rose to his feet and held Mylee's hand to guide her safely across the wooden plank to the shore.

"You're so sweet, Seth," Mylee said once reaching the shore. The willow trees hid the dock from the world on their other side.  Mylee suddenly leaned to Seth and let her lips meet his.  She kissed him passionately for a brief moment.

"I love you, Seth.  I am glad that what happened, happened!  Maybe in another life, we'd be married," she said softly, adding, "Thanks for being my true friend."  She smiled and winked mischievously at him as she disappeared through the willows.  Seth stood in silence, tasting Mylee's sweetness on his lips.  Their meetings on the dock grew further apart as the baby grew inside her.  Only one other time did their lips meet.

"Dad, when the baby comes we're going to wrap it in a blanket and hand her off to you while we take care of Mom," the nurse in the birthing room said to Tony.  Mylee labored and pushed the baby further towards its new life outside the womb with each contraction.

"Uh, it's okay, I am not good at holding kids or anything like that," Tony responded nervously.  The two nurses looked at each other and grinned.  Tony stood at Mylee's side.  He felt her clench his hand at each contraction.

"Okay," the doctor said, "push real hard this time."  Mylee pushed her hardest at the next contraction, feeling herself tear and a sudden feeling of relief overcome her.  The baby, with the help of careful tugs from the doctor, slipped from her body and into the doctor's hands.

"There we go Mom, it's all over." He laid the baby into one of the nurse's arms while he cut the umbilical cord. The other nurse suctioned fluids from its mouth and nose. The baby suddenly cried its first breaths.

"She's healthy, great color, and beautiful, folks! Congratulations," the doctor said after examining the baby and passing her back to the nurse.

"Here you go, Dad!" the nurse said. She handed the little girl to Tony. Tony took the bundle of blankets that held his daughter and peeked into the opening to see her face. He felt magic!

"Not so hard is it, Dad?" the nurse said after seeing a gentle fatherly look come to Tony's face. An aura of love emanated from him. The nurses again smiled at each other.

"She's so beautiful," Tony said after a moment. He was awed by the scene around him. He kissed the baby's cheek and held her close to him. Mylee, her face looking exhausted and still covered in perspiration, smiled.

"Let's show her to Mom, Dad." the nurse said. She took the baby from Tony's arms and held her to Mylee.

[229]

"She is perfect!" Mylee said. She gazed at Tony wide-eyed.

"Poor baby needs to be fed, Mommy," the nurse said. She placed the baby to Mylee's bosom. Mylee took her breast into her hand and aimed the nipple at the baby, who immediately ceased its crying and began suckling for the first time. Mylee looked to everyone and smiled.

"There we go," the nurse said after seeing the baby nurse normally. "We'll leave the three of you alone and let you get to know each other." She turned towards the door, smiled at Tony and patted him on the back. "Call if you need us," she said. She closed the door behind them as they left.

"Lie with us," Mylee said to Tony. She scooted carefully to one side of the bed to make room for him, never disconnecting their baby from her breast as she did. Tony nuzzled carefully next to them.

"Well, here's our little Halley," Mylee said. She carefully folded the sheet back from their daughter to expose her innocent face. The baby remained attached to her breast.

"She is so perfect, Mylee," Tony said. "I can't believe it. They laid in silence admiring their little child. The nurses soon returned to take the baby to the nursery so Mylee could rest.

[230]

"Okay dad," The nurse said, "They are both sound asleep—It's time for you to get out there and hand out those cigars!"

"We'll call you if we need you, but I am sure it will all be fine."


"Wow, it happens fast!" Tony said to Mylee four years after Halley's birth. They watched as she skipped and danced along the sidewalk during their nightly evening stroll. "Seems like she was born yesterday."

"She is so funny," Mylee said, mentioning how she had rarely cried as an infant and now had such a positive outlook on life.

"Mommy, Daddy! Watch!" Halley said. She ran across the lawn. Tiny lights that were built into her shoes flickered. She cartwheeled and then stood looking at them.

"Good job, baby girl!" Tony said. He and Mylee clapped loudly as Halley took a bow. She had learned to do so from watching gymnastics on television—her favorite pastime. Only months later the "look at me" meant to watch her ride her bike. Mylee and Tony again amazed at her aging reaching the speed of light.

"Hey, honey, what's up?" Tony asked after calling his wife just before lunch one day. Mylee held her phone to her ear with her shoulder while wiping the counter with a damp cloth. She left her job to become a full-time mom the year prior.

"Nothing, just cleaning house. Might head over and visit Mom later, that's about it," Mylee replied.

"I was thinking about coming home for lunch and digging into some leftovers," Tony said.

"Sure, come on home. I'll whip something up!" Mylee said.

"Great, I'll be right there," he said.

"Here you go," Mylee said. She placed leftover stir-fried ginger chicken from the previous evening in front of Tony and set a plate out for herself.

"Shop sure is doing good. It's running smoother than I thought. Dad sure helps out when he's around," Tony commented. "It's good to see him and mom getting away in their motor home like they do."

"I knew it would be fine. You're a hard worker and a good businessman, just like your father," Mylee said. She added a few more compliments and some small talk about their daughter. She

[232]

scooped up their plates after they finished their lunch and began to rinse them in the sink.

"Damn pretty wife of mine, you get prettier every day," Tony said. He approached Mylee from behind. He placed his arms under hers and took her breasts in his hands and began nibbling her ear.

"Wanna get lucky?" he whispered while rubbing his semi-erect penis against her. He felt her press herself towards it and she tilted her head to the side to allow him better access to her neck.

"Oh, I guess," she said as she playfully added, "What was your name?" She giggled and turned to her husband and kissed him passionately. She led them to their bed. They scattered their clothes around it and pounced on each other.

"Oh boy, I needed that!" Tony said breathlessly after their mutually satisfying interlude.

"Me too, whatever your name was," she again teased. Tony smiled and shook his head. He began to massage her body.

"What's that?" Tony said with a serious tone.

[233]

"What's what?" Mylee asked. She looked around the bedroom and then to Tony's face to see the direction of his focus.

"This," he said. He removed all but one finger from Mylee's right breast and pressed to a particular place. He took Mylee's hand to guide her own finger to what he felt. Mylee's face paled as she felt a small hard node with the tip of her finger.

"You have to get that checked immediately!" Tony said. His face expressed concern. Mylee's face remained pale but she maintained her poise.

"Probably just a cyst, but I'll call later and set up an appointment to get it checked out," she said dismissively, but unable to fully disguise her concern.

"Yeah, I'm sure it will all be fine," Tony assured her, "but make sure you call today and get that appointment. Okay?"

"I will, I promise," Mylee said. They gathered their clothes and dressed. Tony kissed her and gave her a questioning look. "I will—I will..." she assured him. He returned to work and called an hour later. Mylee had set up the appointment.


"Go to work, honey! I'll be fine," Mylee told Tony a week after finding the lump in her breast. He had offered to take the day off work and drive her to her doctor's appointment. "All they are

[234]

going to do is just set up another appointment for later." She said. "I want to do some shopping while I'm over there anyway, and you need to be here to pick Halley up after school."

"Okay, but call me if you need me, honey," Tony said as Mylee backed the car from the driveway later.

"And what is the reason for your visit today, Mylee?" the white-smocked nurse inquired. She looked as rigid as the creases in her uniform. She smelled of antiseptic from spending her career in examining rooms. She held her pen to the clipboard in her hand as Mylee, who sat submissively below her in a hard plastic chair, answered.

"I found a lump in my breast. It's small though, probably just a cyst or something," Mylee answered. She waited unsuccessfully for the nurse to affirm her positive thought.

"And how and when did you discover this lump Mylee?" the nurse asked.

"About a week ago, Uh, during a self-exam in the shower," Mylee replied.

"Okay, the doctor will be here in a few minutes. Go ahead and put this on," the nurse instructed. She handed her a blue paper-thin gown with the ties to the front instead of the

[235]

rear. She glanced towards Mylee's breast with a concerned look before walking away. Mylee did as instructed and sat alone in the chilly room staring at various posters of the inside anatomy of the female body.

"Good morning, Mylee!" a chipper elderly male voice sounded. A grey-haired gentleman entered the room. He wore the same white stethoscope-adorned overcoat that every doctor wore. He offered Mylee his hand as he seated himself on a padded stool. He scooted directly in front of her.

"So you have a lump, huh?" he said. He scanned the clipboard that he held in his hands then looked at her. "Lie down here and let's have a look." He smiled and laid the clipboard on the stainless steel cart at his side.

"Show me about where it is, Mylee," the doctor said. Mylee located it with ease, having felt it herself so many times since discovering it.

"Here," she said, rolling her fingertip around it.

"Okay, keep your finger on it a sec," the doctor said. He slid his finger to under Mylee's and pressed inward. "Aha, there the little bugger is!" the doctor said. His eyes were askance across the room as he built an image in his mind with his fingertips. He spoke as if it were a little harmless bunny. He probed that entire breast, along with the other, firmly and fully, searching them for any other abnormalities. Mylee laid there slightly humiliated by the process and embarrassed that her nipples had become erect from the rooms cold air. The doctor noticed neither.

"Well, what say we take a little biopsy of it so we can get to the bottom of it, Mylee?"

"Uh, okay," Mylee said

He explained that he would numb it with an injection first and that the entire procedure would be nearly painless. The nurse returned with appropriate release forms and injected the Novocain. The doctor returned within minutes and before long the procedure was over. As he said, it was nearly painless.

"Now, that wasn't so bad, was it," the doctor said. Mylee nodded in agreement. "I will have this to our lab in ten minutes and we could have some information today. I know these things are stressful and I always push the lab for quick results so we know what we are dealing with quickly. Two-thirds of these lumps are benign, half of those go away on their own. The others can be left, or removed if they begin to grow." He smiled and took a breath.

"Luckily, even if it is malignant, we will be on it early and the outcomes are usually very positive when that is the case." Mylee was not expecting the lightning speed of the procedure. The word "usually" in his statement stood out to her.

"Okay Mylee, we'll call you when we get the results back. And so you know, we never discuss these things on the phone so don't be alarmed when we ask you to come in," the doctor said.

"Ah, it will probably be okay," Mylee thought. She was leaving the department store later with some new socks for Tony, two new outfits for Halley, and some bras to replace the old ones that she had been clinging to. She treated herself to a frozen yogurt at the food court of the mall. She sat thinking. She watched as the small children rode their ponies up and down as the merry-go-round carried them in endless circles.

"I didn't have any discharge or weird pain or anything, and I feel good. Besides, two-thirds of the time lumps are just lumps," she reasoned. "This one is so small-- I'm just going to leave it there unless it gets big." She took another spoonful of her yogurt and turned the page of the throw-down magazine that she was reading.

"I think I'll get some Chinese food from Chop-Chops Chow Mein for dinner tonight and treat Tony and Halley. They love that stuff," she thought. She finished her yogurt and returned the magazine to the stand. She tossed her empty cup into the trash and walked towards her car. She was making a mental list of what foods to order at the Chinese restaurant. Her cell phone rang just as she sat behind the wheel of her car.

"Hello."

"Hi Mylee, are you still in town?" the doctor's voice asked.

"Yes, I am," she answered, surprised to hear from him after only three hours.

"We have those results back. Would you like to discuss them today? Or, you can come back tomorrow if you would like?" he said.

"No, I'm here, I can swing by right now if you would like. Oh, unless you're closing" she said after realizing it was getting late in the day.

"No, right now will be fine, Mylee, I'll see you in a bit," the doctor said. He hung the phone up as Mylee's was still pressed to her ear.

[239]

"Whew, sounds good or he would have wanted me to come in right away," Mylee thought as she drove toward the doctor's office. "I hope that one old Chinese guy is cooking at Chop-Chop's tonight—he's so much better than that lady."

"Hi Mylee, glad you were still in town. Come in and take a seat," the elderly doctor said. This time he led her to his office, complete with bookshelves, family photos, and a huge cluttered wooden desk that Mylee guessed was older than the doctor who sat behind it.

"Well Mylee, that little bugger wasn't what we were hoping for," he said. "It is malignant and we are going to have to treat you, but at least we got the little bugger early, which is the good news," he said. He again made the cancerous tumor seem less threatening with his pet name for it.

"You sure?" Mylee questioned.

"Yes Mylee, we are certain," the doctor said with a more fatherly tone. He rose and walked around his desk to Mylee's side and placed his hand on her shoulder.

"It is a somewhat rare and more aggressive form of the disease-- I won't bore you with the long name at this point, but it is still highly treatable," he said. "Mylee, because of it being rather aggressive, I am recommending a double mastectomy as well as both radiation and chemotherapy."

Mylee's mind was struggling to grasp the opposite of what it was wanting to think. Reality momentarily eluded her.

"Mylee, are you okay?" the doctor said. He noticed her distant look and the paleness that had come to her face.

"Oh, I'm okay," she responded. His voice had made her snap out of the thought of leaving her daughter motherless.

"Mylee, this is going to be fine," the doctor said as he again placed his hand on her shoulder. "We just have to get this taken care of right away-- nip it in the bud-- get rid of that little bugger. You will be fine!" he reiterated.

"What do we do next, doctor?" she inquired, knowing from being a nurse that taking action quickly was best. An image of her naked and breast-less self appeared in her mind.

"Mylee, I would like to arrange an appointment with Dr. Raj right away. He is the absolute best surgeon that I have ever known for such procedures. I'd like to call him and have him call you right away if that would be okay with you," the doctor said.

"Sure doctor, whatever you think." She said. She sat listening, as he explained the details of the various treatments that she faced.

[241]

"Are you okay to drive, Mylee? I can drive you home tonight and you can have someone come for your car tomorrow. I don't mind a bit and it is only a half hour away," the doctor said after their talk.

"No, I'm okay. I need a little time to think anyway. But thank you so much for the offer," Mylee said.

"I'll be fine. I will be waiting for Dr. Raj's call. Thank you." she said. The doctor walked her out of his now closed-for-the-day office, keeping his arm on her shoulder the entire way.

"You sure you're okay to drive Mylee?" he asked again. Mylee nodded with a smile and walked towards her car.


"Why me! What did I do to deserve this?" Mylee screamed while pounding on the steering wheel of her car in the empty parking lot. Her car was hidden from the doctor's office by the shrubbery. "Why me?" she again questioned. She sobbed uncontrollably and laid her head on the steering wheel between her forearms. Her tears rained to the floor of the car. Pain set into her palms as bruises began to form on them from being pounded on the steering wheel. "It's not fair!" She sat alone watching the shadows from the trees grow long. A man roared into the parking lot with a noisy sweeping machine resembling a military tank. He stared impatiently at her as he passed.

"I have to go home," she thought. She forced a composure into herself, realizing that her daughter and husband would be worried if she were late.

"I need to get Chinese food," she thought, not having planned to cook. She began focusing on how to appear normal when she arrived home. Thoughts raced through her head. She phoned her order into the Chinese restaurant to avoid contact with any Edgewater residents. Half the town brought food home from it once a week it seemed.

"Damn, I wish I had asked the doctor!" Mylee lamented as she drove back towards Edgewater. "I don't even know when I start chemo, how long it will take, how long I will be in the hospital after the surgery!" She began realizing that the doctor had discussed much of these points with her and that her mind had failed to register them.

"I'm probably going to lose my hair. I'm not going to wear a stupid looking wig," she continued thinking. "I wonder how bad my breasts will look when they are done? No nipples? Hopefully,

[243]

there won't be huge scars. I wonder if they do the reconstruction right then or later?"

"I wonder what is Tony is going to think about them not being there? This sucks!" she said. She again hit the steering wheel with the heel of her hands, this time feeling the pain immediately from them already being bruised.

"I'll probably be sick with that chemo for months! Who's going to keep up the house? I have to take care of Halley." Her eyes filled with tears as she thought of her daughter.

"What did he mean by me having a more aggressive form of cancer? Oh, great!" she worried. "Damn, I wish I had asked! I don't know anything! I'll call the doctor first thing in the morning before I tell Mom or anybody."

The towers of the bridge that crossed the river into Edgewater appeared in the distance.


"Hi honey, what did the doctor say?" Tony asked as she entered the door.

"Ssshhh," she said quietly while holding her index finger to her mouth and glancing towards their daughter. She set the Chinese food on the counter.

"Okay," he mouthed silently back to her. He also glanced towards their daughter. She was engulfed in a cartoon show. His face showed concern.

"Mommy!" Halley said loudly after noticing her, running to her with her open arms.

"Baby doll!" Mylee replied. She lifted her to kiss her and then twirled around in circles. They both laughed.

"Brought some Chinese food," Mylee announced as she sat her back to the ground.

"I just want fried rice and broccoli! I don't want any of those worms!" Halley said. She was referring to the chow mien noodles that she identified as such since the first time she laid eyes on them.

"You want to eat here or watch TV?" Mylee asked. Halley opted for the latter and vanished to set up her TV tray.

"Here you go, baby," Mylee said as she sat the rice and broccoli in front of her.

Mylee motioned to Tony towards the bedroom with her head.

"What is it, Mylee?" Tony asked anxiously after closing their door.

"I have cancer!" Mylee said. Her chin began shaking through a frown that had formed on her face. She struggled to contain her tears.

"How do they know? Don't they have to do some tests?" Tony asked. His face became frighteningly pale.

"They did Tony. I have to have surgery, radiation and the whole nine yards." She said. "They are 100% sure. They did a biopsy." Tony took her tightly to him, nuzzling his head against hers.

"It will be okay," he whispered. He stared blankly behind her as he held her.

"What else did he say?" Tony asked as his fears gave way o questions.

"He said they caught it early. He told me not to worry too much," she said, omitting the part about it being an aggressive orm of the disease.

"That's good!" he said, "I've read that it's one of the most urable types of cancer if it is caught early. That teacher, Mrs. osa, and that one lady at the flower shop both had it over wenty years ago and they are cured." A look of hope appeared n him and he nodded to Mylee.

"Tony, I don't want Halley to know for a while. I need a little time. I'll talk to her when I get this figured out a little better. Okay?" Mylee said, looking at him. Tony nodded in understanding. "The same with my parents—at least until I get a clearer picture from the doctor." Tony again nodded.

"I'll call the doctor tomorrow about the treatment and stuff. For now, let's just act like nothing happened, okay?"

"Okay," Tony assured her, as they heard their daughter scream, "I'm done!" from the front room. Mylee left to pick up her plate.

"Are you crying, Mommy?" Halley asked as she lifted her plate from the tray.

"Stupid allergies honey! I hope you don't get them when you're mommy's age." Mylee said. Halley smiled and turned back to her TV show.

"I'll be in the garage. I have to clean my workbench," Tony announced while passing quickly and looking away from Mylee and Halley.

"I'll be okay Tony. I'm not leaving you guys!" Mylee said after finding Tony crying in the garage. She took him to her and let him cry on her shoulder.

[247]

"Will you tell Dad, Mom?" Mylee asked after having told her mother of her cancer two days later. She was unable to face her father shattering into tears.

"I'll tell him, honey," her mother replied through her sobs. She cuddled Mylee while feeling angry at the world. "I love you so much. I just know that it is all going to be fine honey-- I feel it!"

"I know it will, Mommy," Mylee said, calling her "Mommy" for the first time in many years. "Make sure Daddy doesn't worry too much, okay?" Mylee asked. She pictured how her father's entire life seemed to have been spent loving and protecting their family.

"I will, Mylee. He will be fine. He is a strong man. You don't worry about us, honey." her mother said.


"I just have to deal with this," Mylee said to herself while driving home from her parent's house. She had talked to the doctor earlier that day. "A week in the hospital, three months of radiation and six months of chemo. I got this!" "So what if I am bald! Everyone in town already knows that I have cancer anyway by now," she reasoned.

"I just have to make it the three years!" she thought. She was thinking about what the doctor said about her type of cancer.

[248]

"It usually rears its ugly head within three years if it is going to come back," he had put it. She recalled the doctor mentioning that there was only a one in five chance that it would come back. "Only", Mylee pondered. "It is what it is--I just have to do it!" She lifted her chin and drove.

"Screw it, sis, I'm coming home to be with you! They will do fine around here without me for a few weeks," Mylee's twin sister Karlina told her after Mylee informed her about her cancer and upcoming surgery.

"When is that surgery?" Karlina asked again. She was surprised that it was to be so soon.

"Next Monday," Mylee answered, "The surgeon said 'the sooner, the better'."

"Okay sis, I will be there to help with Halley and I can stay as long as I want. I've already made enough to retire on and if this bank doesn't like it, they can shove it. I'm sick of this crap anyway." Mylee's sister said while speaking of her investment banking career.

"Thanks, sis," Mylee purred. She sat thinking of how close she and her sister had always been, never expecting her to have to carry such a burden for her.

"If you need anything at all, you call us, Mylee," one of the two friends that came to visit her the next day said after hearing of her condition through the small-town grapevine.

"Okay, you guys," Mylee answered. She was humbled by the number of friends that had called or come by, as well as the many that smiled caringly or hugged her as she shopped at the local stores.


"Come on baby girl, let's walk the long way home today," Mylee said to Halley after walking to meet her after school. She saw the curiosity growing in her daughter as the many visitors came and went and knew it was the time to tell her.

"Next week, honey, Mommy has to go into the hospital so the doctor can fix me up," Mylee said. A look of concern overcame Halley's face. "But I will be out of the hospital in just a few days and I don't want you to worry," she added before Halley had time to respond.

"But Mommy, really sick people go to the hospital like Uncle E.," she replied nervously. She was referring to her great uncle that had gone to the hospital the year before and had passed away from a stroke.

[250]

"No honey, most people just go in to get stuff that needs to be fixed, fixed!" Mylee said. "Mommy's going to be fine!" she added with a large smile on her face.

"Mommy's got a disease and they have to operate and then give me medicine for a while that will make me lose my hair and feel sick, but then I will be good as new," Mylee told her.

"Mommy," Halley asked as she stared into her mother's face with own face contorted in fear, "Are you going to die?"

"No, no, no baby girl! I am just going to be sick a while," she assured her. "But you are going to have to be my nurse sometimes," Mylee said. A sudden relaxation came over her daughter and then a look of curious excitement as she began imagining herself in a white uniform and being her mother's nurse.

"I'm going to be the best nurse in the world for you, Mama!" she said. Her eyes became wide with excitement.

"I know you will, honey!" Mylee said. She dropped to one knee to take her daughter into her arms. "I couldn't ask for a better nurse to watch over me." Mylee fought to contain her tears. She kissed Halley's cheek and rose to her feet.

"Come on, let's go cook dinner for Daddy," Mylee said with a relieved tone. They walked hand-in-hand towards their home.

"Now you can't worry while Mama is sick so Daddy doesn't worry. And you have to be a big girl and help Daddy keep the house clean, okay honey?" Mylee said as they walked.

"I will, Mama, and I won't let Daddy worry at all! I promise, Mommy!" Halley replied. Mylee saw the young lady coming out in her.

"Thank you, honey," Mylee said. She patted her lovingly on her back.

"Grandma and Auntie Karlina will be picking you up from school most of the time, Honey, so your dad can work. They will be helping us until I feel better, okay?" Mylee said.

"Auntie Karlina is coming!" Halley cried out excitedly. "I love Auntie Karlina!" Suddenly adding, "Oh, and I love Grandma too."

"You be a good girl for Mama and help everybody out, okay honey?" Mylee asked as they rounded the corner to their house.

"I will, Mama, I promise," Halley said.

[252]

"The procedure should take about three hours and she will be back in her room where you all will be able to see her" the doctor, dressed in blue scrubs complete with the blue elastic banded cap said to Mylee's family. She was being strapped into the gurney for her trip to the operating room. Her entire chest was painted orange with an antibacterial solution and she wreaked of antiseptic.

"She will be a little groggy from the anesthesia for a while. Then we want her to rest, and for you folks to get some rest as well, so at some point we will have to ask you to leave." the doctor instructed. They all nodded in unison.

"You can follow us to the surgery waiting room upstairs and I or a nurse will keep you updated on our progress," the doctor said. Two identically clad male nurses unlocked the wheels to Mylee's gurney and began rolling Mylee from the room. The doctor walked ahead and disappeared into an elevator.

"Okay folks, this is as far as you are allowed," one of the nurses announced after stopping in front of two heavy swinging metal doors.

"I love you, sweetie," her mother said as she kissed her cheek. Tony held one of her hands and her father the other.

[253]

"See you soon, baby," Tony said. He leaned and kissed his wife on her lips then smiled at her.

"You'll be okay, honey," her dad said. He was unable to hold his tears back any longer. His tears dribbled to her face as he leaned to hold her in his arms.

"We have to go, sir," the nurse said after a few moments. Mylee's mom pried her father from Mylee.

The nurse entered a code into the keypad at the side of the doors. The lock clanked and the doors swung inward. The nurses rolled her forward. Mylee's family stood solemnly as the solid metal doors closed behind her.


"Okay, Mylee, here's how it is going to go," the anesthesiologist that came to her side said after introducing herself. She gave a detailed explanation of the procedure. Mylee's tears dried and she became focused on her operation.

"How you doing, girl!" a kind voice sounded. He was a nurse that she hadn't met before. He was black and had a soothing and positive nature. He held her hand as he introduced himself. She could see his smile through his mask.

"Hi Mylee, it's me, Dr. Raj, under this Halloween suit! You doing okay?" the doctor said as he entered the operating room.

[254]

"Good," she replied as they slid her from the gurney to the nearly-ice-cold operating table. They arranged the rhythmically beeping machines to within clear view around her.

"Okay, let's take a head count," Dr. Raj said. He called out "anesthesiologist."

"Ready!" a reply came.

"Assistant surgeon," He called out, again hearing that person answering "ready!", until every person in the room had chimed in the same.

"Okay," Dr. Raj said, "Here we go!" All of them stepped back from the table except the young woman anesthesiologist that Mylee guessed to be close to her own age.

"Okay Mylee, count back from ten to zero for me," she instructed. She began to squirt the contents of a syringe into Mylee's IV.

"TEN, NINE, eight, seven, si...", Mylee counted. She sank into a deep coma not halfway through her count.



"Mylee! Come on, honey! Time to wake up!", the young anesthesiologist said three hours later. Mylee began to hear the sounds of the machines beeping around her and her eyes began to focus.

"There you are!" the anesthesiologist said with a warm smile, greeting Mylee as their eyes met.

"It went perfect, Mylee," she said. "We'll be taking you to see your family in just a few minutes! They are all outside waiting for you and they know you are fine."

"There's our girl," her mother said loudly as they wheeled her into her room. All of her family had gathered there to wait. Her twin sister had arrived during the operation.

"Hey, Sis! I love you!" Karlina said to her sister as she kissed her forehead. Mylee smiled, recognizing her voice through her half stupor.

"Hi, honey," her dad said. Tears of relief streamed down his cheeks. He was trying not to break out in a complete bawl.

"Hi, baby," Tony said. He stroked the hair from her forehead and smiled gently.

"Hi," she said, smiling at him and rolling her head across the pillow to greet everyone with the same smile.

"I have a surprise for you!" Tony said. He suddenly lifted Halley, who held a single yellow rose in a blue cellophane wrapped vase with a little stuffed bear tied to it.

"Hi, Mommy! I got these for you myself," Halley said while sporting an ear-to-ear grin. Mylee's focus on the rose caused her entire surroundings to come clear.

Thank you, Pumpkin!" Mylee said. She gave Halley a huge smile. The entire family smiled at once.

"I'm going to be the best nurse ever, Mommy!" Halley said. Tony held her close to the bed and let her hug and kiss her mother.

"I know you will, Babygirl!" Mylee said.

The doctor came in and told them it would be best for Mylee to get some rest and for them all to come back in the morning. They all said their goodbyes and left Mylee alone in her room.

"Well, that's that," Mylee thought as she lifted her head slightly. She saw only the contour of bandages where her breasts once were. She laid her head deep into the pillow and cried herself to sleep.

# CHAPTER 16

.

"Isn't she beautiful?" Layla said while lying in the hospital bed with their newborn baby. It laid nursing her breast. Ian laid at the edge of the bed with his head resting on his elbow staring at his daughter from inches away.

"I can't believe how sweet and beautiful she is," Ian replied. He petted the baby's pink cheek with the back of his index finger. "I think I saw her smile!" Layla lifted her head to look. "I love the name Erica. I think we chose the perfect name!" Ian said, "Your dad would be so proud."

"Yes, he would." She said. She gazed again in awe at their baby while thinking of her father.

"Pfft," Ian and Layla heard come from their daughter, unsure from which end.

"Like grandpa, like granddaughter," Ian said after remembering Layla's finger pulling stories. They chuckled together. The baby startled briefly, then continued nursing.

[259]

"She still there?" Layla teased, seeing Ian perched in his wheelchair beside the crib one day. Layla was amazed at how Ian spent every free minute of every day huddled by her side.

"She is so beautiful!" Ian cooed. His face was gentle.

"Well come eat," Layla ordered. She watched as Ian tore himself from her side. This same ritual repeated itself many times until Erica had outgrown the crib, began to walk, and then run.

"Great day today," stay-at-home-parent Ian said to Layla. He had taken the role of the daytime parent, allowing Layla to resume her nursing job.

"Went for a walk to the park. I'm a little sore, but gets better every day." He said. He was referring to the calluses that were building at the nubs below his knees where his new plastic legs were attached. "She sure loves that swing!" he said. Layla smiled at him.

"Making chicken stir-fried with fresh vegetables and ginger for dinner," Ian announced while holding a colander full of freshly picked produce from their garden up to her.

"You don't have to cook for me every night, Ian," she said, "I'm not a cripple!" Their eyes met and they roared with laughter.

[260]

"Yeah, I know, but I want to eat good food!" Ian teased. Her eyes rolled and she shook her head.

"You're lucky I love you!" she said, shaking a threatening fist at him with a grin.

"I've got the dishes, you go read to your daughter," Layla said. She saw a smile come to his face.

"She's asleep," Ian informed Layla a short time later as she replaced the dishes into the cupboards. He embraced her from the rear and cupped her breasts in his hands.

"Hurry up Mommy, Daddy has a big surprise for you," he said. He pushed his already erect penis into her buttocks and kissed her neck.

"Big?" she teased. Ian gave her breasts a playful punishing squeeze and chuckled.

"Well, I guess—if I have to..." Layla said playfully. She giggled as she drug him to their bedroom using both hands. They enjoyed a nearly all-night sexual session, an oft-repeated routine that they both looked forward to.

"Daddy, breakfast time!" Erica announced first thing in the morning.

"It's Momma's turn this morning, baby! Momma made Daddy work hard last night around the house after you went to bed and he is exhausted!" Ian said while looking playfully at his wife. She again was rolling her eyes with an "I ought to kill you look" on her face. She arose from bed to make her daughter breakfast.

"Mommy said to tell you to get your lazy butt up," Erica screamed through a half-guilty-for-using-a-bad-word grin.

"What did you say, Nuttybutt," Ian said. He swooped her into bed with him and tickling her until she screamed for mercy.

"Go tell Mamma butt that I'm on my way!" he said. He put his daughter on the floor and launched her to tease her mother on his behalf. Ian strapped on his legs. His pace quickened as the aroma of bacon wafted through the house.

"Bye, daddy!" Erica chimed as she was leaving for kindergarten with her mother. Ian gave her a kiss as he strapped her into the backseat of their car.

"Bye honey bunny!" he said. He blew her a kiss through the car window. He sighed a deep breath, wondering where the time had gone.

"Mom's picking her up from school, Ian," Layla informed him.

"Okay, I might walk over and have a beer or two with Seth after I get home then."

"Call me and I'll come pick you up," Layla replied, thinking of his legs.

"Thanks," he said, "Drive careful." She threw him a kiss and smiled. He walked towards the corner to catch the bus to the community college, where he pursued the classes needed in his quest to become a police officer. The local force, at the community's urging, had promised him a job.


"Hey, honey! Hop in!" Layla said, picking Ian up at Seth's a couple hours after her work.

"Why are you driving this?" Ian inquired. Layla was picking him up in his pickup equipped with hand controls built for the legless.

"I like driving this truck," she said, "It's easy once you get the hang of it. Not only that, let's say we were somewhere and I HAD to drive it? I need to stay in practice.". Ian nodded in agreement.

[263]

"Mom kept Erica for dinner so we'll swing by and pick her up on the way home," she said. Ian again nodded his approval.

"We've got it pretty good," Layla said reflectively as they were driving to her mother's.

"What do you mean?" Ian replied.

"Oh, you know, I just love having our family. You're in good shape and we are all healthy. I have a good job and with your pension our finances are good. I just feel grateful for it all," she smiled at Ian and patted his leg then returned her hand to the pickup's hand controls.

"Yeah, I know Layla. It's hard to imagine....," Ian replied, stopping himself mid-thought. Layla let it lie.

"Maybe we'll catch a movie tomorrow night," Layla said on one Friday night while giving Ian a ride to Seth's for their monthly poker game. "I think I'll go visit Mom a while and pick you up on the way home. Drink your little heart full of beer," she instructed. She rarely ever saw her husband drunk.

"You know, I think I will partake of God's nectar instead tonight while I'm taking those guy's money!" he said. He lifted a bottle of Napa Valley cabernet wine from his bag. Layla shook her head and smiled, knowing he came home the previous month with zero money in his pockets. She looked ahead into the distance and sighed a content breath.

"What is it, Daddy? What is my surprise? Can I open it now?" Erica screamed after waking up one Saturday morning. She had barely slept from the excitement of being told that her parents had a surprise for her the following morning.

"You go get it, Mommy," Ian told Layla in a monotone voice.

"No, you get it, I don't want to have to get up. I'm drinking my coffee," Layla replied. They saw the frustration and excitement building within their daughter.

"Come on! Get it, Daddy!" Erica said as she jumped into the air and landed hard on both feet. Her fists were clenched in frustration and she wore a half-smile on her face.

"Aw, it's just inside that closet. Go get it yourself and you can open it," Ian said, acting bored with the moment. Erica looked confused at their lack of interest. She glanced at them over her shoulder as she walked to the closet.

"DADDY! MOMMY!" she screamed. She fell to her knees crying. "Aaahhhh!" she exclaimed as a tiny mottled-colored miniature Australian Shepherd puppy with one blue eye and one brown eye bounced out of the closet and directly into her arms.

"Mommy! Daddy! Can we keep him?" She looked back at them with her arms full of puppy and her eyes as big as saucers. The puppy devoured her face with its kisses, licking as if it were trying to erase it. Her eyes begged them through the lapping.

"That is your present, baby. That is your puppy! Unless you don't want to keep him!" Layla teased. Erica's eyes widened to saucer size. Her hug became one of ownership.

"I love him!" she screamed. Her face was on fire with excitement. "Thank you, Daddy! Thank you, Momma! Thank you! Thank you! Thank you!"

"His name is "Blue boy," after his one eye. I'll call him Blue," she said. The puppy nuzzled her neck and began nibbling her ear as if scratching a flea. She roared with laughter. "Look Mommy, look Daddy, it's eating my ear!" she screamed through her giggles. Ian and Layla sat holding hands and watching.


"I'm eating your ear!" Erica would say daily as Ian scooped Erica into his arms. She nibbled on his ear with rapid and tiny nips, mimicking what her dog did to her—and only her. Ian would nibble her back.

"What you do, Blue?" Ian would say lovingly to the dog each night as it cuddled in his lap while he watched TV. When Ian rose to retire to his bed for the night, the dog would trot and lay beside Erica until the morning. It was their family's dog.

"How's our favorite neighbor family?" the neighbor from two doors down inquired one day. Ian, Layla, and Erica passed them at the front of their house while walking the dog as they did each evening. He and his wife marveled at how happy and content their family was after all they had been through.

"Great, Bill, how about you folks?" Ian replied while smiling warmly. Layla mouthed "hello" to the elderly missus.

"And how's little Miss Pretty and her baby?" the neighbor said to Erica, eliciting a shy smile from her. Blue pawed gently on the neighbor's leg and accepted gentle pats from him.

"Come on, Blue!" Layla said to get the dog down from the neighbor. They continued on their way. They walked a different route daily for years, hardly ever missing an evening regardless of the weather, for years.  Erica loved the dog more as those years passed.

"Come on, Daddy!" the just-turned-eight Erica prodded one day. "We're going to be late for practice!"  She stood at the front door, anxiously tossing the ball time after time into her mitt.

"I'm ready, Pumpkin," Ian said, throwing the coaching bag with the balls and bats over his shoulder.  "Mom's going to meet us there after work so you better shape up!"

She smiled and rolled her eyes.

"I wonder where she gets that from?" Ian thought.

"Load the dog in the back of the truck, honey," Ian said. He saw the dog bouncing behind their screen door in anticipation. The dog would lie patiently during the entire practice, only to frolic wildly with all the kids afterward.    Ian and Layla never missed a game.  None in their family ever noticed the envy of their family's bond in many of the other parents.  Erica grew and their life evolved.  Ian's love for his family and theirs for him did not.

"Honk the horn, Daddy," Erica said. She wanted him to blow the boat's loud horn as some locals passed them on the river during one of the many weekend outings.

"Hoooooonk, honk, honk!" the horn bellowed.

The other boat responded in kind as it occupants waved and smiled at them. Ian sat at the helm with Layla beside him sporting an ear-to-ear grin and having much more fun than she had thought she would when Ian had talked her into buying their new boat.

"Catch anything?" Erica screamed to the other boat. Her hands were clasped into a megaphone in front of her. Its occupants were unable to hear a word she said over the drone of the two boat motors. Ian held up his hands in front of him and spread them apart, giving the international "catch anything?" sign. The man in the rear held up a stringer of striped bass that looked to be the limit. Ian gave him the 'thumbs up' sign.

"I Might have to see if Seth and Abel want to do a little fishing this weekend!" Ian said to Layla, raising his eyebrows in succession a few times. Layla nodded a "that's a good idea" back to him. She saw the anticipation on his face.

"The last one in is a rotten old carp fish!" Ian announced after tying their boat to a small delta islet. The island flooded at every high tide but had a sandy little beach the moment it began to ebb. Ian launched himself, prosthetic legs removed, into the water. Erica followed closely in her bright orange tight fitting life preserver, even though she was a strong swimmer.

"Pee EW!" Ian and Erica teased Layla. They both held their noses indicating she was the "rotten carp." They treaded water while Layla dipped a toe into the water to test its temperature.

"Man overboard!" Ian yelled signaling Erica to join him in sweeping their extended arms full speed into the water to soak her mother with the cold water.

"That's it! I'm 'gatoring' you!" Layla said. She jumped into the water, keeping only her eyes and nose above it to stealthily chase them.

"Aaaiiiii!!!" both Erica and Ian screamed in feigned fear. They paddled frantically from her. The dog leaped from the boat from the excitement and joined the chase game. It barked and kept a 'dog-smile' on its face the entire time it played with them.


"Here baby girl, you drive," Ian said. He stood from behind the steering wheel of their boat on their way back to Edgewater.

[270]

"No, Daddy, you drive, I don't know how," Erica said nervously. She saw that her dad had abandoned the helm of the idling underway boat.

"You better learn quick then Babygirl! Somebody has to steer this thing!" Ian said. He stepped behind the driver's seat and crossed his arms. Layla sat still, staring into the distance. Erika reluctantly took the helm after carefully assuring herself that her dad was close by.

"See, it's easy!" Ian said as he watched his daughter's nervousness ease. "If you want to go faster, just push this forward a little," Ian said. He leaned to the side of her and pushed the throttle forward slightly.

"Not too fast, Daddy!" Erica screamed.

"Well pull it back to slow down—you're driving!" Ian said. She slowed it. Then she sped, then slowed, repeating it several times per minute and once frightening herself with too much throttle. She snapped her face to Ian when it happened. He stood firm and let her fix it.

"Honk the horn, honey!" Ian screamed as they passed a boat. He saw his daughter glow with pride as she did and as the other boaters saw her at the helm. She steered near other boats to make sure they saw her. Ian rarely captained the boat again.

"She looks like my dad," Ian whispered to Layla. He saw the excited and adventurous look on her face as they explored every turn of the delta's sloughs. She bit her tongue at the side of her mouth as she steered.

"She does," Layla whispered back with a warm smile. She saw his father in both them.


"What are you thinking?" Layla asked after noticing a distance, and tears, in Ian's eyes.

"Aw nothing really. A little flashback to some old pals-- Feeling lucky actually." He looked at Layla, saying, "Thank you."

"No, thank you, Ian," Layla said. She slid closer to him on the bench seat of their boat and kissed his forehead. "I love you more than the world. We will always be together and I will love you every day, I promise." She said it as if renewing her wedding vows. Ian smiled and one lone tear fell to his cheek. Layla kissed it away.

# CHAPTER 17

"Hmm, let's see what I can do...," Samantha's dad thought as he browsed an area of the internet unknown to the typical user. He again sat in the small creek-side camera-free coffee shop forty minutes from Edgewater.

"Weird how they call this 'newsgroups!'" he thought. It contained zero news. It was mostly used by people pirating software and stealing audiobooks and movies. Buying drugs and sharing child porn was especially one of its main uses.

"Wonder why they don't just call it 'Pervertville'!" he thought while shaking his head in disgust. The results began to appear on his screen from a software program that he had written that traced child molesters as they set up their mislabeled sites on this vast network. "Dark web, now that's more like it," he thought as he considered what those in his field called it.

"Oh great!" he thought, as sites labeled "Antique Dolls," "Physics of motion," and a plethora of others appeared on his screen. All of them were sites where child pornography was shared among perverts. All of them knew what they were and had the passwords to enter them thanks to their like-minded sicko pals.

"This is sick!" he thought. He'd found such sites thousands of times for the government and turned them over to the appropriate agency, but never actually looked at their contents in detail as he now was.

"How can anyone look at this shit!" he thought after seeing innocent children, including diapered babies being sexually abused. He continued perusing the sick sites, carefully comparing the results of his scans to the list of known pervert sites being surveilled by the government, all of which were known to him due to his work.

"Oh, that sicko morphed his site again," he commented to himself. He saw that one particular site that had been under surveillance for months had moved its content to a new area. It had established a new innocuous name and had changed its password, all of which was traced by Barry's software, making the entire move transparent to law enforcement.

"Those sick bastards are all going down," he whispered to himself while gloating. He reveled in knowing that, thanks to his efforts, over two hundred perverts who regularly visited the sicko site was going to be raided soon and brought to justice.

"Okay Shitbag Smith, let's see where you are," Barry thought as he clandestinely delved into Smith's desktop police computer. Smith sat sound asleep with his arms crossed in front of him. His head was tilted downward, exposing all three of his chins. "There's your tax dollars at work, folks," Barry thought, shaking his head in disgust. "Oh well, just so you are there," he thought. He shifted his computer hacking efforts to Smith's home computer.

"What do you know, Shitbag's computer is on. He sure likes making my job easy." Smith left his computer online twenty-four hours a day, uncaring of the energy wasted and only concerned with not having to do any extra work if he decided to check his e-mail or play online poker.

"Okay," Barry murmured. His voice was obscured by the sound of the rippling creek next to the coffee shop patio.

"Create new file, filename file.ext.exe, file location, program files, Win.exe," Barry typed. He installed a program to destroy every bit of evidence that Shitbag's computer had been hacked. He designed it so it would do the same after each of his visits. It also allowed him to alter the times and dates of entries and events in Smith's log files as well as destroy evidence of it ever being used while Barry controlled it.

"Now Shitbag, now for the dagger to your chest and career," Barry thought. He created a picture file under the "Example gifs" folder that comes with every computer. He named it x.exe. sys, thinking that it would be an appropriate heading for the content that he planned to place within it. Its complex name would also be scary enough to discourage Shitbag or others from ever clicking on it.

"Smith, this is going to steamroll and you aren't even going to know what hit you," Barry thought. "Have fun in prison, asshole!"

"Here we go!" Barry said. He brought up one of the worst child porn-sharing sites that he had gleaned from the millions of sites. He knew the FBI was monitoring it and that its users were soon to be raided.

"Should have used the TOR browser Shitbag!" Barry mused. He began downloading pictures of prepubescent girls being raped and molested by old men. He stored them in the newly created picture file on Smith's computer.

"Next," Barry thought. He visited another child porn site, and then another, and another, downloading more disgusting images. He altered their download dates in the computer's brain to spread them over a period of years.

[276]

"You're so screwed, Shitbag!" Barry thought. He had just put Smith on the pervert police's radar several times, with one sites sure to be raided in a matter of weeks.

"Here we go," Barry said. He delved into Smith's personal picture folders. He perused pictures of the river, foggy roads, and typical delta scenes. "Figures," Barry thought, seeing none showing his ex-wife or family.

"These I'll put right here," Barry thought. He created a folder and named it "Fun stuff". He inserted pictures of Sam as a youngster, unclothed and playing in a small plastic pool in front of their house. He added another of her in a revealingly tight see-through shirt at the public swimming pool just as she was sprouting breasts. He added four others that he had sorted from the suitcase of memories. .

"Now this," he continued thinking. He placed several other pre-teen sexually provocative pictures of girls whose faces were hidden, but who resembled several local girls, into the folder along with another of Sam and three of her friends in tiny bikinis at the local park.

"Now…" Barry thought. He manipulated the dates the files to look as if they had been accessed over the years on a somewhat regular basis, up to and including just days prior to Sar

[277]

being arrested on the drug counts. He then manipulated Shitbag's files to indicate that Smith had attempted to delete his browsing history after visiting each porn site, showing that his intent was to hide his activities.

"There! The shit is going to hit the fan!" Barry thought. He exited Smith's computer and sat watching his installed program erasing any evidence of it ever being tampered with. He shut his own down that did the same. He leaned back in the chair and sipped his latte and stared at the creek. He breathed deeply and a grin came to his face.

# CHAPTER 18

"How's Mylee?" Seth asked Tony, after going to Tony's auto parts store for a part he didn't need.

"She's doing better, Seth," Tony said, "She's frustrated and bored from being trapped at home. She can get out of bed now, and that helps, but she is still weak." He rang up the cash register with Seth's purchase.

"You ought to go by and see her, Seth. I know she would love the company and you can save me the grief of having to listen to how boring her day was!" Tony said.

"Maybe I will, Tony. I'll grab her some candy. That'll cheer her up," Seth said.

"Yeah, that might work. That or a bottle of wine!" Tony said. He looked at Seth and smiled while shaking his head. "Not being able to have her evening glass is another of her biggest gripes." Seth laughed.

"Okay, I'll swing by and say hi," Seth said. He began to feel anxious.

"Mylee home?" Seth asked her sister Karlina, who had answered the door.

"Yep, she's here. Good to see you, Seth, give me a hug, it's been a while!" Karlina said. She opened her arms and hugged him. "She's in her room watching TV, go on in. I'll be in for my cut of that candy in a minute!"

"Mylee?" Seth said, lightly tapping on the door.

"Is that you, Seth?" she said. Her voice sounded stronger and more chipper than he had expected.

"It's me, I'm just here to ream your butt for not telling me about this sooner!" He said. She sprang to a crossed-legged position atop her bed with a huge grin as he entered. He noticed the flatness under pajama top.

"I know, Seth. I feel bad. I got overwhelmed by all of this," she said. I was thinking about you the whole time though."

"Mylee, I know! I can't imagine what you have been going through! I have been worried sick about you!" he said. He took a seat at her side on the bed.

"Is that candy?" she said. She ripped the box from his hand and started ripping at its ribbon. She looked up to him again. "Oh, and flowers too?" She left the flowers in Seth's hand

and continued manhandling the candy box. "You're so sweet Seth!"

"Here, I'll take those and get a vase," Karlina said as she entered. She took the flowers from Seth and reached into the candy box as its lid popped off and grabbed two pieces before Mylee could react. She threw one into her mouth and left the room with a teasing smile.

"If you are going to be here a while Seth, I'll run to the store," Karlina said after re-entering the room. A generous portion of one of the candy nuggets filled her mouth.

"Sis! I am fine. I don't need a twenty-four-hour babysitter, damn it!" Mylee said. She gave her sister a scolding smile. Her sister ignored her and smiled back.

"I'll be here Karlina, take as long as you want, I have nothing better to do than sit here and antagonize your sister," Seth teased. Mylee rolled her eyes and playfully slapped his arm.

"Back in a while," Karlina said as she flitted from the room. Seth awed at how similar their mannerisms were in addition to their identical looks.

"Yum," Mylee said, reaching for a particular piece in the center of the candy box.

"Oh, no, not that one!" Seth screamed, yanking the box from her and taking the one she wanted from the box.

"You brat!" she said with a fake scold on her face. Seth retrieved the piece she wanted and lifted it to her mouth. She jokingly snapped at his fingers.

"I really have been worried sick about you, Mylee," Seth said. His green eyes bled sympathy. He took her hand in his. "You know I love you, right?" Seth said. He looked up at her.

"I know you do, Seth. You are the best friend I have ever had. I trust you," Mylee said. "I thought about you when they were taking me in for the operation for some reason. It gave me strength." Seth sat at her bedside, hanging on her every word. "But I'm going to be fine now Seth. You quit worrying, okay?" She hugged him with her eyes.

"How are you feeling other than physically, Mylee? I worry. You must have some pretty odd feelings about it all," Seth delved. Mylee's eyes sank to the mattress.

"Every time I look down at myself, I kind of feel like a freak," Mylee said. She bowed her head further into herself. "Seth, I have no nipples and there are some ugly scars!" She lifted her head to him. Seth saw tears welling in her eyes.

[282]

"Mylee, you are the most beautiful person I have ever met. You are more beautiful today than ever. I hate to break the news to you, sweetie, but you happen to be more than just a pair of nipples!" Mylee smiled and felt her face blush.

"Besides, unless you are planning to run the streets of our fine town naked, nobody will even notice," he teased. Mylee's eyes rolled as she grinned. "Besides Mylee, I've read that they can make them good as new these days with that reconstructive surgery stuff. Don't worry, they will be good as new in no time." Her eyes dried and her posture straightened. "Matter of fact, you can resize to a Dolly Parton look if you want!"

"Right!" she said sarcastically, again rolling her eyes. They laughed then Seth became more serious.

"Mylee, I have money saved that I will never use and you are welcome to all of it you want to help you get through all this." Seth said. Mylee smiled.

"Thank you Seth, but our insurance should take care of most of it. You save your money for when you get old—you might need it." She pictured his humble lifestyle.

"Well, I'm just saying if you need it, I have it." Seth confirmed his statement with his eyes.

"I really am feeling a lot stronger." Mylee said. "I'm dreading the chemo and stuff. I hate the idea of being bald, mostly for Halley's sake, you know, the kids teasing her and all."

"Mylee, Halley is a strong girl with a huge heart and keen brain! She will be fine and would kick your butt if she thought you were worried about her instead of yourself," Seth responded. Mylee noticed the similarity of Seth's and her daughter's grins.

"Hey, this is a bump in the road, girlfriend. This will be over before you know it and you will be back to your pain-in-the-butt self in no time!" Seth said. He caressed her hand. Seth changed the subject to town gossip and food.

"Sounds like your sister is back," Seth said, hearing the refrigerator and cupboards opening and closing. "I better let you get some rest. I just wanted to come by and say hi!" He rose from the edge of her bed. "Next time I'll bring a bottle of wine and drink it in front of you!" Mylee gave him a flash of her middle finger.

"Seth," Mylee said, grasping his hand and pulling him to her. "Thank you for caring for me." "Kiss me," she whispered. She placed her hand on the back of his neck and pulled his lips to hers. They kissed passionately, only stopping when hearing her sister's stirring in the kitchen cease. Mylee smiled mischievously as he rose.

"Thanks for coming by Seth, you are my very best pal." Her sister entered the room with a bowl of soup. "We've sure had a lot of fun together!" she said, winking at him. Seth smiled and rolled his eyes at her. Her taste filled his mouth.

"All righty then!" he said, "I'll be back to see you soon. Call me if you need anything." he said. He immediately glared a 'YOU BETTER NOT!' look after he had said it. He saw the corner of her mouth rise.

"I'll see you later too Karlina—try to put up with her crap!" Seth said. He gave Karlina a hug. Karlina kissed his cheek and smiled at him.

"He's kind of cute," Karlina commented to Mylee after he left the room. Mylee smiled.

"Damn it!" Seth thought. He kicked the ground in frustration as he walked to his car.


"I have your hair, Mommy," Halley said a few weeks later. She held what little was left of her mother's hair away from the toilet. Mylee heaved bile and then strings of blood. The chemotherapy sickness weakened her to a shell of herself.

[285]

"Thank you, baby," Mylee said, heaving into the toilet again and glancing up at her daughter. Saliva drooled from her mouth.

"You'll be okay, Mommy," Halley said. Mylee's sister watched from the bedroom.

"I'm okay, baby girl," Mylee said, as the sickness gave her a temporary reprieve and let her return to bed.

"I'll get you some water Mommy," Halley said, having heard the doctor tell her how important it was that she stays hydrated. .

"Here, Mommy," Halley said, handing her the glass of cold water. She climbed into Mylee's lap and both sat silently with their bodies joined at nearly every point.


"You okay, Mylee?" Mylee's father asked while checking on her. As he did each afternoon, he scanned her for subtle changes, good or bad.

"I'm good daddy," she said. She watched as Halley entered her room and climbed into her father's arms.

"Good baby. You're doing great!" he said, as he began tickling his granddaughter. Mylee found their play therapeutic.

[286]

"Anything we can do for you Mylee?" her many friends that stopped by each day would ask. "Just let us know." The town pulled together as one. Seth often relieved Tony of the task of driving her to her treatments so he could tend to his business. Seth needed to help.

"How do you feel, Mylee?" Tony asked on one of his many visits during each day.

"I'm okay, Tony," she answered. "Not much of a wife to you right now, am I?" Tony's face melted into compassion. He smiled a loving and scolding smile. Mylee smiled back.

"Is Halley eating okay and everything, Tony?" she inquired. She stared intently at him as he answered.

"She's doing great! Eating well and doing well in school!" Tony replied. He noticed Mylee's body relax as she nodded.

"Thank you, Tony," Mylee said, her weak voice cracking. Tony leaned to her and kissed her forehead.

"I got this baby, you just rest and get better," Tony said. He ignored the vomit smell and kissed her on her parched lips.

"I knew you could do it, honey!" Mylee's dad said. They sat having coffee one morning a month and a half after her chemo and radiation had ended. "You are a trouper. And did I mention hard-headed!"

"Wonder where I got that from." she teased back. Her strength had returned to where she could do housework, walk her daughter to school and spend time at the gym.

"Boy, Halley is sure happy! Poor thing was sick with worry over you, honey," her dad said.

"Whew, Dad, that was touch and go for a while. I wasn't sure whether the cancer was going to kill me or that stupid treatment," Mylee said. She looked up at him. Her face displayed disgust at what she had been through.

"Well, it's all over now, Mylee!" her dad said. He rose from his chair and kissed her on the forehead. Mylee felt the roughness of his just-shaven whiskers, just as she had during his very-morning kiss as a child. "I'll see you later honey, I have a very important golf date I have to make." He grinned and batted his eyebrows then smiled as he exited the front door.

Mylee's gathered strength as each day passed. Weeks later she felt much like her old self—except when she looked down.

[288]

"Hey honey, I'll be in in a minute," Mylee said. She heard the loose change in Tony's pants pocket rattle to silence as he dropped his clothes to the floor. Mylee had bathed and shaven every part of her body, determined to reintegrate sex into their marriage.

"Hmm," Tony thought, smelling a slight cinnamon scent in the room and seeing the flicker of the candle on Mylee's nightstand.

"Here I go," Mylee said to herself. She turned to examine her breast-less side profile and new negligee in the bathroom mirror. She double checked her makeup, took a deep breath and turned off the bathroom light. She slipped into the candlelit bed beside her husband.

"I love you, she whispered into Tony's ear. She kissed his neck as he laid on the edge of the bed turned away from her.

"You awake Tony?" she whispered.

"Not tonight, Mylee," Tony said coldly. He re-nestled himself away from her at the side of the bed.

"What is it, Tony? Talk to me. I need you to love me," Mylee pleaded. She raised herself to one elbow over him. The candle behind her silhouetted her image on the wall. "Please, baby." She reached and began massaging his groin.

[289]

"Not tonight, Mylee!" Tony again said, removing her hand with his own. He rolled to a more face down position to prevent her from fondling him again.

"What is it?" Mylee begged as she began to cry. "Please Tony!"

"I can't Mylee, it's so ugly!" Tony exclaimed. "It's just so ugly!"

"So that's what I am, just a freak!" she exclaimed. She rolled from Tony and to her knees. Her face became beet red in anger and tears spewed from her. Her teeth clenched.

"You inconsiderate bastard!" she screamed. She pushed his shoulder, nearly knocking him from the bed as he tried to turn towards her. "Screw you! I hate you!"

"Please Mylee, you'll wake Halley up!" he said. Mylee quieted. Her feelings raged.

"Screw you, Tony! All I have been through. As much as I've loved you! Now, this!" she said. She tore the top blanket from the bed to cover herself on the couch.

"I'm sorry, Mylee. I shouldn't have said anything. It's just hard," Tony said. "I was just kind of waiting for the reconstruction." Mylee glared at him in disbelief.

[290]

"Screw you Tony!" she said while gathering the blanket in her arms. She blew out the cinnamon candle and left to the living room couch. She cried herself to sleep.

"Bastard!" Mylee thought, waking the following morning to the sound of Tony locking the door behind him while leaving for work an hour early. "Chicken!" Mylee thought. "I'd better get up so Halley doesn't realize we were arguing. Hopefully, she didn't hear us last night."

"It will get better, Mylee," Tony said over the phone, calling her just before lunch. "I am just not ready for it all right now. I was hoping for the reconstruction to make it all easier."

"Yeah Tony, this has sure been hard on you. I'm glad it was such a walk in the park for me!" Mylee said sarcastically.

"I didn't mean it that way Mylee," Tony said.

"How else could you mean it, Tony?" Mylee said angrily, adding, "Whatever!" as she slammed the phone into its cradle.

[291]

"Sorry I missed dinner, Mylee; it being inventory time and all," Tony said that evening. Mylee sat on the couch, covered with the same blanket as the previous night. Halley slept in her room.

"Why don't you come to bed?" he asked.

"For what, Tony?" Mylee said in an uncaring tone.

"It will all work out, Mylee, we just need time and we shouldn't drag Halley into this." Mylee nodded submissively in agreement.

"I'll be in in a while," she said coldly. She turned her attention back to the television.

"Goodnight, Mylee," Tony said gently from his same face-to-the-wall-on-the-edge-of-the-bed position.

"Goodnight," she replied, laying quietly and listening to her husband's breath louden as he drifted to sleep.


"Bye-bye, my little angel!" Mylee said after walking Halley to school the following morning. Their hands were joined the entire time, except when she held Halley's backpack to let her practice her cartwheels on some of the lawns they passed.

"Bye, Mommy!" Halley said over her shoulder. She released her mother's hand and her attention became focused on her classmates. They were screaming her name in greeting from the swing set. Mylee stood and stared, happy to see the glee in her daughter as she joined her friends.

"Air is starting to get brisk," Mylee thought, wrapping her sweater around her more tightly as she walked from the school-grounds. She noticed the leaves on the trees adopting their fall colors. She decided to walk the long way home while the weather still allowed it.

"Part of me sees Tony's point," she thought as she walked. The chill left her as the sun rose in the sky and the breeze over the river shifted to away from her. "It isn't pretty. You don't see scars like that every day." She looked down at her flat front. "He is a good guy and he's been through a lot with this too. I probably should have had them fixed. After all, it has been a while and I have had time. We have our family and that's all that matters. This is a no-brainer, I'll just get them done!"

She walked briskly along the river and turned up the last street in town. It ran perpendicular to all the others. The gentle slope towards it from Main Street for several blocks gave it a distinctive feel of the town's boundary. It was.

"I'll call him when I get home and see if he wants to come home for lunch," she thought. "I need to let him know that I love him and understand so he doesn't feel hurt." She strolled up the tree-lined street. A row of houses, all built a uniform distance from the street and each of them well-kempt, showed their nearly-fifty-year-old age.

"Wish I had brought my phone!" she thought. She could walk by the market and get some fresh lunchmeat and bread if he could make it to lunch. She paced forward, feeling the heat from her chemo-weakened leg muscles as they strained under her, her body never having fully recovered.

"Oh, that's Tony's pickup at Jerry's," she remarked to herself. She saw his truck at the shop in the alley behind the generator repairman's house. She turned up the hill towards it.

"Those garbage men!" she exclaimed. She shoved a garbage can to the side of the alley that had been left nearly in its center after being emptied. "They have Tony blocked in—Idiots! He must have got here early."

"Hmm?" Mylee sounded. She discovered the main roll-up door facing the alley closed and the regular walk-through one locked as well. "Jerry must have slept in. Well, it is early, they are probably inside having coffee." She ascended the steep stairs at the back of the house to its back door.

"Uh-uh-uh," a guttural rhythmic grunt sounded from within as Mylee reached the top stair. Her stomach sickened and her heart began to race. Her eyes gained focus through the glare of the windowed back door.

"Oh God, no!" her mind pleaded. Her tears began to mercifully blur the horrendous vision of her unclothed husband savagely thrusting himself into a woman who stood open legged and bent forward over the back of the couch. Her mind reeled, ricocheting from shock, to hurt, and then to disgust. It evolved into unchecked rage.

"That son-of-a-bitch!" her mind screamed to itself! The veins on her neck pulsated as if about to burst. Her face blued with anger. She tried the doorknob. It was unlocked. She entered behind them unnoticed and stood watching.

"You motherfucker!" she screamed. Her teeth gritted in anger as she hit Tony with the heels of her opened palms using the entire weight of her body. The brute anger-driven force disjoined him from the generator repairman's wife and nearly knocked him to the ground. She spun him around to face her. Hi eyes widened in shock. His fully erect and wet penis bounced between them.

"You no good fucker!" she said. The woman rose and was forced to smear her oversized breasts across Mylee's non-existent ones to retrieve her clothing from the table behind her.

"We are through! I mean done! Go ahead and stay and fuck this slut!" Mylee said, screaming at Tony but briefly turning her disgust to the disloyal wife. The wife cringed in shame. Her body language showed no argument with Mylee's characterization. Mylee turned and stomped to the rear door, down the steps, and to the alley. She stopped briefly to give her husband, who had come to the door, the middle finger before disappearing from sight.


"Oh god!" Mylee cried. She braced herself on one of the empty garbage cans. The oversweet reek of a nearby honeysuckle-covered-fence combined with the vision of her husband's infidelity caused her to vomit her stomach's contents until only bile was left.

"Oh please, god!" she again pleaded to the air above her. She wandered from alley to alley, crying and hiding from everyone, strewing pockets of bile as she did.

[296]

"What is it, Mylee?" Seth screamed. His face became contorted in terror as he ran towards her. He saw Mylee dry heaving and nearly unable to walk. She gasped for air between her pitiful sobs. Her body had guided itself instinctively to him.

"What is it, Mylee?" Seth asked again, demanding an answer with his tone. He took Mylee into his arms, feeling her full weight collapsed onto him. He cradled her toward his house.

"Mylee, please! It's okay sweetie, you're with me. I have you, whatever it is," Seth said while holding her to his heart. He brought her to his lap as he sat on the couch and placed his cheek firmly to hers. "Is it Halley, Mylee? Are you sick? Please Mylee," he pleaded.

"I have you, Mylee," Seth whispered again. He felt her body begin to unstiffen. "It's okay." He kissed her gently, time after time, on her cheek and forehead, hugging her between each one. Her sobs quieted.

"Okay, what is it, Mylee?" Seth asked calmly. Mylee lifted her head from his shoulder.

"Is it Halley—Is she okay? Seth asked. Mylee nodded that she was.

"Good," Seth said. He probed further, "Your dad? Mom, Tony?" He saw her frown and nearly break into tears as he got to

[297]

Tony's name. "Is it Tony? Is he okay?" Seth asked. A look of anger appeared on her face.

"What is it, Mylee? Did he hurt you? I'll kill that son of a bitch!" Seth said.

"He thinks I'm a monster!" She said. She suddenly jumped to her feet and ripped her top and bra upward exposing the scars and nipple-less patches of skin where her breasts once were. "Because of this!" She stood still and facing him. Tears gathered in her eyes as she continued exposing herself to him. She waited to see him repulsed. Seth rose to his feet and took her to him.

"I told you Mylee, you are the most beautiful person in the world and he can go fuck himself!" Seth said. He crouched to her and kissed every part of her breast area, every scar and both patches that once were her nipples. "You are a beautiful angel. Every last part of you is beautiful!" He held her at arms-length and gazed at her. She believed him. She believed in him.

"Tony can go screw himself!" he said. His anger grew.

"He doesn't have to Seth, I just caught him screwing that generator guy's wife when I went to his shop!" Mylee said. Seth pulled her top down and covered her.

"That fucking pig!" Seth said. His eyes glared through her as the vision of Tony screwing that big-titted skank, who he had heard had fucked every married man in town, appeared in his mind. "Mylee, he is a pig! This has nothing to do with you, he always has been a pig!"

"Mylee, you can stay here, I will stay with you, I will go kick his ass, I'll do whatever you want!" Seth said.

"I'm done with him, Seth! I'm just going to have to figure out how to make this as easy as possible on my daughter," Mylee said. Her composure became nearly restored.

"I have to go home for Halley and I'll figure this out as I go, but I know that this marriage is over. I should have figured Seth, leopards don't change their spots." She lifted her eyes to his. "He is dreaming if he thinks I will ever have anything to do with him again! I have a doctor's appointment tomorrow for some blood work and I am going to be gone all day. I'm going to have Mom watch Halley tonight and tomorrow, and I'll have time to think."

Seth sensed an angry undercurrent swirling within her. He reasoned that she wanted her daughter gone to shield her from the foul language, screaming, and scolding that Tony was in for that evening.

"Good, Mylee! You do what you have to do and know that I am here for you a hundred percent!" Seth said.

"Thanks, Seth, I'm going to be alright. I'm going to go get Halley's things together for Mom's tonight while that asshole is at work. I may be back if things get ugly," she said. Seth rose and escorted her to the door. Mylee paused before opening it and kissed Seth passionately.

"I love you, Seth," she said, as she turned and opened the door. Seth ripped her back to him, kissing her more passionately than ever before. He released her and she stood tall as she walked out the door.


God! How am I going to tell Halley?" Mylee thought as she walked towards home. "Her little heart will be broken." Hopefully he will just move out and let us have the house and make it all go smoothly for her sake." She suddenly recoiled to the rear. She nearly stepped in front of a car at the intersection.

"This is all his fault! Maybe he should have to tell Halley!" she thought. She had second thoughts while considering not being there for her daughter when she found out.

"Why would any man flush their family down the toilet like this?" she thought. "What a pile of garbage!" Her mind drifted to Seth. "Damn!" she lamented. "I always knew he loved me. I just wish..."

# CHAPTER 19

"Hey guy, I'm on the way!" Debbie informed Abel on the phone, calling nearly forty-five minutes before he had expected.

"I'm ready when you are," Abel replied. His worn and oil stained jeans were replaced by factory faded new ones. A flannel shirt took the place of his usual t-shirt. He reached to his face, verifying that he had removed all of his abrasive whiskers in case Debbie kissed him again.

"There she is!" Abel thought to himself as Debbie's car parked in front of his house. She sprang from the driver's seat and danced to his front door in one of her many playful gaits.

"Hi babe!" she said as Abel opened the door, not waiting for her to knock. She grabbed the handle of the screen door and flung it open in her direction. She jumped to her tip-toes and smeared a generous amount of bright red lipstick on Abel's lips.

"Oops," she said, removing a hankie from her bib overall pocket. She wetted it with her saliva, held the back of Abel's head for support, and dabbed the lipstick from him. She kissed him

[303]

again, leaving as much evidence of her on his lips as before, but left it to stay this time. She laughed at it.

"Ooh, you smell good Abel," she commented. The fragrance of the cologne that the lady at the drug store recommended that morning wafted from his body. Abel had applied it as instructed by the young female drug store clerk.

"You look pretty," Abel complimented. She wore a tight-fitting black blouse tucked under the bib of her overalls that displayed her near-perfect profile. The bib was pushed outward in front by her breasts.

"Thank you! Let's hit it!" she said. She tossed Abel the keys to her car, grabbed his hand and skipped backward down the driveway in front of him. She towed him to the passenger door where she stepped to the side to allow him to open it for her. She plopped in in her usual mannor.

"Ahh," Abel said, sliding the driver's seat backward. His contorted body found relief as the seat adjusted to his much larger frame than Debbie's. Debbie laughed at his predicament while sliding across the seat to position herself as close to Abel as the console would allow.

"Hang on, where are we going?" Abel said. He had put the car in drive before realizing that Debbie had said they were

[304]

going out of town to one of her favorite restaurants but hadn't shared its location.

"Over the bridge and to the left," she sang gleefully to the tune of 'To Grandmother's House We Go'. She giggled freely at her own antics. Abel smiled and shook his head.

"Here? Are you sure? Looks pretty scary!" Abel said as Debbie instructed him to turn off of the levee. He turned at the next street after passing a row of hundred- plus year-old dilapidated structures. Each had a run-down residence atop it. Abel reasoned that the homes were likely above where the flood waters would be if the levee were ever to break. He couldn't help but think that the bottom of each building had sat in those flood waters many times in their long history.

"Yep, pull down to the first road and take a right," Debbie said. Able noticed an anxiousness building within her. She sat erect, looking down the ancient brick street as he turned. It was lined with century-old bright-colored storefronts.

"Who'd have known?" Abel said. He was surprised at the appearances of the fronts of the buildings after seeing the rear of them. "I've driven past this place a hundred times, but I had no idea it was an actual town."

"Park right there," Debbie ordered, pointing to a vacant curbside on Abel's right. Abel let an oncoming car pass on the narrow street to allow him to progress around a parked car and to the vacant parking spot. The street curb's height blocked the passenger door so that Debbie had to climb over the console and exit through Abel's door-- a task she accomplished with ease.

"Come on!" she said, grabbing Abel's hand with both of hers and walking backward to tow him towards a small run-down storefront. An old orange cat sunned itself in one of its two large bay windows. Faded red curtains shrouded its interior's view from the street.

"Pineapples Café," she said. She laughed and pointed to those exact words painted on the face of both matching windows. The words on each window framed a many-years-old hand-painted pineapple.

"Jingle, ding, doink, dong, jingle," a red cloth ribbon tied to ten different bells sounded at more of a rattle than a chime as they entered the door from which they dangled.

"Back here," Debbie chimed. She led Abel to a rear table that looked as if it were already occupied. There was a half glass of water sitting in front of a pulled out and turned chair.

[306]

"DEBBIE!" a voice sounded. An elderly and portly grey-haired Mexican woman with an unusually wide smile appeared between two stained curtains that blocked the view of the building's rear. "Pineapple! Pineapple! Debbie is here to see us!" the old Mexican woman announced over her shoulder to the kitchen. She let the curtains fall closed behind her and began wiping her hands on her well-worn apron. Her smile grew as she neared Debbie. She opened her arms expecting, and receiving, a hug from Debbie.

"Oh you look so pretty!" the Mexican lady said after sweeping her eyes from head to toe and examining her. "You need to eat more," she scolded.

Abel recognized her as the typical caring Mexican mother that considered all babies and people who were not obese as too thin. Her eyes then shifted to Abel. She scrutinized him carefully as if ascertaining his suitability for her surrogate daughter.

"You got a boyfriend now, Debbie?" she chimed with her heavy Mexican accent, still scrutinizing every detail about Abel.

"Yes, Trini, this is my boyfriend Abel," Debbie replied without hesitation. Able was surprised at her characterization of him.

"Pineapple!" Debbie screamed as her wide eyes shifted focus. A frail-looking Chinese man of barely five feet appeared through the once-white-now-yellowed curtain from the kitchen. Debbie threw her arms around him, nearly lifting him off his feet with her hug. The old Chinese man began to glow and his face reddened from her attention.

"Debbie's got boyfriend!" Trini said, shortening her sentence and changing its tone as if speaking to the Chinese man in his native language. She pointed to Abel with her eyes.

"Hi sir," Abel said. The old Chinese man greeted him with a humble bow of his head. A warm smile came to his ancient face. The pupils and irises of his eyes were greyed and matched what was left of his hair. Abel surmised he was nearly a century in age.

"Pineapple," the old man replied. He offered his ancient wrinkled hand in friendship to Abel after wiping it on the more-clean inside of his white apron.

"I cook!" the old Chinese man said. He turned and disappeared back into the kitchen. Trini, his lifelong waitress, explained he had several phoned-in orders to prepare.

"You want menus, Debbie?" Trini asked, pronouncing the first E in Debbie's name as a long A. She half-heartily reached towards a stack of menus that were well beyond the length of her short over-round arms.

"I know what we want," Debbie answered, as Trini expected. She rolled off an order of items that sounded foreign to Abel.

"Sound okay?" Debbie asked, looking towards Abel after finishing her order.

"Sounds perfect!" Abel replied. He had no idea of what she had ordered.

"Look," she said after taking Abel to the kitchen. She peeled back the yellow curtains to show the little Chinese man hovering over a pair of side-by-side giant woks, each three feet across, with a large faucet protruding from the wall between them.

"Psst!" Debbie said, attracting Abel's attention to a bright red hunk of pork resting in an oversized oven. The oven was flavored with, what looked to be several decades of smoke and seasonings. They were caked to a depth of nearly two inches over its internal entirety. "Wait till you taste it, Abel!" she said with a big smile. She licked her lips and returned them to their table. The old Chinese man never realized their presence. He busied himself flinging a myriad of noodles, meats, and vegetables into the air from each wok while huge gas-driven flames roiled underneath them.

"Oh, I have the bad gout in my toe," Trini said, sitting with Abel and Debbie for nearly their entire meal. She removed her foot from her hand-made Mexican sandal to show the swelling and redness. Abel noticed that the worn shoe had long ago molded itself to the shape of her foot. The shoe looked as if the foot had resided in it for a decade or more. She appeared uncaring that they were in the midst of eating their BBQ pork, chow mien, and the rest of the wide array of dishes that Debbie had ordered.

"Oh damn," Trini said as the bells on the door again rattled. She loathed the idea of her incessant talking being interrupted to wait on another customer. She held her finger to the air signaling them to wait for her return and settled the new customers.

"He's good-looking," Trini said about Abel. She talked as if he weren't present. She drug out the sounds of the O's in "good" to dramatize her statement.

"Yes, he is!" Debbie agreed, still chewing the remnants of her last bite. The aroma of paper wrapped chicken filled the air as

[310]

she tore into another one and released its flavored steam into the room.

"You need time before a baby," Trini said. "You make sure you use rubbers!" She said it as though she had just told them to be careful driving home. Abel's face reddened as the other patrons examined both him and his date. They seemed not to approve of the loose sexual relationship that Trini had implied. Debbie, however, soaked in Trini's devotion and smiled at her somewhat inappropriate motherly guidance. A flash of light came through from the front window as the orange cat spread its curtains and jumped to the floor. It disappeared towards the back of the building.

"I love you, Pineapple!" Debbie said after finishing her meal. She approached him from his rear as he continued to stir his flavorful concoctions in the giant woks. She kissed him on his weathered cheek. Pineapple hugged her while holding a two-foot-long spoon in one hand and an equally long Chinese spatula in the other. He smiled a broad smile this time, exposing the near toothless interior of his mouth. He turned back to the woks and continued to stir them incessantly.

[311]

"Bye, Trini!" Debbie said.  The elderly Mexican waitress ignored the incoming customers to give her a huge hug after spewing motherly advice about using sunscreen on her fair skin. She again interjected the "rubber" comment as part of her goodbye, this time raising the heads of the new customers who had just entered.

"You give me a hug too," Trini said.  She grabbed Abel and hugged him before he had time to react. Abel hugged her back, barely able to fit her portly body in his arms.  "You make sure you love my Debbie," she scolded as she released him from her bear-like grip.

Debbie butted in on Abel's speechless behalf.  "He does and he will!" she said.  She smiled at Trini and threw Abel's arm over her shoulders.  She wrapped hers around his waist and led him to the front door.

"Let's walk through downtown," Debbie said.  She laughed as she saw Abel turn his head in each direction and notice that the "downtown" was only two blocks long.  Nearly half of the storefronts were curtained off and being used as residences.

"I love this place," Debbie said.  She motioned with her head towards two old men across the street who were sitting on well-worn wooden chairs and playing a dominos type of game.

[312]

"Careful!" Debbie said, keeping Abel from falling over the two-foot high curb at the edge of the sidewalk. She led him to the nearby concrete steps at the corner.

"Nying, yang, gyeegow yang!" the two old men yelled as two young teen skateboarders skated down the center of the street. They seemed to be chewing them out, but quickly returned to their game. The teens smiled respectfully, seeming quite used to the scolding.

"It's like stepping back in time here," Abel commented. He saw an elderly Chinese woman who exited her tiny herb shop begin sweeping the sidewalk. Her broom was worn half to nothingness. An equally aged broom-clad oriental woman from one of the other shuttered shops joined her in moments. The rattle of their foreign-tongued chatter filled the air. The smell of Pineapple's Café scented the entire downtown. The fresh fruits and vegetables that were displayed on outdoor carts in front of some of the stores began being rolled inside for the night. The high levee's shadow darkened the streets and signaled to all that the day was coming to a close. Debbie held herself close to Abel as the evening wind pierced through her clothing.

"Here," Abel said to Debbie. He stepped in front of her and offered his hand to help her down the two uneven steps from the curb at the end of the street. She took it and stepped down and replaced his arm around her.

Only two businesses remained open-- Pineapples and a small bar with about twelve seats. Four of the barstools were occupied by elderly Chinese men who were slamming dice cups to the bar and had cigarettes dangling from their lips. The others stools sat vacant.

"Here, let me pull away from the curb!" Abel said to Debbie, not wanting her to have to traverse the console again.

"No, I've got this," she said. She paused to kiss Abel before entering the car. "I love being with you Abel! You make me happy!" She climbed clumsily over the console to the passenger seat and plopped into it with a satisfied sigh.

"You make me happy too," Abel responded as he took his seat behind the wheel. Debbie smiled warmly at him and slid close to him. She cradled his upper arm in her arms and laid her head on his shoulder.

"That was a wonderful date!" Debbie said while rising from the seat of the car after Abel had opened her door. She fell into his arms on the street in front of his house. Their bodies were obscured from sight by the darkness afforded them from a huge shade tree at the street's edge. It blocked the waning

[314]

moon's light. Debbie devoured Abel's lips with hers. Her tongue reached deep into Abel's mouth. Their warm fluids comingled into one flavor.

"You are a beautiful man, Abel," she whispered as she pressed herself to him. She began rhythmically massaging herself against him. She felt him harden. "Feels good!" she whispered as she continued breathlessly massaging herself on him. She sighed in pleasure as her eyes closed and her mind drifted to fantasy. Her thrusts reached a manic pace as she suddenly exploded into a violent orgasm, discharging what seemed to Abel as cups of fluid and soaking herself to her knees.

"Look what you did," Debbie breathed, smiling sensually, her eyes partially open and her stomach continuing to spasm. She stepped away, letting Abel see her. "I do that sweetie," she said."

Abel stood in awe as Debbie leaned to him for support. Her entire body was weakened from her orgasm. Her strength soon returned.

"Felt so good, babe," Debbie said, turning her back to the car and sitting on the lip between the seat and the door opening. She unzipped Abel's pants and took his penis into her mouth in one continuous motion.

[315]

"Oh, uh," Abel groaned as Debbie bobbed wildly near his groin. He began visioning his mother. Terror set in him as his hardness melted to a flaccid pile of flesh in her mouth. "I'm sorry!" Abel cried in embarrassment. His face reddened to the color of blood. His eyes filled with tears, and his entire body shook in shame.

"It's okay, Abel. It happens, sweetie!" Debbie said lovingly as she rose to her feet. "It really is okay Abel, you are with me and I love you." Abel was unable to face her as she spoke. He stood in unbearable shame. Her soft words were all that kept him from running away. "I love you" she repeated. She took Abel to her and combed his hair with her fingers. She kissed his cheek between each stroke. "Baby, whatever it is, we will work through it. I promise. I'm never leaving you for any reason!" Debbie told Abel. Torrents of tears poured from his eyes.

"It's no big deal," she continued. Abel snorted loudly as he gulped a huge breath of air. He sighed heavily as he exhaled it. "Let it out," Debbie coaxed. She began to bear all of Abel's weight. Able cried into her embrace.

"I guess I'd better go inside," Abel said. He was unable to face Debbie. He held his eyes aimed at the ground.

"Abel, look at me," Debbie said gently. She placed the side of her folded index finger under Abel's chin and raised it so his eyes would meet hers. A loving smile came to her face. "Do you love me Abel?" she questioned.

"Yes," Abel said, expressing love verbally for the first time in his life.

"Then trust me, Abel, this is a nothing issue and I just want to be with you forever," she said, adding, "Ever since I met you, I saw a beautiful man, both inside and out, and my whole being wants nothing more than to be with you forever." She placed her lips on his, tasting a mixture of his warm saliva and salt from his tears. She guided him to his bedroom. She laid him on the bed, removed his shoes, and pulled his pants off. She laid beside him.

"I love you," she whispered, repeating herself softly until he drifted into a much-needed sleep.

"I love you boyfriend!" the note on the nightstand read. Debbie had arisen early to make it to her morning shift at the Riverview restaurant. The note continued, "I will call you later. I get off at two. All my love!" It was signed with a perfect image of Debbie's lips in freshly applied brilliant red lipstick. A lone dandelion, gleaned from Abel's front lawn, adorned it.

"So this is what it feels like..." Abel thought, lying back to his pillow and staring at the ceiling.

"Pick a hand," Debbie said, smiling mischievously after finding Abel in his garden after work. She held both of her hands behind her back. Abel hesitated.

"Pick a hand," she ordered again.

"Right," he said.

"Congratulations sir, you won!" she announced. She brought her empty right hand to in front of her and read from an imaginary document.

"You, sir, have just won an all-expenses-paid ferry ride to San Francisco with the prettiest woman on earth!" Debbie said. She held her hand rigidly in front of her with her thumb extended to point at herself as that woman and laughed.

"It's going to be a blast! Have you ever done it?" she asked. She silenced herself and waiting for Abel's reply.

"Nope," Abel responded, "I didn't even know they had ferries there." He examined the picture on the ferry ticket that she produced.

"Well, should we get ready to go, or do you have another hot date lined out for the day?" Debbie teased.

"NO!" Abel said.

"Okay then, I'm going to run home and change and I'll be back in forty-five minutes." She put her hand behind his head and pulled his lips tightly to hers. "Love you!" she said as their lips parted. She made Abel feel like nothing had happened.


"Honk! Honk!" Abel's heard in less than twenty minutes. He gathered his wallet, cell phone, and some loose change and headed to her car.

"Get in, big boy! I'll drive," Debbie said sporting her usual broad smile. She spoke to Abel across the passenger seat through the half-rolled-down passenger window. She patted the seat with the palm of her hand as she spoke. "If we hurry we can catch the next ferry! I know a shortcut!" she said. She drove slightly over the speed limit all the way and weaved through backroads and streets to the ferry terminal. She drug him at her usual breakneck pace to the ferry.

"Isn't it neat?" Debbie asked, hurriedly scurrying Abel to the rail at the front of the multi-level ferry boat as it left the dock.

"Yeah, it is," Abel replied. He shuddered as the alien-like craft's fans filled its rubber skirt and lifted it to a hover. It began gliding across the chops in the water as if they weren't there. Seals sunned themselves amongst the saltwater-tolerant flora and boulders on the shores as they passed. "It's like a lost world", he said.

"I love this," Debbie said. She wrapped Abel's arm around herself to use as a shawl to shield her from the cool bay breeze. She closed her eyes and lifted her flared nostrils into the air, taking the full aromas of the saltwater bay into them. She licked her lips as if she had tasted it.

"I'm flying!" she said, holding her arms to her sides as if she were a gliding airplane. She dipped one arm while raising the other as if performing acrobatics while giggling like a child. Her jet black wind-blown hair began shimmering in the sun. Abel saw her change her focus to the distance.

"Look!" she exclaimed. She grabbed Abel's arm and positioned him to directly face the Golden Gate Bridge in the distance. It framed Alcatraz Island as if ready to swallow it. San

[320]

Francisco's image grew in front of them as they neared it. The ferry glided to the dock without a bump and its giant fans let it settle next to the gangplank.

"Now you're going to see why I told you to wear tennis shoes," Debbie said after disembarking from the boat. She drug Abel at a hurried pace across the six-lane street. He tripped on the streetcar rail at its center. The pedestrian light counted down the few seconds they had to cross. The organic saltwater smell evolved into a mixture of exhaust fumes, cotton candy, hot dogs, and other street vendors' wares. The traffic quieted and the air became still and odorless as Debbie steered them to the end of a dead end street.

"Are you kidding?" Abel said. He stood staring up a steep hillside, its stairs switch-backing from side to side through a jungle of flowers and ivies, reminding him of the 'Jack in the Beanstalk' tale.

"Come on!" Debbie commanded. She got behind Abel and began pushing him forward with both hands as if forcing him over an upside-down cliff.

"Okay, okay," he said. She grabbed his hand, leaped to his side and began tugging to set a rigorous pace up the several hundred stairs. They passed the slope's inhabitants, many of whom were lugging sacks of groceries to their stair-side homes by this one and only access.

"How are you folks today?" a nude couple greeted. They stood facing Abel and Debbie as they readied to enter their hot tub on their trailside patio.

"Great," Debbie responded, stopping to chat about the beauty of the trail with them. She invoked an invite to join them which she politely took a rain check for. Abel shifted his eyes to the architecture and surrounding flora as he waited and they soon continued their ascent.

"I thought I was in shape!" Abel said as they reached the top. He leaned forward and placed a hand on each knee to catch his breath. Debbie laughed and pointed out the round Coit Tower then led him to a west-facing pedestrian viewpoint. He watched as she seemed to soak in its panorama.

"Down we go!" she said, guiding Abel through the Italian district. She referred to it as 'North Beach'. Abel saw no beach in sight.

"Check it out..." She said, dragging him from the center of the shoulder-to-shoulder Asian crowd and into a long and narrow shop filled with live fish, frogs, turtles and beasts that he had never seen before. A Chinese man dropped a fish "accidentally"

[322]

onto the sidewalk, letting it flop wildly and barking in his native tongue to advertise the freshness of his wares. Old Chinese women negotiated ruthlessly over pennies worth of fresh produce nearby. They stopped to enjoy a beer at an old Irish pub in an alley among the downtown high-rise offices. Before long and without warning, and to Abel's amazement, the ferry terminal appeared again before them.

"Well, are you worn out?" Debbie said as they arrived full-circle to the ferry terminal.

"I'm good." Abel responded. His feet throbbed like hammer pounded thumbs. They flashed their round trip tickets and boarded.

"Let's go up top," Debbie said, leading Abel towards the top deck of the ferry. She stopped at the onboard bar as they passed it and purchased them each a plastic cup of red wine. They traversed a circular steel staircase to the roof. The evening's darkness was illuminated by a never-ending array of lights in the the skyline. They sat in the front row in the open air.

"Thank you, sweetie," Debbie said, nuzzling her body to Abel's, then sipping her wine. Abel watched her sit still, seeming to absorb the surrounding lights.

[323]

"I love you," Abel said.  Debbie replied silently by pressing her lips to his.  They sat quietly and closely for the hour-long return.

"Let's go to my house for ice cream," Debbie said, turning left towards her house from the bridge's exit in Edgewater before hearing Abel's reply.  "I have Huckleberry ice cream with chocolate syrup!  I didn't even know they made huckleberry ice cream," she exclaimed, adding, "My whole family used to go camping and picking huckleberries when we were kids up in Oregon!"

"What's the heck is a huckleberry?" Abel inquired.

"They grow wild on a bush," she said, adding enthusiastically, "But wait until you taste them."  Her eyes fixed ahead as she imagined their flavor.  Abel saw her lick her lips and swallow in anticipation.

"Here," Debbie said, handing Abel a bowl with a generous amount of both ice cream and chocolate syrup.  "I'll be right back!"

Abel sat on her tiny jungle-like patio that was hiding behind her second-hand-furniture filled house. He imagined a nineteen twenties movie set as he had walked through it.  Each furniture

[324]

piece was un-faded and seemed new, despite its sixty plus years of age.

"Mmm, it's killer!" Abel said. His eyes skewed upward as he sampled the huckleberry treat for his first time. He was surprised that its flavor was still detectable through the chocolate that smothered it. He tasted another bite as he looked over the patio. Breezes coaxed soothing songs from the many wind chimes. They seemed to be carefully hung in key locations so as to capture the wind without tangling.

A softball-sized water feature that balanced a tigers-eye type marble in its flow sat atop a driftwood stand. The striped gem was held captive by the gurgling water's motion. The water cascading from under it and back to the tiny pool below it mimicked the sound of a distant mountain brook. Abel soothed to its song and dance. "Leave it to her," he commented to himself.

"How's the ice cream?" Debbie said, returning with her own bowl equal in size to Abel's. Her bib overalls were now traded for pajama bottoms and a t-shirt. Abel noticed no other garments under them.

"Great!" Abel replied as Debbie made room for them bot in an oversized soft padded large round chair made for one. She

[325]

summoned Abel to beside her with a hand that had abandoned a spoon in her mouth for that purpose. She folded her legs under her and used Abel's side for her backrest. She snuggled her body next to him, as if making a nest, and fed herself another oversized spoonful from her bowl.

"I found that in an old junk pile next to an abandoned house a couple of years ago," Debbie said. She pointed to an old hand-pump with the top of her spoon like a teacher using a pointer stick in the classroom. "Those I got one day when I saw some people in an old VW bus parked alongside the road and I stopped to help, thinking they were broken down. Turns out they were there digging those out of a vein of them," she said, again using her pointer to guide Abel's attention to a half-dozen nearly-foot-long perfectly shaped crystals. "They were cool people! They let me use their tools, I ate lunch with them and still call them once in a while," she said, smiling at the memory.

"Did you have fun today, Abel?" she asked. She cocked her head to look over her shoulder to see his response.

"It really was a nice day. One of the best days ever!" Abel said. Debbie showed a satisfied smile and turned back to her original position. She took another large spoonful of ice cream after gathering the chocolate syrup that had sunk to the bottom of the bowl.

[326]

"Sure smells good out here," Abel commented, sensing the aroma of vanilla filling the air.

"Oh, that is the jasmine! I love jasmine!" Debbie said. She leaned to the edge of her chair with an odd excitement and placed her empty bowl on the table. She stood and cupped the white flowers from an oversized clay pot in her hands. "Don't tell anyone, but I stole a cutting of this from down in front of the city hall," she said. She smiled mischievously as if someone would care.

"I have a movie picked out for us tonight," she said while taking Abel's empty bowl from him. She extending her hand to tow Abel from his cushiony chair. "It's 'Pretty Woman,' have you seen it?" she asked. She leaned back to offset Abel's weight as she pulled him to his feet.

"No, I haven't watched many movies actually," he responded. "I love to watch them, I just never had anyone to watch them with." Debbie paused. She felt a sadness.

"You'll like it!" she said. She led him again to the retro-adorned front room and to the overstuffed couch that sat directly in front of the television. "I'll get a blanket." She retrieved a thick down comforter and snuggled next to Abel after spreading the blanket evenly across them both. The air inside cooled from the brisk delta breeze wafting through the open patio screen. The aroma of jasmine trailed them into the room.

"I cry every time! I've seen this movie a thousand times." Debbie said, dabbing her eyes with a tissue as the movie came to an end.

"Have you ever had a massage, tough mechanic man?" Debbie inquired. She positioning herself at the edge of the couch, anxious to hear his response.

"No," Abel answered. Her face livened with excitement.

"They are really good for your lymph system, your immune system, and your overall health," Debbie explained, offering her hand to Abel. "Come on, I'll show you."

She took Abel's hand and led him to her bedroom. He watched as she removed several neatly folded stacks of laundry from an odd-looking bench-like table. She positioned the table towards the center of her room.

"Take off your clothes, lie down with your nose and mouth in that hole, and just cover your bottom with this towel," she instructed, handing Abel a sterile looking white towel. "I'll be right back!" Abel listened, as a soothing oriental-type music blended with the sound of ocean waves gently washing across a gravelly beach began filling the room. He disrobed and laid on the padded table as instructed.

"Okay, I'm back," Debbie announced. She lit a lavender candle and let it be the only light in the room.

"No, don't lift your head! Just relax," Debbie said, seeing Abel begin to stir. She immediately removed the towel he had placed over his butt, leaving Abel wondering why she had bothered to have him put it there in the first place.

"Hang on, I hate getting this oil all over my clothes," Debbie said. Abel saw the t-shirt and pajama bottoms she was wearing fall into his view through the hole in which his face rested. A slightly-warmer-than-body-temperature oil began pouring over his back, followed by the firm and soothing strokes of Debbie's hands to spread it. She found every one of his muscles with her fingertips. Her thumbs kneaded deep into them for nearly an hour.

"OOOHH", Abel moaned.

"Feel okay? Not too hard?" Debbie inquired. Abel moaned again as a reply.

"Okay, turn over," Debbie instructed over the sound of the music. Abel hesitated for a moment and then complied. Debbie repositioned herself at the head of the table. She massaged every facial muscle as well as the lobes of his ears. She leaned, bare-breasted, over Abel to pull and tug on the muscles in his chest and front shoulders. Abel noticed that her snow white skin made her light pink nipples seem to glow. He closed his eyes, but her image remained.

"I'll try not to tickle you," she said. She shifted herself toward his feet and spread the warm lavender-scented oil over them. She shared generous amounts of oil to his legs, then his chest and to every part of his body. Her own body was drenched in it as well. She massaged each leg carefully, moving rhythmically higher on his body with each stroke until she could reach no further.

"Hang on a sec.," she said. She moved to Abel's side and mounted his body like a horse. She applied her entire weight onto her hands and dug deep into his chest. She then slid her hands to behind his neck and pulled its muscles towards her. Abel moaned as his stress abandoned him.

"Geez! Your muscles are tight!" she said. She applied even more pressure and worked her thumbs to his breastbone. Her hairless and oil covered body slid in every direction over him as she massaged him. She felt Abel harden under her.

"Feels so good," Abel said. His eyes remained closed. Debbie retrieved the bottle of oil from the nightstand and squirted it generously between them. She continued to massage his chest but was aroused by Abel hardened between her legs. She felt his stomach spasm with each glide over him. Debbie cradled his penis in her labia and fell forward, aiming her nipple at his mouth. His lips parted to accept it.

"I love you, Abel," she said, watching him nurse her gently, continuing to massage him with her full body the entire time. She withdrew her nipple from him, sat over him and slid downward. She felt him sink into her. She placed both hands on his stomach for support and raised and lowered herself upon him.

"You're so beautiful!" Abel said after opening his eyes and seeing her over him. He watched as her upper arms penned her breasts outward and to each other. She milked Abel with her pelvis. Her eyes were shut and her head was tilted to the rear. She unknowingly bit her lip at each downward thrust.

"Get on top, baby," Debbie whispered, rolling them to allow herself under him, never allowing him to slip from her as she did. "Feels so good!" she cooed. Abel began pounding her. Sweat poured from them both.

[331]

"OH ABEL!" Debbie screamed, her entire body clung to him as Abel moaned loudly and convulsed in orgasm. They collapsed to each other, their bodies spent.

"Oh, sorry!" Abel said, realizing that he was crushing Debbie under him.

"It's okay," she said, hugging him to her.

"That felt so good," she whispered. "Now, that wasn't too hard, was it?"

"Harder than last time!" Abel answered. Their eyes met and they erupted into laughter.

"Kiss me," Abel said.

Debbie rolled him to his back and sealed her lips to his. She snuggled to his side and they drifted to sleep in each other's arms.

"I'm going to marry that man," Debbie thought, delivering coffee warm-ups from table to table the following morning with a more than usual glee in her cadence.

"What are you grinning about?" one of the regular customers asked. Her face reddened as if she were caught with her hand in the cookie jar.

[332]

"Oh, just thinking," she replied with an ear-to-ear grin.

"Wonder why she likes a guy like me?" Abel thought the following day after Debbie dropped him off at his house.

"She could have anyone. She is the most beautiful person in the world!"

"I never want to lose her, I know that!" He laid his keys on the table and found a mirror. Her lipstick was smeared across his face. Her essence filled the air. He closed his eyes and tilted his head back and inhaled deeply to enjoy the last bit of her magic aroma before showering.

He awoke the following morning and laid thinking.

An odd and painful guilt suddenly overcame him. He sluffed to a chair in fear. He skipped his usual breakfast that day.

# CHAPTER 20

"EDGEWATER POLICE CAPTAIN ARRESTED IN CHILD PORNOGRAPHY STING!" the headline of the read-by-everyone-in-Edgewater Herald Newspaper announced in gigantic print at the top of its front page. Most people already had heard the raging gossip in town and craved for more juicy tidbits.

"FBI nabs seventy-three for sharing and uploading child pornography, including Capt. Mike Smith of the Edgewater Police department," the byline under the main heading read. "Police Chief held on a no-bail federal warrant in Sacramento" another accompanying article informed.

"It figures," Barry overheard a local patron in the coffee shop say to his friend. Both held newspapers open in front of them. They shared the sick details back and forth as they learned them.

"He always struck me as a fucking weirdo!" one man said. He was passing judgment on Smith immediately, as is common to every person accused of child molestation. "What a piece of crap!", his friend added.

"I couldn't agree more my friend!" Barry thought as he listened, knowing that Smith was just that, albeit not for what he was accused of. "How's it feel, Shitbag?" Barry celebrated. He savored the thought of Smith rotting in jail-- or getting a homemade knife jammed into his heart.

"Police chief kept isolated from other inmates!" Barry read on an inside page.

"They will get to you Shitbag! Hope they issue you some Vaseline!" Barry smirked.

"Captain Smith denies all charges," a tiny headline buried deep into the paper read. The article was quick to explain that nearly all of those accused of child molestation routinely denied their charges and that most were eventually convicted.

"You're down, Shitbag!" Barry thought as he closed his paper, uninterested in the balance of the small town weekly gossip it contained.


"I'm going to kill that son of a bitch!" Captain Smith promised himself after figuring out that Barry had orchestrated the ruse that landed him in prison.

[336]

"That no good hippie fucker," Smith thought, "I swear I will kill that fucker for this!" he steamed while pacing in his small, dimly-lit, dried-urine-smelling cell.

"I was set up! I'm not a pervert! I'm a law enforcement officer for Christ's sake, I'm one of you!" Smith announced to a guard walking by. The guard glared at him with disgust.

"You are not one of us, you sick fuck! I hope you rot in hell so my daughters never have to see you on the street!" The guard said. He walked away, leaving Smith to begin living his life of being known as a sicko. His own attorney was unwilling to listen to his unbelievable and convoluted conspiracy theory, having heard every child molester that he ever represented come up with similar bizarre and unbelievable stories.

"This is bullshit!" Smith screamed to the judge in the federal courtroom as he was being arraigned on further charges. His computer, after having been forensically examined by authorities, caused them to charge him with several more felonies since his initial arrest.

"Sir, you open your mouth disrespectfully like that again in my courtroom and I will charge you with contempt of court!

[337]

You are in enough trouble, mister!" the judge said angrily. The judge recorded Smith's face in his mind so he would remember him well when it came time to sentence him.

"Now sit down and keep your mouth shut, mister!" the judge further admonished. His face was red with anger and had a look of pure resolve to follow through on his promise if Smith opened his mouth again.

"Sorry, your honor," Smith's attorney said. He pushed Smith to his seat with an admonishing look on his face. "It won't happen again!" He glared at Smith with an "if-it-does-you-will-be-looking-for-a-new-attorney" look and glanced at the judge to show his contempt for his own client in order to save face for his further appearances in front of him on other matters.

"You tell him to shove it up his ass!" Shitbag Smith screamed at his attorney a month later, who had brought him an offer from the federal prosecuting attorney to serve just seven years for all the charges that had mounted since the beginning of his case.

"Look, Mike," the attorney explained, "the evidence is overwhelming! It was downloaded to and from your computer on many occasions. They have traced the traffic to your home. You need to take this deal or you will be in here for your entire life. It

[338]

is the best we can get! Take the son of a bitch!" the attorney said forcefully. Smith's face contorted in anger and his teeth began grinding to the point where they were squeaking aloud.

"Mike," the attorney told Smith calmly, "I can promise you a minimum of thirty years if you don't take this plea. I have done this for twenty-five years and I know when I am going to lose, and this is one of those times. Please listen to me!"

"But I didn't do a fucking thing!" Smith said. His body slumped into the wooden holding cell chair. He raised his head looking for sympathy in his attorney's face. It had none.

"Well Mike?" the attorney impatiently asked, standing cross-armed in front of him awaiting his final answer.

"Oh fuck it! Every motherfucker in this world will always see me as 'Chester the Molester' anyway! My fucking life is ruined!" Smith said, finally adding, "Go ahead and set it up. And tell that scumbag judge to go fuck himself for me!"

"Okay, I'll set it up," the attorney said as he began gathering the legal papers and lined yellow pad that he seemed to always have in front of him. "You made the right decision, Mike." Smith grunted in anger and waved the attorney from the holding cell with the back of his hand without saying another word.

"In the interest of justice, I'm going to dismiss this case with prejudice!" the judge said. He slammed his gavel to his desk and dismissed all charges against Samantha.

"I am so sorry for this injustice young lady." The judge said. He ordered her released from prison immediately after seeing evidence that Smith had taken nude pictures of her and other girls and had stalked her much of her life. The judge had erased his every doubt of Smith's guilt, seeing his computer records, credit card receipts, the picture of him threatening Sam in the back of the police car, and the rest of the evidence. He believed Sam's every word about him throwing the cocaine baggie into her hands to gain her fingerprints.

"We did it Sam!" Barry said to his sobbing daughter as he took her into his arms in the courtroom.

"I told you the truth would come out, Sam," Barry said for the benefit of the judge, who was standing to leave the courtroom. Reporters from the local papers swarmed the attorneys for comment after Sam and her father refused their pleas. Their headlines smeared Smith's reputation further the following morning.

"That's really good news!" Trish said while smiling earnestly at Sam. "I really am happy for you." She began to tear.

"I am not just leaving you, Trish. I love you, and I will see you every weekend! I promise!" Samantha vowed. She took her to her arms and kissed the tears from her cheeks and held her. Sam worried, thinking back to her gangster cellmate and hoping Trish wouldn't have to bare someone like her.

"You will be out in a year Trish. It will ...!" Sam said, stopping herself mid-sentence.

"Hey, we will spend most of our lives together as best pals, I promise!"

"And don't worry when you get out about needing a place to live. Andy has a little farm and I'm sure you can stay with us a while. I'll talk to him!" Sam said. Trish smiled.

"Kiss me," Samantha said, taking her into her arms again and hugging her. Trish cried into Sam's chest.

"Hey girlfriend, it's all going to be good, trust me," Sam said. She heard the guard approaching down the hallway. "I love you, and I always will-- and besides, I'm not done with these yet!" she added. She playfully reached with both hands and massaged Trish's nipples between her thumbs and forefingers. Trish smiled through her tears.

[341]

"There's my girl! My free girl!" Samantha's dad said. He lifted her from her feet and swung her in a circle as he hugged her outside the prison gates.

"I am so sorry for all of this Sammy and I am so sorry it took so long to get you out," Barry said. He whispered in her ear as he hugged her and before handing her off to her boyfriend. "Let's keep all this between me and you forever, okay Sam?" He pushed her back slightly to make eye contact and impress how important it was that no soul ever know of their ruse. She affirmed their pact with her eyes and a slight nod. She turned her attention to her boyfriend as they walked towards the car.

This fucking ice pick is going in your fucking head next time you fight us, you child molesting prick!" a huge framed, overly-muscular, shaved-headed Aryan gangster said as he stood over Smith. Smith laid on the prison shower's floor in a pool of blood.

"You're our bitch now!" he said. He peered down at Smith while zipping his pants closed. He replaced his striped prison shirt and covered his full body jailhouse tattoos. Smith cowered below him. His anus was torn savagely from being raped by the huge gangster and four of his friends, all of whom participated in the beating.

"I'm going to torture that fucking hippie prick and his little whore daughter in ways they will never imagine when I get out of this place! I swear they are going to fucking pay!" Smith thought laying still in bed that night. His hate and yearn for revenge grew after each time he was raped. The rapes were unrelenting. His nights of plotting revenge could not be counted.

# CHAPTER 21

"Tony! I told you! We are through! Our marriage is over!" Mylee screamed into her phone. "You better think of what you are going to tell your daughter, you selfish prick!"

"But..," Tony tried to interject. Mylee calmly, but loudly, cut him off.

"Tony, save your selfish breath! Go fuck yourself, better yet, go fuck one of your girlfriends!" There was a sigh on the other end of the otherwise silent line.

"Halley is staying with Mom tonight and you can find somewhere to stay. Matter of fact, you should look for a permanent home, maybe one of your girlfriend's houses. I don't give a shit as long as I don't have to look at you!" Mylee said. Her voice grew angrier with each word. Tony tried again to speak. She silenced him mid-sentence with the "end call" button on her phone. She ignored his many calls the rest of the night. She called her mother to ask her to pick Halley up at school, saying she had to leave early the following day for her doctor's appointment and

[345]

that Tony would be gone that night. She supplied no further explanation, nor did her mom expect one.


"Zip it, dickhead!" Mylee said. She pinched her thumb and forefinger and ran them across her mouth as Tony tried to talk to her the following morning as she backed from their driveway.

"Please?" he mouthed through her shut car window. His arms were splayed out from his sides in a begging manner. Mylee shifted to forward and drove past him without a glance. She held her middle finger in the air beside her head as she passed him.

"What a pile of garbage!" she thought as she drove away. Visions of him behind the married woman as she bent over the couch appeared in her head. "Fucking pig!"

Mylee relived her husband's sex scene, her daughter's pending trauma, and the thoughts of her own humiliation in the town for the entire drive to her appointment. She sobered to her reality as she entered the door of the fluorescent-lit sterile smelling doctor's office.

"Oh, come on back, Mylee," the stoic, past-middle-aged, blue-gowned nurse said to Mylee. She glanced at the clock, seeing that Mylee was perfectly on time for her appointment. Mylee assumed that this was a ritual of hers. An elderly couple in

[346]

the waiting room both looked from their magazines and over the top of their glasses at Mylee. They too studied the clock.

"Hi, Mylee," the doctor greeted warmly as he entered the examining room. He shook Mylee's hand and took a seat on the black vinyl-topped stool in front of her chair.

"Mylee, don't be alarmed, it's probably nothing, but your last blood tests from a couple weeks ago show an elevated white blood count." Mylee's body stiffened. "I want you to walk across to the last office on the end of the building across the way so we can get a couple pictures of your body just for safety's sake," he continued.

Mylee shook her head in compliance.

"As soon as he's done, we'll take a look and you are on your way! It'll probably only take an hour or so," he added. He patting Mylee on the knee as he rose and passed her off to the nurse. The nurse walked her to the door and pointed out the location in the building across the parking lot, telling her that she was expected.

"Okay, just lie still for a few minutes for us, Mylee," the calm young radiology technician instructed. He carefully positioned Mylee, who was clad in an open-backed gown, on the narrow table that was part of a large space-aged looking machine.

He vanished behind a wall and reappeared behind a thick wire-meshed window several feet from the door where he had exited.

"Here we go, Mylee," he said through the speaker above the machine. His voice sounded much more distant than it was. The huge machine began to rattle and growl. She and the table began to move at a snail's pace through its round hoop. The noise became louder with each inch of movement. The technician was focusing on dials and screens. Mylee laid still staring at the ceiling.

"Okay Mylee, that's it!" the technician said after reappearing from behind the enclosure. He helped her from the sliding table. "Go ahead and get dressed and I will send the scan over to your doctor in a few minutes." He escorted her to the adjoining dressing room, and to the exit after she had dressed.

"Okay, Mylee," the grey-haired bespectacled doctor began after Mylee was again led to the examination room. "I reviewed the results of the scan with the specialist that reads them and we found several areas of concern."

Mylee began to shake inside.

"Mylee, I'm not going beat around the bush," the doctor said. He glanced to the floor and then directly into her eyes. A sadness and look of dread overcame his face. "Your cancer has returned. It is in your liver, your lungs, and your brain," he said. He looked to the floor again and then back to her.

"Mylee, we can treat you, but no matter what we do, we are talking a few months – tops. The treatment would be terrible and of little use. I don't recommend it." he said. "Mylee, I am so sorry."

Mylee began shaking uncontrollably. The doctor stood from his stool and took her seated body close to him. She soaked his white coat in both tears and sweat.

"How long?" Mylee asked, looking closely at him to listen.

"About four months, Mylee, maybe six with treatment, but it would make you very sick and, as I said, I don't recommend it," the doctor said.

She nodded in understanding. She became calm. "I don't want the treatment." She said. She looked into the doctor's eyes, who confirmed her wishes with a single nod.

"There won't be much pain, Mylee, and what there is we can control and keep you comfortable," he said. "I'm so sorry Mylee. I wish there was someth..." he began to say as Mylee interrupted.

"It's okay doctor. It isn't your fault. It isn't anyone's fault It is what it is." she said with a broken smile.

[349]

"Come on Mylee, I'll drive you home and my assistant will follow us in your car," the doctor said as he rose.

"No, I'm okay. I want to think and I am fine to drive" she said as she forced herself to composure. Her voice became strong and she stood. "I really appreciate everything you have done," she said. She smiled sincerely. She saw the pain in him.

He fought back tears as he escorted her to the door of his office. "Call me in a couple of days, Mylee, just so we can chat and I want to order some pain medications for you in case you need them. Have your husband or family call me anytime Mylee, and I mean that!"

Mylee reflected on Tony and her situation as the doctor mentioned him. She shuddered in disgust.

"This sucks," Mylee thought as she took her seat in her car. He emotions mimicked the many she had as when she first found out she had cancer—except the ones of finality. "This is really screwed up!" she screamed angrily to the steering wheel. Thoughts of her daughter's life without her began racing through her head. She pictured her daughter dressing for the prom, having her first period, going on her first date, getting married and having kids without her.

"It's so fucked up!" she screamed again as she drove. Her daughter's face kept flashing before her. Each time it showed a different emotion and each time Mylee cried louder. Edgewater's bridge towers appeared in the distance. Her body had drained its tears and was allowing relief from her feelings. A strength grew within her as each mile passed.

"Mylee, we need to talk," Tony said as she parked her car in their garage.

"About what?" Mylee said. She was fighting to not blurt out to him that Halley wasn't his daughter. "Yeah Seth's, Tony. A good man—a real man! That's her daddy," she thought about screaming to him. She had mulled it for half the drive back from the doctor's office.

"I love you, Mylee, I always have and I am so sorry!" Tony said. His face looked tired--as if he hadn't slept for a month. His clothes were unkempt and wrinkled. "I am such a piece of shit!"

"Tony, you are a piece of shit! That is the only thing you said that I can agree with. You don't love me and you never have. You don't even know what love is!" Mylee scolded angrily. Her face was painted in disgust.

[351]

"But Mylee, I don't want to lose you! I don't want to lose our family!" Tony begged. Mylee sat staring at him, the look on her face evolved to one of amazement.

"Tony, you need to realize that you have ruined all of that! I have no interest in ever having anything to do with you again! You need to get that through your head!" Mylee said. Tony's body slumped into a standing wad of nothing.

"Tony, for our daughter's sake, we do need to talk though," Mylee said, unsure of what she planned to say next. "But you have to understand that it isn't about you and me, but only her." She stared at him. "Tony, I just got back from the doctor and the cancer has spread. I only have a few months to live." Tony's face saddened. He fought to hold back tears. He opened his arms in front of him and stepped to take her into them.

"No, Tony!" Mylee said. She pushed him, and his arms, back from her. "I told you, Tony, this is about Halley, not us. Thanks to you, everything is ten times more complicated now. Halley is losing me and I hate tearing her family apart at the same fucking time!" "Goddamnit! You would have to fuck everything up!" She looked at him with complete contempt. His eyes sank to the ground. His stomach churned painfully wanting to discharge its contents.

[352]

"For now, I think it is best that we both be home with our daughter and act like everything is normal," Mylee said, grasping for thoughts as she spoke. "I will tell her you are sleeping on the couch because my medicine is not good to be around for boys. She can sleep with me."

"But we can work this out, Mylee," Tony said, grabbing her arms with his hands and staring into her face.

Mylee twisted her arms from him angrily. "Tony, goddamnit! I told you! It is over. If you are going to live in our house, I don't want you touching me, trying to kiss me, or talking to me, except for just dealing with our daughter. Do you understand me, Tony?" He froze from the iciness in her voice. "I mean it, Tony. It is either this way or I will tell her about my cancer and about how you put your pieces of ass over both of us!"

Tony nodded submissively. Mylee demanded and received an audible answer.

"I understand," he said. Compliance was scrawled on his face.

"I'm saying nothing to my parents, my sister, or anyone about what you have done, for the sake of Halley. I'll be dead soon and hopefully you won't be dragging your harem of sluts to

[353]

our house and screwing them in front of her," Mylee said warningly. Tony cringed.

"Now go to work, Tony. If I were you, I'd clean up first. You look like shit!" Mylee said. She disappeared into the house, losing herself in the kitchen until Tony showered and left for work.


"Guess what, baby girl?" Mylee said to her daughter later that week as they walked the long way home from school.

"What, Mommy?" Halley answered, their hands joined and their arms swinging as they walked.

"Honey," Mylee said after setting herself on one knee in front of her, "Mommy's going to get to be your angel soon".

"What do you mean, Mommy?" Halley said with a look of terror and confusion. Her smile was replaced by an unstable frown and her chin began to quiver.

"Mommy's going to heaven to be your angel forever in a few months, Baby," Mylee said. She took deep and controlled breaths.

[354]

"Are you going to die, Mommy?" Halley asked as tears streamed from her face. She paled and her entire body began vibrating.

"Honey, Mommy's cancer came back, and this time the doctors can't fix it. But it's going to be okay, honey," she said. She released her grip on her daughter's arms and took her trembling body to her own. Halley began wailing at the top of her lungs.

"I'm not leaving you, Baby," she said as she cried with her. She felt guilt from her lie. "I will be your angel and I will see everything you do. I can't answer in words from heaven, but you can pray to me every night and I will hear every word you say, I promise! I'll find ways to let you know I am there, Honey. I love you so very much and so does your daddy. Grandpa and Grandma and Auntie Karlina all love you and it's all going to be okay, I promise." She paused and let her daughter cry.

"I'm not going away real soon, Babygirl. We have a lot of time left to love each other" Mylee said. She felt a slight relief come to her daughter. Her sobs turned to sniffles, and again to sobs as their eyes met. Mylee held her and soothed her. Mylee felt relief. Death was the easy part.

"Thank you for loving me and Halley so much, Sis," Mylee said to her sister at her bedside. Her sister sponged her with a towel and smiled. Her cancer, after just two months, had advanced to where she was unable to walk. Now, a month later, her breathing was shallow—and even shallowed more by the pills that kept her body-wide pain in check.

"Mylee, I will be with Halley every day of my life, I promise. I'll love her as my own. I will show her your picture every day and tell her how much you love her and we will both pray to you every night," her sister told her. "I'll make sure that she never forgets you and knows that you are always there with her. I promise you that!" She stroked Mylee's pale sunken-cheeked face. Mylee smiled weakly. She began slipping towards unconsciousness as each second passed. Her daughter had laid in bed with her for nearly an hour earlier, loving her for what would be her final time in life.

"She's almost gone," Karlina solemnly announced as she left her sister's room. She sat and took her niece's broken hearted body into her arms. Halley hugged her as if she wanted to climb into her.

Tony, who had sat silently alone at the kitchen table since the morning, disappeared into Mylee's room. In only a minute he reappeared and walked from the house bawling. His face had paled and his mind seemed absent. He looked at no one. Seth glanced to him with scorn. The family looked to each other, unsure of its meaning. Mylee's father and mother looked at each other with fear. Seth rose to his feet and rushed to Mylee's side. He saw her breathing.

"Hi my love," Seth said as he sat softly beside her. She opened her eyes and a weak smile came to her face.

"I love you, Seth," she said, unable to speak in more than a whisper.

Seth fell over her with his tears gushing. He kissed her parched lips, moistened them with his tongue, and kissed them again.

"In the drawer," Mylee whispered. She directed Seth's attention to the drawer of the nightstand with her eyes.

"Here?" Seth asked as he placed his hand on the handle. He slid it open. It revealed three envelopes. One was addressed to Halley, one to Karlina, and the last to him. She tried to speak. Seth put his ear to her mouth to hear her weakened voice. He sensed her soul leaving her.

"Give them to them to open when the time is right," she whispered. Seth leaned back from her. Confusion showed on his face.

[357]

"When is that, Mylee?"

Mylee smiled trustfully and mouthed, "You'll know."

"Hold me, Seth." She whispered as her eyes fell closed.

Seth lifted her into his arms and pressed his face to hers. She whispered her last words;

"I love you, Seth."

She took a deep breath and became limp in his arms.

Her passing was announced by his wails.

# CHAPTER 22

"Hey Andy!  How are you?" Sam said, able to hug and hold her boyfriend for the first time since being imprisoned.

"I'm great, sweetheart.  I am just so glad to have you back.  I have been missing you so badly for so long!" he said.  He lifted her from her feet and hugged her.  He sat her in front of him and stared.

"I can't believe it, Sam!" he said.  He kissed her again and stood in disbelief.

"I've missed you so much too, Andy," she whispered as he held her.

"Wait until you see the farm and the cabin," Andy said.  He knew that the many pictures he had shown her through the thick glass window couldn't match seeing the real thing.  "It's everything that you told me you ever wanted."

"I can't wait!" Sam said.  She felt herself being infected by Andy's excitement.  Images that he had shown her flashed in her mind.

"Let's get out of this place," Sam's father said, glancing at the prison's gates with a sickened look.

"Amen," Samantha said. Andy opened the front passenger door for her. She placed her hand on the door and looked back toward the prison. She sighed deeply, turned, and sat into the car. Andy closed her door and seated himself in the rear.

"How was Trish? You know, with you leaving and all?" Andy inquired.

"Sad that I was leaving, but happy that I was," Sam said, fighting back tears. "She gets out pretty soon. She is a great person, an honest and decent person. She doesn't belong in that place! I promised her I would come see her every weekend, and I'm going to do it! I feel so sorry for her!"

"Well tell her if she needs a place to stay when she gets out, she is always welcome with us!" Andy said.

"Thanks, I will tell her. I love you," Sam said. She glanced back at him. She began to recall all the reasons that she had fallen in love with him. She looked deeper toward him. She became aroused. She realized an awakening coming over her. Andy sensed her looking at him and turned from looking out the window to her. She smiled seductively and licked her lips. He smiled back the same.

"It's everything we've ever dreamed of, Andy!" Samantha said the following morning. Having arrived at their property after dark the night before, she was unable to see it. "I so love it!" She had slept more sound than anytime that she could recall. She had enjoyed wonderful intimacy with Andy before dozing off.

Sam sipped the fresh ground coffee that Andy delivered to her when she awoke. The morning sun warmed the entire room through its ceiling-height bay window as she dressed. Wisteria flower clusters cascaded from the trellis just outside. "It's like heaven, Andy," she said after walking towards the window and staring outside. She looked over her shoulder at him. Her eyes were wide with excitement and the grin couldn't leave her face.

"Come on, Love", Andy said. He offered his hand to her and led her outdoors along a grape trellised path to a perfectly manicured garden. Sam stood speechless. An array of fruit trees lined the side of the garden. A coop of chickens scratched and fluttered worry free in their cage at its rear.

"I can't believe it, Andy," Samantha said, her eyes glazed with amazement. Andy smiled, his body expressed accomplishment. She kissed him.

"Here", he said. He led her to a porch swing on the elevated front porch that overlooked the meadow. The grove of oak trees surrounding it acted as their property's foyer. A doe browsed in the distance. Andy left and soon returned with another cup of coffee for them both and nestled beside her on the made-for-three swinging bench. They sat in silence, sipping coffee and rocking. The aroma of the fresh herb garden below the porch saturated the air around them. Their days continued much the same, except Andy left for work in the mornings. Sam assumed much of the gardening duties, except they enjoyed them together on every weekend, excepting the time each weekend she visited Trish in prison as she promised. Sam's life became tranquil. Her love grew.


"What do you think?" Sam asked Trish after retrieving her from the prison a year later. They walked hand in hand through the garden and then the entire property. Andy was at work.

"It's all so beautiful Ba..." she replied, stopping herself mid-sentence.

[362]

"Hey, it's okay. It's just us." Sam said.

"I just didn't want to...." Trish began before again being interrupted.

"I know, but it's nothing," Sam said. She squeezed Trish's hand and they continued their walk.

"Andy is a good man, Trish. He told me to invite you to stay with us and he meant it. Don't feel pressured to move on anytime soon, okay?" She looked to Trish's eyes. Trish nodded humbly. After showing Trish the garden, they unpacked her meager belongings into one of the brightly colored spare bedrooms.


"Andy, if Trish ever gets on your nerves or you want more privacy or anything and you want me to ask her to move out, I will. I love you and you have already been more patient than any husband that I can imagine." Samantha said one evening as they laid in bed. Trish had stayed with them for several months.

"Hey, I love Trish. She shares in all the work, there is no nicer and polite a person, and she never misses a day at work. She always pays her fair share of our expenses. I honestly enjoy having her around!" Andy said. "She's like wife number two!" Samantha smiled and let out an inaudible sigh of relief.

"I really enjoy her too, it's nice to have company around here, especially with the baby coming and all in a few months," Sam said.

"Then let's just leave perfect alone!" Andy said. He smiled warmly at Sam. She rolled him to the top of her and gave herself to him, just as she did on most nights. They slept in each other's arms.

"Damn!" Samantha thought, feeling so dishonest for letting Andy live in her lie. She laid in bed the following morning after he had left thinking. She loved tow people.

"I should have just told him! He deserves the truth!" she scolded herself. "It's just not fair! It's got to happen."

"You awake?" Sam said as she pushed Trish's already ajar bedroom door open with her shoulder. She held a freshly brewed cup of coffee in each hand.

"Yup," Trish said, already sitting up in bed and resting her back on the pillows propped against her headboard. "Just soaking in the morning sun!"

[364]

"It is so nice today!" Sam said while handing Trish one of the steaming cups. She leaned and kissed her good morning and sat beside her on the bed.

"Andy had to go in early today?" Trish asked. "I heard him leave quite a while ago."

"Yeah, he wanted to do some catching up on some bridge design project they are on," Sam told her. She set her empty cup on the nightstand beside the bed and nestled herself against the headboard beside Trish in the sun.

"How's our little baby?" Trish asked, caressing Sam's two-month-along slightly-rounded stomach in a gentle and circular motion.

"She's good", Sam said. She took Trish's hand and relocated her caresses to her bare breasts under her nightgown.

"Feels good" Sam whispered. She lifted her gown over her head to expose her fully nude body. She slid downward on the bed and laid flat on top of the bedspread. The sun soaked into her entire body. Trish followed her and took Sam's breast into her mouth.

"Feels good," Sam moaned. Trish stood and disrobed. She reentered the bed, this time laying her head between Sam's open legs.

"Wait", Sam said, instructing her to turn herself so Sam could take her to her mouth as well. Their eyes were shut and their visions became only their fantasies. They were silent, except for the wet sucking sounds and moans they elicited from one another.

"Oh! I'm going to cum!" Sam moaned loudly. Her body began to convulse and she pressed Trish's mouth to her. She heard a sound to her side. She peered through her squinted eyes towards the bedroom door as Trish erupted into her own ecstasy. Her husband stood still, then disappeared from its opening, shutting it quietly behind him.

# CHAPTER 23

"What are you thinking?" Debbie asked. She noticed Abel to be in a distant place as they walked along their usual riverfront route one evening.

"Oh, nothing really," Abel responded in a melancholy way. He smiled thankfully towards her.

"BRRR", she said. She cloaked herself with Abel's coat as they walked. He wrapped her with his arm to hold it in place.

"Come spend the night with me, Abel," Debbie said, tiring of them living apart. "We need to spend every night together." She shifted her eyes upward to him. He smiled.

"Sounds good to me," Abel said, seeming to agree to both her propositions. Abel walked quietly. He sighed a contented sigh.

"You're a magic woman Deb. I am so glad we met," Abel said. He paused and looked at her.

"Thanks, Abel," Debbie said. She kissed his cheek. They continued toward her house.

"Here," Debbie said. She handed Abel a glass of wine as he sunk into her pillowed couch. She sat beside him with her own glass and set the bottle on the coffee table in front of them. They sat quietly, finishing the bottle of wine while watching a weekly serial drama that they both had come to enjoy.

"Come on!" Debbie ordered, her face flushed from the red wine. She offered Abel her hand to help him from the overly deep divan. She leaned away from him to counterbalance his weight as he rose, then led him to her bedroom. A flickering candle was its only illumination.

"Hang on. Be still," Debbie ordered. She disappeared into the bathroom. She reappeared clad in a sheer black nightie. Her bright red lipstick had been freshened and was uncharacteristically lined in black highlighter. It brought a surreal look to her ivory teeth and snow white skin. Her hair was strewn wildly forward as if combed with her fingers. Debbie stood six inches taller, elevated by black-laced, knee-high leather stiletto heels. She stood upright and firm.

"Now, don't move!" she ordered. She lifted Abel's shirt over his head and ripped his arms violently upward in doing so. Abel reached to unbutton his pants.

[368]

"I said to hold still!" she said. She slapped his hands to his sides. She unfastened his pants and yanked them and his underwear to the ground in one motion as he stood facing away from her bed.

"Sit!" she ordered as if he were a dog. She pushed his hobbled-by-his-pants body to the bed using both her hands. She freed his legs from his pants and underwear with a firm yank, leaving him lying completely nude on top of the bed. She took his soft penis into her mouth and hardened it, then stopped, raised herself over him and studied him. Abel laid confused and began to shift himself to his side.

"Lay down," she said sternly. Abel complied, and laid back to the center of the bed. His still erect penis laid across his navel. Debbie stroked it at intervals, preserving its hardened state for several minutes, never stroking it more than once at each touching. Able felt uneasy.

"Good boy!" she said. She still glowed from the half bottle of wine as she tore her nightie from herself. Her breasts were harnessed into thin leather bridles that cinched each outward. The restriction caused them to discolor and the veins to protrude. Her nipples were pinched in tiny adjustable vices.

"You want me?" she asked with a nasty look on her face. She straddled him and forced him into her dryness. Abel's penis skin peeled painfully backward. Abel felt her juices mercifully relieve his sting. She began rising and falling on him.

Debbie moaned as her body responded to the enjoyment of her darkest fantasies for the first time in years. She'd longed for the time to reach a comfort level with a man to allow such a freedom. Abel began to unnerve.

"Get up!" Debbie ordered. She suddenly stopped and withdrew Abel from within her. She dismounted him and flopped flat, face up, on the bed. She splayed her fully extended legs to their widest. She grabbed Abel's testicles with her hand and squeezed them. He winced in pain. He began to soften.

"You get down there and eat my pussy now!" she ordered with a meanness in her voice. She threw Abel's testicles painfully against his own thigh. Pain shot through his stomach.

"I said now! You get down there and eat it now!" she again ordered. She rose to him and grabbed him behind his neck. She violently forced his face to her crotch. She squeezed the back of his neck in punishment for his hesitation.

"Nooo!!" Abel screamed. His face became contorted in hatred. Debbie's face became his mother's. Reality abandoned him. His soul exploded.

"I'll kill you, you fucking whore!" Abel screamed. He mounted himself on top of her and wrapped both hands around her throat. Debbie's face began to show terror. Abels face became eerily blank. Every muscle in his naked body squirmed and tensed. He began to wretch her life from her. His teeth clenched to the point of shattering. His thumbs dug into her airway until it collapsed.

"I hate you!" he screamed. Tears scattered in every direction as his head shook in anger. Debbie's eyes reddened in streaks and her pupils dilated more at each second's passing. She felt life creeping from her body.

"I'm sorry Abel—I'm so sorry", she began to think. She saw his deep pain manifesting itself within him as her life drained from her. The panic left her. "I understand, Abel..." she thought.

Abel saw a smile come to one corner of her mouth as she became limp in his hands. Her pupils rolled to the back of her opened eyes.

# CHAPTER 24

"Come on, Daddy! Let's go!" Ian heard his now eight-year-old daughter scream. She stood rushing him to hurry and get the chainsaw to cut their Christmas tree, an annual ritual that she cherished each year the weekend after Thanksgiving.

"Alright, alright, I'm coming," Ian said. He grabbed the gas can and the saw and strapped them to the back of the pickup bed. The sleds and snowman materials had already been loaded the night before at his daughter's prodding.

"Ready, Hon?" Layla asked her husband as he climbed into the passenger seat of their truck. She smiled at their daughter's annual anxiousness.

"Ready Freddy!" Ian playfully responded while smiling at his daughter. Erica grinned as she saw her father's childlike playfulness begin. She sat strapped into the elevated young child's seat behind them with her arm wrapped around their dog. The dog seemed to be smiling.

"We're off," Layla said as she manned the hand controls of Ian's truck. They headed up to the hour-away snowy

[373]

mountains in search of the perfect Christmas tree. Layla was always amazed that her husband and daughter managed to find that very perfect tree each and every year--according to the two of them.

"We did it, Honey! We found the perfect tree again!" Ian told his daughter. She began glowing with pride. Layla rolled her eyes and smiled at Ian. He tied the tree to the bed of their truck after strapping the gas can and chainsaw into place.

"I'm worn out!" Ian said to his daughter, adding, "You sledded me out!"

Erica laughed loudly, thinking of the many times she begged her father to drag her to the top of the hill for her to sled down. He always rode with her. Their loudest laughs came on their crashes. Their next stop was always the little mom-and-pop mountain store that sold gallons of hot chocolate to the many visiting children and their parents. Ian feigned sleeping as they arrive at it.

"Daddy! Wake up, it's hot chocolate time," Erica screamed. Ian continued to fake sleeping. "Daddy!" she again screamed, this time at the top of her lungs and kicking the back of his seat.

"Hot chocolate!!!" Ian screamed, now feigning his awakening and screaming as if it were the highlight of his life. Erica cackled a hard laugh. Layla smiled, enjoying the two of them playing. They all sat near the huge rock fireplace at the end of the restaurant and sipped through their cups of hot chocolate. Ian sat petting the old black lab that lived there with the elderly couple who had owned the place for his entire memory. The old man let Erica feed two logs into the fire. The old couple met them at the door on their way out and hugged them all.

"Somebody is tired," Ian said, pointing to the back seat of their truck where Erica had dozed off. Her head laid against the side of the car seat, barely rolling as they rounded the mountain corners. The dog slept curled around her.

"My legs are killing me! That walking in snow is hard on the ol' nubs!" Ian said. He leaned forward and removed each one and quietly sat them in the back seat so as not to awaken his daughter. "That was a great day!" Ian said quietly to Layla. A look of contentment came over his face.

"It was, Ian," Layla said. Her face showed appreciation. Layla stared ahead and rounded the icy corner ahead of her. Ian pulled his pants above his leg's ends to examine the source of his pain, thinking that it might be worse than he thought.

"Damn," Layla said suddenly. Ian looked to her, seeing a look of panic in her face. Ian followed her intent stare forward, seeing two teenaged boys in a raised, wide-tired pickup sliding sideways at them. Layla hit her brakes and swerved to the side of the road to avoid them. Her tire left the roadway and slammed into a huge rock. The car spun in the direction of the oncoming pickup and violently collided with it. Erica snapped awake from the impact. Both she and Layla began screaming in terror as their truck flipped onto its side and then onto its top. It slammed into a tree. The seatbelt was unable to compensate for Ian's legless body and allowed him to be violently ejected from the car's window along with their dog. They slammed to the rocky ground at the side of the road.

"Oh God, no!" Ian pleaded as he regained focus of his surroundings. His right forearm was broken and bent unnaturally backward and nearly all of the ribs on that same side were shattered into pieces. He watching his truck careen through a curtain of sparks as it spun down the road on its top and come to a stop a hundred feet away.

[376]

"Please God!" he begged at the top of his lungs. He saw flames growing from the rear of the overturned truck where the gas can was strapped. He began crawling franticly towards his family. His pain was suppressed by his terror. He squirmed and rolled, fighting any way he could towards his pickup. He saw his wife dangling upside down and unconscious behind its wheel.

"DADDY! HELP ME! DADDY!" he heard his daughter scream as she looked towards him. She hung from her seat and blood trickled from her nose. Her terrified eyes begged him as the flames began to spread more rapidly. They began billowing through the broken rear window near her.

"I'm coming, baby!" Ian screamed as he began crawling wildly towards them. He was screaming in terror. A loud hiss sounded from the rear of the truck and the gas can exploded.

"DADDY PLEASE! DADDY PLE...." Erica tried to scream. She fell silent. Ian screamed and fought towards her.

"Come on guy, it's too late," a man's voice sounded. The man and another man from a passing car lifted him and carried him from the flames. Ian fought them savagely and screamed "IT'S MY FAMILY!" He collapsed in emotional pain and watched the flames rise to the height of the surrounding trees. He

[377]

watched as the flames melted his truck, and his family, into the pavement. He finally lapsed into a merciful coma.

"Son, it's Mom and Dad," Ian heard as he began to regain consciousness the following day. His body was covered in bandages. None of it was without pain. He opened his eyes to see his father and mother standing at his side. Their faces were engraved with grief.

"It's us, son," his father said, forcing a smile through his sadness. He watched his son disappear in terror as the events of the previous day began to fill his consciousness.

"Are they gone, Dad?" Ian asked. His face begged to hear different than what he knew. His eyes filled with water.

"They're gone, son," his father said as he looked to the floor. His mother began crying and was unable to speak. Each took a side of his bed and wrapped him in their arms and withstood his pitiful wails until his body gave in to exhaustion.

We're sorry.", "You'll see them in heaven," Ian heard over and over as every person in town filed past him at the funeral. He saw the grief and compassion in all of their faces. None consoled him. He could only stare blankly at them.

[378]

"Ian, look at me," Seth said seeing the pain in his friend. He grabbed each side of Ian's head between his hands and forced him to look at him. "Ian, you have to do what your girls would want you to do!" Seth said forcefully. "Ian, you have to live! I love you. Your parents love you. Everybody loves you!" He forced Ian's head upward to stare in his eyes. "You have to do this for your wife and daughter, Ian, you can't let them down. Come stay with me a few days and let's just be pals, okay?" Seth pleaded. "Please Ian, do it for your baby and wife." Seth hugged him and kissed him on his forehead before reluctantly releasing him to the other mourners.


That night, Ian told everyone that he wanted to be alone. He insisted. He sat alone in his bedroom and flipped through his family albums. He saw his wedding day and the glow of happiness on Layla's face. He saw Erica in his arms on the day of her birth. Then her baptism. Then each birthday, including her last. The day she got her dog. All of it was blurred through tears. He lay on the bed with his head propped up on the pillows. His wedding pictures hung on the walls with the many family portraits. He could see Layla's clothes neatly hanging and her shoes arranged on the floor through the closet's open door. He felt relief from knowing that he would not be the one who had to empty her belongings from his life.

Ian was ready to feel the relief of the bullet from his pistol tearing through his brain. Even though tears cascaded from his cheeks, he began to feel a warm relief overcome his body as he lifted the gun from the bed. He positioned it against the side of his head in such a manner that his death would be certain. He closed his eyes and saw his wife and daughter. He put his finger on the trigger.

Ian suddenly felt the bed jar. His daughter's dog had jumped onto the bed with him. The dog seemed desperate and serious. For the very first time ever, the dog squirmed to Ian's ear and began to nibble it--exactly as the puppy had done to his daughter a million times and how his daughter had done to him an equal number. The dog nuzzled Ian's face and licked his tears dry. It nibbled his ears again and whimpered. Ian heard his daughter begging. Ian began to bawl and his mind began to fight with itself. Erica was pleading "Daddy no!" in his mind. He could take no more. He took a deep breath, wailed pitifully, and began to squeeze the trigger, hoping to be with his family again in seconds.......

[380]

Made in the USA
Monee, IL
07 August 2020